THE DESPERATE WIFE

C. L. JENNISON

BLOODHOUND
— BOOKS —

www.bloodhoundbooks.com

Print ISBN: 978-1-5040-8597-7

To Richard, for being absolutely nothing like the dastardly men I write about

PROLOGUE

July 1988

'LOOK, AUNTIE KATHY, IT'S MUMMY!'

From her chair at the wooden kitchen table, five-year-old Ava proudly held up the carefully drawn picture and Kathleen Kennedy smiled indulgently while drying her hands on a tea towel. The little blonde girl, who was small for her age, was practically camouflaged by the mountain of craft paraphernalia covering the tabletop. Her mother's birthday was two days away and they had spent the afternoon creating themed decorations in preparation for the big day. Kathleen loved looking after Ava on Friday afternoons for her friend Christine next door. It had been a standing arrangement for nearly a year now, and had done wonders to ease Kathleen's loneliness since she lost her husband. Not to mention the sadness at not having any children of her own. She had grown to adore Ava over the months and was also pleased she could help Christine out while she had some adult time to herself.

1

'I've never seen your mummy in a purple-and-orange-striped dress, but I like it!' said Kathleen, crossing over to Ava. 'Now, we're going to have to clear some room on the table or you'll have nowhere to eat your tea. Can you help me pack your crafts away?'

Ava nodded, pigtails bobbing, and slid off her chair. Kathleen bent down for the big plastic box on the floor and as she placed it on one of the chairs for Ava to easily reach, movement through the window caught her eye: a dark-haired man hurrying down Christine's garden path and out the gate into the passage. Kathleen blinked and, ghostlike, he was gone. She smiled wryly to herself and turned her attention back to the little girl.

An hour later, after Ava had finished eating the tea Kathleen had cooked her, followed by two scoops of ice cream topped with sprinkles, they made their way, hand in hand, past the apple tree and through the gate in the fence separating the neighbouring properties. As they approached Christine's back door, Kathleen noticed it was ajar. Despite the pleasant July afternoon, it was unusual. A faint warning bell began to ring in Kathleen's head, and she stopped, keeping hold of Ava's hand so the child didn't run inside.

Kathleen bent down to speak to Ava. 'Silly Auntie Kathy forgot to bring the birthday bunting we made for your mummy. Will you run back to my house and get it, please?'

Ava nodded compliantly and skipped back through the still open gate. Heart skittering, Kathleen hurried to the door, pushed it open and shouted Christine's name from the threshold. This was the usual time she brought Ava home and Christine normally intercepted them en route. She strained her ears, but no sounds came. Although it was still warm, she shivered. She shouted again, venturing into the boxy porch. The closed door straight ahead led to a utility cupboard and the door to her left led to the kitchen. It was also partially open but from what she could see, nothing looked untoward.

Conscious that Ava would come running back any second, Kathleen shouted Christine's name again and ventured into the kitchen. Rounding the countertop, she was surprised to see strewn flowers and shards of glass in a puddle of water on the quarry-tiled floor. But what she saw beyond that, partially obscured by the legs of the kitchen table and chairs, was Christine's half-naked body. Ripped stockings. Gaping mouth. Vacant eyes.

Kathleen clamped one hand over her own mouth and gripped the edge of the countertop with the other. Struggling to comprehend the macabre scene, she could do nothing except stare in shock as the surreal moment stretched around her. Suddenly, a high-pitched scream jolted her out of her frozen state, and she turned in horror to see Ava standing behind her, the birthday bunting slipping from her small hand and coiling on the cold hard floor.

CHAPTER ONE

AVA

June 2018

AVA LOVED HEARING Ali's now-familiar laugh. She watched as he reached towards the screen and splayed his fingers in front of the camera, as though they were separated by an impenetrable force. They were, really. She mirrored the gesture, less afraid of showing her growing feelings now, reluctant to sever their connection despite the digital clock in the top-left corner counting down the minutes into seconds. She stared unblinkingly at his image, desperate to imprint every detail of him onto her memory.

'Goodbye, *habibti*,' he said.

'*Habibti?*' she asked.

'It's a Saudi Arabian term of affection. My father used to say it to my mother all the time. It means "my love".'

She gasped, surprised, and felt a reciprocal bloom of warmth in her heart. A feeling she hadn't experienced in a long time.

'Until tomorrow,' he said.

Then he was gone, again, leaving behind a grey rectangular void where his two-dimensional form had been only moments before.

Ava sighed with disappointment as she habitually checked her watch – a present from her dad passed on from her beloved mum – and logged off. The evening stretched ahead of her like a long, dark tunnel. Something to get through until Ali filled her permanently dreary life with sunlight once more. Their last tutoring session – if they could still be defined as tutoring sessions – had flown by as usual. They were the perfect escape from her mind full of worries and head full of memories. She was becoming addicted to him. She looked forward to their daily online sessions immensely; it was hard to believe they only met three months previously, in her very first week as an online English tutor. She had made a new year's resolution to try to expand her tiny life, to find a purpose greater than just being Rex's wife, but it had taken her until March to finally pluck up the courage to create her profile.

In the hours she and Ali spent talking she could forget about her broken marriage, her dwindling confidence, her abject shame and disappointment about the way things had turned out, despite her best efforts. Instead, she immersed herself in her insular, online teaching life and ignored the whispering voice warning her she was venturing into dangerous territory, again. Blurring the line between student and teacher, in reverse this time; older but no wiser. Their dynamic was slowly shifting into something unprofessional and potentially dangerous but, for now, Ava was stubbornly refusing to acknowledge it to herself. But she knew, deep down. She might not have crossed the line yet, but she was teetering on the edge of it in blustery conditions.

Ali was so different to any man she had ever known, not just culturally, but in the way he spoke to her, and listened, as though she was worth listening to. It was a shockingly basic but heady combination. He'd even noticed her bruises – they were getting more and more difficult to conceal – and although she kept trying her best to pass them off as her own clumsiness, avoiding his doubtful and concerned laser gaze through the screen, she suspected he knew the truth by now.

Rising from her desk in her sparsely furnished but immaculately decorated home office, Ava stretched her lean, petite body upwards, feeling her squashed spine click with relief. Five sessions in a row had sufficiently tired out her overactive, anxious brain, and she would repeat the process tomorrow. And the day after that. She had nothing better to do, after all.

She enjoyed speaking with her other students, as well as Ali. The variety of extremely well-educated personalities she taught was still eye-opening. She often felt like a fraud as an online English teacher. Her students' general knowledge often far exceeded her own and she had no business teaching her mother tongue to these articulate, often trilingual men and women doing their utmost to better themselves and their situations when she hadn't completed the final year of her English Language and Literature degree herself. They all had one goal in common: to inhabit England and add to its infrastructure with their honest intentions. Those against immigration were clueless to the potential they were stifling with their narrow-minded views of 'foreigners'. That's how Ava saw it, anyway.

In amongst the plethora of new and regular intelligent, ambitious students she had been teaching for the past three months, there had only been one flashing incident – in the early days. Not bad going. At the time, Ava had briefly considered not reporting it. It had been so long since she had actually laid eyes on an erect penis that her curiosity was piqued. She did the right thing though, after dithering for a few red-cheeked moments, and banned and blocked the perpetrator. Nothing inappropriate had happened since, unless her increasingly flirtatious conversations with Ali counted as untoward. It wasn't as if anything was ever going to happen though; he was thousands of miles away in Saudi Arabia and she was here, in the UK. And married.

Heading downstairs into her stark, shiny kitchen, and turning on the lights, her brain nonetheless conjured up images of Ali's chocolate-brown eyes and his sexy, playful grin, her imaginary vision obscuring the reality of the beautiful, empty space beyond. The six-seater table positioned below the sky lantern was never eaten at or sat around, surrounded by friends or family, drinking coffee and sharing news. The designer fridge was devoid of tacky holiday magnets or children's drawings. The flooring, lighting and units had been chosen by Rex without her input. The designer kitchen most people dreamed of brought her absolutely no joy whatsoever.

Despite her guilt at flirting with a man other than her husband, she needed the images of Ali to counteract the miserable memories of Rex and the life they shared, if 'shared' was the correct definition. She needed her undefinable relationship with Ali to make her feel *something* again, especially if that something was hope.

Leaning against her pristine granite worktop, her thoughts flitted from Ali to her mum and dad, as they often did. Her fingers subconsciously stroked the face of her mum's watch – the last precious gift she had received from her dad before she had lost him to cancer just over three years earlier. She clutched onto memories of them both tightly.

Her mind circled back to Ali. Was she genuinely falling in love with him, or just the idea of him? Did it matter either way? He made her happy, which was more than Rex did, or ever had.

Ava smiled sadly as she remembered her dad's words after she first met Rex, before she'd even acknowledged to herself the true motive behind choosing him. She realised now she had simply latched onto the mediocre interest he had shown in her, then clung on for dear life, ignoring all the red flags. Heartbreak and grief had obscured her vision, skewed her judgement and made her do stupid things.

'He's a man of few words but I think your mum would have liked him. You're due some good luck, my darling girl.'

She had agreed wholeheartedly; she really did deserve it, after the tragedy of her mum's demise and then the disaster that was Blake. She thought her dad had deserved good luck too but look how that turned out. Now she was virtually alone, and her life was even more of a mess than it had been before. The adage was true; money couldn't buy you happiness, especially not when it came in the form of an inheritance following her loving parents' deaths. She was perpetually perplexed as to why she had been served so much undue misery in her lifetime.

A vibration jolted her out of her maudlin reverie. The sharp text was a variation on a theme, flashing above a couple of missed call notifications. Ava stared at the phone she had left on the island, as though petrified a hologram of the message's sender was about to appear right in front of her. She closed her tired eyes against the prickling tears threatening to pierce and rubbed her temples to ease the tightness that always accompanied contact from her husband. She knew how much he hated waiting for a reply from her, from anyone. There'd be hell to pay later.

She deliberated whether to call or text him back. He'd warned her about calling him at work, but he'd phoned her twice so it must be urgent. Composing herself, she opted to ring.

'Where the fuck were you?' he asked immediately, as

though he'd been staring at his mobile, waiting to pounce upon it the instant her name appeared, like a hunter would its prey.

Caught off-guard, she began to stammer a reply, 'I... I...'

'Never mind,' he said, cutting her off. 'I need you to bring me my Armani shirt. Come to the showroom. Text me when you're outside and I'll come out to the car.'

'Now? But... but why? It's already teatime.' She regretted the words the instant they left her mouth. It wasn't her place to question him.

She heard him huff out a heavy sigh. 'What are you – the speaking clock? I don't have time for your dopey, bullshit questions, Ava. Yes, now. I've got to go out again tonight. Hurry the fuck up.' He hung up.

She dithered for a moment, phone clasped in her right hand and fingers clenched into a fist in her left. Squeezing her eyes shut she suddenly threw back her head, gritted her teeth and squealed from the depths of her stomach, into the empty space of her showroom-worthy kitchen. Then she opened her eyes, plucked her car keys from their home on the hook, and did as she was told.

CHAPTER TWO

REX

REX FLICKED his wrist and his mobile clattered noisily onto his immaculate desk, empty except for a computer and a phone. Streamlined, just the way he liked it.

'Fucking dopey bitch of a wife.'

He sat back, drumming his manicured fingertips onto the padded arms of his ergonomic chair, resisting the urge to stand up and punch something, silently praising himself for his restraint. There were customers in the showroom, and he needed to remain composed, projecting the 'impressive sales manager in the corner glass office' persona. But he was wound right up. His jaw tightened and his heart pounded, his internal warning bell signalling trouble. Ava always made him feel this way and it usually took one thing to calm him down. God, he needed to see Poppy.

If his hair hadn't been full of products and styled just so, he would have run his hand through it in exasperation, but he settled for propelling himself out of his chair and bouncing on the balls of his expensively shod feet instead, like a boxer, trying to out-hop his annoyance. It was ironic that Ava had driven him to using his fists for anything but sportsmanlike pursuits. What the hell was she doing questioning him over a simple request? It wasn't as if she had anything more important to do than bring him his shirt, or anything else he needed, whenever he needed it. Certainly not that shitty little tutoring job she did for pin money even though she had more than enough in the bank. What a waste of goddamn time.

He strode to the buffed glass door and yanked it open, hoping to catch the attention of the giggly dolly bird on the service reception; he felt like a proper drink but would have to settle for a flavoured Nespresso from the coffee machine. He tutted when he saw she was with a customer and deliberated getting it himself, just for something to do, then thought better of it; he'd wait for her to finish. And where was Jason with that fucking Vantage update? Smoothing his silk tie against his starched black shirt, he sat back down and stilled his chair, staring out towards his staff and his showroom, but not really seeing anything at all. His brain was spluttering dangerously.

He thought back to when he first got himself entangled with his dopey fucking bitch of a wife nearly four years ago. Entangled being the operative word – she fell for him, literally, and ended up clumsily contorted on the floor at a party that Rex absolutely did not want to be at, almost dragging him down with her. Rex wryly observed that she had been dragging him down ever since and congratulated himself on being able to see the humour in a shit situation. He had guessed she was that type immediately – a leech – but she was attractive, he supposed, in an obvious way. She was also profusely apologetic in her tipsy state, all smoky eyes, fishnet tights and inviting cleavage, albeit smaller than he preferred. He had been forced to act in a gentlemanly manner, as his mother had always taught him to, so they had chatted awkwardly for a bit, and she had flirted and stayed leaning against him in a suggestive, helpless way for much longer than was necessary, whilst others around them came and went. He had watched the others with envy, desperate to extricate himself yet show himself to be honourable at the same time. After all, appearances were everything. He later suspected she had orchestrated the whole thing. Before he knew it, she had wangled her way into his life, and he found it easier to just keep seeing her amongst his regular rotation of hook-ups. Plus, it made his mum happy to see him appear to be settled with a 'nice' girl.

His runaway train of thought was derailed by Jason striding purposefully towards his office, sales ticket flapping and white teeth stretching into his dimples.

'Hit me, Jasey,' Rex instructed as his top minion stuck his head through the doorway.

'Second test drive this week,' confirmed Jason, cocking his fingers and 'shooting' his boss.

'Good lad.' Rex returned the gesture, their playful routine down pat for his best sales-target hitter, his own role cast as the cool boss. Jason would convert that test drive into a sale, and it'd mean a nice little bonus all round. Not that it'd make that much difference, mind you. Only getting his hands on the rest of Ava's huge inheritance, and keeping the fancy house in the process, would give him the life he really wanted. Fucking hell, she really was plaguing him today – all his thoughts kept boomeranging back to her!

As he watched Jason carefully reverse the Aston Martin from its spotlit pride of place, he silently fumed, giving his brain permission to rake back over his spousal misfortune and the sorry sequence of events that led to the pathetic proposal. It wouldn't have happened if it weren't for her goddamn father getting goddamn cancer. Six months from diagnosis to death. Ava had been utterly broken and he had been stuck in an impossible, emotional bear trap. He had grown more resentful by the day whilst Ava pawed at him like an abandoned puppy, desperate for attention and affection, while his mother pecked at him about settling down properly too. He was sure Ava could sense his desperation to withdraw from her, yet she seemed to relish the challenge of trying to regain his interest, not realising that she never really had it to begin with.

Her proposal had caught him unawares and he heard himself agree to it while imagining his mum's elation to the news – a misguided, impulsive reaction he had regretted every day since. Once they were married, Ava became even needier. She lost even more weight until her hip bones jutted out and her best feature – her face – lost its youthful dewiness and became papery and gaunt. She stopped instigating sex after he refused to even entertain the idea of children (not that he really wanted her, but he usually enjoyed banging her roughly from behind, pretending she was someone, anyone else). She was a mess!

But Poppy was different. Poppy was nubile and immaculate and effervescent, always bubbly and upbeat. Poppy had never accused him of secret phone calls, or meetings, or attempted to lay sly little traps to catch him out. She was nothing like Ava. With Poppy he was his true self, his best self – powerful and revered and completely in control. They had found each other again after all these years and all he had to do now was solve one major problem and life would be great. Successful, solvent and great.

His phone pinged with a notification: Poppy had posted a new photo. He cast a cursory glance around the showroom, moved his phone below his desk, opened the Facebook app and was greeted with the sexiest image yet – Poppy in a black, low-cut, cropped sequinned top, all Bambi eyes and glossy pout. He felt his dick twitch and opened their long message thread, typing what he felt.

Simply stunning. xxx

He waited a few moments for a reply, imagining her seductively biting her lip as she read his compliment, but none came. He knew she was either playing coy or deliberately making him sweat, turning him on. He *was* sweating; she was like a drug, and he needed a fix, quickly. He also needed to extricate himself from his marriage sooner rather than later. It was time to finesse his escape plan.

CHAPTER THREE

EADIE

EADIE WAVED off the make-up girl once she had finished applying her liquid eyeliner and surveyed her reflection. She was pleased with what she saw in the illuminated dressing-room mirror and felt a little bubble of happiness wriggle upwards inside her, feeling an almost physical pop as she held her phone aloft to take a selfie. Immaculate make-up, a professional blow-dry and a tight designer dress which held her ample curves in place perfectly... this was a moment to remember.

Eadie pressed her thumb to the screen a few times, taking shots whilst fractionally changing her expressions and angles of the camera – everyone knew the perfect selfie was at least a 10:1 ratio. With her porcelain complexion and stunning features, she was practised in the art of capturing her very best angle but the narcissist in her enjoyed the process.

A few minutes later, she caught sight of someone watching her while allowing the make-up girl to apply a final dusting of powder to her already immaculate T-zone and resisted the urge to roll her heavily false-lashed green eyes. As a plus-sized model and Instagram influencer she was always getting pestered, mostly by men. This man looked as though he was about to enter the room but then seemed to change his mind and carried on down the hallway. A moment later he doubled back and leaned against the doorframe, shoulders hunched and hands shoved into his pockets.

'Hello,' he said simply, dimples visible in a face that seemed to smile as a default setting. He extracted a hand and pointed at himself. 'Ethan.'

'Hello,' Eadie echoed after a pause before blotting her blood-red lips on the tissue the make-up girl was holding. The air was charged with something indecipherable; Eadie was surprised by how great-looking he was but absolutely did not want to give him any encouragement whatsoever. He looked like a 'good boy' and good boys served no purpose for her.

'All ready for the show?' he asked, nodding in the general direction of the studio.

'Err... clearly,' she replied, wearing a wry expression.

'Right.' Ethan smirked, looking down at the floor before meeting Eadie's beautiful, black-rimmed eyes in the mirror. 'Are you planning on sticking around afterwards?'

Eadie pursed her lips and thought about her answer to a question so obviously laden with a deeper meaning. Despite her misgivings about good boys in general, she felt strangely flattered and amused by him.

'Depends on whether I win or not,' she answered.

'Cool.' He nodded. 'I might see you later then,' he said, giving her a cheery wave before backing into the corridor behind him.

'If you don't want him, I'll have him,' said the make-up girl, staring after Ethan.

Eadie did roll her eyes at that.

———

Three hours later, trembling violently, she stared at the producers – had they really won? The show's titles were still running on the giant screen in the corner of the studio and her three teammates' reactions ranged from giddy to shell-shocked.

'Oh my God, oh my God!' middle-aged Clifford from Ireland repeated. Glamour puss Mirelle from Worcester was making a low squealing sound through gritted teeth, fists clenched. Gorgeous Ethan from Leeds was still punching the air forcefully, gleefully.

The producers were talking at her, but the sound didn't carry properly. Besides, she was double checking the maths in her head: £500,000 divided by four was indeed £125,000 each! Added to her healthy savings pot – sponsored posts paid pretty well these days – this extra jackpot meant she could finally launch her Eadie Lee product line.

Back in the green room the four winners clustered together in a clumsy group hug, overawed and overexcited, still.

'I can't believe it. I just can't believe it...' Clifford was like a stuck record of winner clichés. Mirelle had calmed down slightly and now broke out of their celebratory circle to rifle through her bag for her phone, leaving the room to make a call. Ethan breathed out heavily, ran his hand through his glossy chestnut hair and smiled cheekily at Eadie.

'Fancy a drink?' he asked. 'I'm buying.'

Clifford and Mirelle declined to join them – Clifford was eager to make his triumphant return to his wife and children in Ireland, and Mirelle tottered off on her sky-high heels, proudly proclaiming she now had a 'hot date' lined up for the night – so Eadie and Ethan headed off to a nearby 'trendy' London establishment by themselves. They stood in the jam-packed bar against a tall, sculptured table holding brightly coloured, bubble-gum foamy cocktails that Eadie had chosen by stabbing randomly at one of the images in the twelve page artfully illustrated drinks menu.

'Cheers, winner,' Ethan toasted, clinking Eadie's glass then holding her gaze as they took their first delicious sips in unison, arms entwined like newlyweds. Whatever they had chosen to drink would have tasted wonderful given the fact that they were both considerably richer than they had been a few hours previously.

Eadie marvelled at how strange and unexpected occurrences can change people's personalities immediately – giddy was definitely not her default setting and Ethan was definitely not her type – and she felt another lovely bubble of happiness begin to wriggle inside her.

'Cheers yourself.' She laughed, a high-pitched tinkle, the sound taking her by surprise.

'So what made you want to go on the show?' he asked.

'Exposure and money,' she said honestly.

He nodded, raising his brows and pulling the corners of his mouth down. 'Me too. I'm an actor slash model,' he said, making a karate chop gesture on the word slash. 'But times are hard. Or they were, anyway. Better now, though. In fact, my mate Ryder bet me I wouldn't apply to go on a game show, so I did. Won a tenner from that bet too. So, what are you going to do with the money?'

'Plastic surgery,' she said.

He almost choked on his drink. 'Why? I mean, look at you.' He gestured up and down her curvy frame, like he was a magician showing off his assistant.

'Futureproofing,' she said, taking a sip of her drink, enjoying his reaction. 'I'm joking,' she admitted as his expression remained incredulous. 'I want to create my own make-up and haircare range, and now I've got the capital to make a start. What about you – what are you going to do with the money?'

He ran his free hand through his hair and scrunched his face up in thought. 'Well, I could be sensible...'

'Are you prone to sensible behaviour?' asked Eadie.

He laughed and put his hand in his pocket. 'How do I answer that? If I say yes I'm boring, but if I say no I'm risky.'

Eadie took another sip of her drink, licked the foam off her top lip and stared him right in the eyes. 'Risky turns me on.'

'Shall we risk another drink then?' he asked, winking.

———

By dawn, Eadie was enjoying a delicious dream – she had won the grand prize on the UK's most popular game show followed by copious, insanely expensive cocktails and a night of surprisingly adventurous sex with a hot guy called Ethan in the nearest, fanciest hotel they could find to stumble into at 2am.

In her dream, Ethan had effusively declared, 'Sod the expense, I'm a fucking winner!' The dream was so realistic she could still feel the hot guy's warm, physical form pressed against her in the comfiest bed she had ever slept in. She felt as though she was lying on a giant marshmallow and strangely, she could also feel the sensation of soft lips against her neck...

Eadie slowly peeled her eyes open and clocked the fancy, oversized chandelier at the same moment as her hangover kicked her ruthlessly in the forehead. She groaned and the hot guy misread it as encouragement and nestled in closer.

'What the fuck?' screeched Eadie, pushing against Ethan with all her strength and holding him, literally, at arm's length. She had one eye screwed shut, but she recognised him as the hot guy from her dream.

'Hey, beautiful.' He smiled, seemingly unfazed by her outburst, or the sight of her first thing in the morning after a night of heavy drinking. He appraised her as though she was even more striking than she had been the night before, as if her smudged make-up, bruised red lips and tousled black hair gave her a sultry film-star look rather than a dishevelled air. She squinted back at him, calculating how quickly she could get him out of the room, her sight, her life.

Why was he even here? She never normally allowed them to stay over. There had never been anyone she had wanted to share her bed with for more than a few kinky hours, winnings or no winnings. He obviously mistook her frozen stare for a classic hangover daze and moved towards her again, but she nimbly slipped from the bed, reaching deftly for her phone, her clutch bag and the emerald-green sequinned midi dress she had been wearing the night before, before heading to the en-suite bathroom, slamming and locking the door behind her.

'Hey babe, you okay?' he shouted from the bed.

Babe? she mouthed to her reflection, screwing up her face in disgust. No, this was not going any further, hot guy or not. Resisting the urge to check all her notifications, as she usually did first thing, she clicked on her photo app and saw the evidence of their wild celebration. She scrolled through image after image after image of the two of them, of blurry cocktails, of fingertips covering the camera lens, of naked flesh. Her memory knitted fragments together, slowly filling in the blanks between the pictures on her phone, until she remembered it all: meeting Ethan before the show, their big win, their salacious night together celebrating their big win, Ethan footing the bill for this crazily extravagant hotel despite having already booked their own respective rooms elsewhere...

Eadie sat down on the closed toilet lid and took a moment to appreciate the luxury bathroom, relishing the notion that luxury bathrooms would feature more often in her future after her good fortune the day before, hopefully with a range of hot men. Choosing to stay, she showered at a leisurely pace using the sublime-smelling toiletries, reapplied her make-up using the miniatures she always kept in her bag, and blow-dried her bobbed hair, fully expecting Ethan to have gone by the time she emerged. Before posting her daily selfie online she felt compelled to check again. Smiling to herself, she closed her clutch bag. It was still in there – a cheque for £125,000.

Back in the room, she was surprised to find Ethan snoring gently in the bed. She looked at him objectively for a few moments before sighing, slipping on her heels, collecting her jewellery, and leaving the room without a second thought. She had things to do and money to spend and this particular hot man did not feature in her plans. Not today, anyway.

CHAPTER FOUR

ETHAN

Ethan tapped his foot impatiently on the bank's blue carpet tile, desperate to tuck all his money up for the foreseeable. His immediate money troubles were sorted thanks to the handsome cheque he clutched in his hand; he was afraid to let go of it on the off chance it might get plucked from his pocket or fall unseen from his wallet before he had the chance to deposit it safely.

His phone vibrated in his back pocket as he shuffled forward in the queue for the lone cashier. Although he wished it signalled a text from Eadie, he didn't need to check it to know that Ali had messaged again. Despite his mild irritation at Ali's frequent communications, he smiled to himself – his once-upon-a-time foster brother was always looking out for him. Ethan genuinely wanted to help him, to fund a trip back to the UK like he had promised, but he now realised he needed to be realistic too. Yes, £125,000 was a massive amount but once he'd paid Ryder back and helped his dad out with those final reminders, as well as whisked Eadie off on the all-inclusive holiday he was going to surprise her with, there wouldn't be that much left for a few little flutters, never mind plane tickets. He felt a lurch of positivity – a windfall and a new woman in the same week – followed swiftly by the familiar itch he was so incredibly desperate to scratch. Perhaps Ali was right to be concerned.

They had met as children when Ethan was six and Ali was a shy, skinny eight-year-old who had been fostered by Ethan's parents, Bruce and Pam, when Ali's own parents had been killed in a terrible traffic collision. Ali, unable to speak much English, and mired in grief and confusion, hardly uttered a syllable for weeks. Ethan felt immediately protective of him and adopted his foster brother role with heartfelt responsibility. All the friendly gestures and stilted attempts at communication helped keep Ethan occupied too, especially in the following months when his mum and dad's interminable cycle of arguments and silent treatments seemed to increase dramatically.

'Next please,' called the harassed-looking cashier from behind the fibreglass window. Her corporate uniform gave Ethan air hostess vibes and his brain created an instant connection to the holiday he'd been daydreaming of. He imagined an exotic tableau – him and a bikini-clad Eadie in an Indonesian infinity pool, sipping cocktails which tasted even better than their celebratory drinks after their big win. God, she was something else...

'Next!' repeated the cashier impatiently, interrupting Ethan's sweet reverie.

'Sorry,' said Ethan, stepping towards her and sliding his cheque through the arched gap. 'Paying in, please.'

The bespectacled cashier – Linda, according to her name badge – looked at the cheque, asked Ethan to insert his debit card and type in his PIN, then turned her beady eyes on him, her expression curious.

'Do I recognise you?' she asked, impatience seemingly dissipated.

'You might. I'm an actor, I've been in a couple of adverts and stuff on the telly,' replied Ethan, always thrilled to meet anyone who had not only seen but remembered his work.

'No, I've seen you in something recently, ooh, what was it?' she asked, taking off her glasses and letting them hang on their chain around her neck. She clicked her fingers. 'It was that teatime game show, wasn't it? I watch it every day. You won, didn't you? Well, I suppose that's what this is,' she said, gesturing to the cheque.

'I certainly did, and it certainly is.' Ethan beamed at her.

'Now, I need to ask this. Would you like to book an appointment with one of our investment advisors, Mr Harrison?'

'Oh. Do I need to?' Ethan replied, his head still full of curvy Eadie in a teeny bikini somewhere tropical.

'We always suggest the option with a deposit of this size. We offer a range of investment possibilities. They help keep your money safe from temptation.'

'Temptation?' he asked.

'Oh yes,' she said, suddenly serious. 'I saw a programme once about lottery losers – jackpot winners who end up blowing the lot! You wouldn't want that, would you?' She leaned forward and raised her brows, regarding him through the glass.

Ethan paused for a moment, an internal battle already secretly raging – his devil voice vying with his angel voice. Linda patiently waited for a response, much more patiently than she had dealt with the previous customers just minutes before, unaware of the chain reaction she had set in motion inside Ethan.

Ethan stared back whilst an almost physical ache began within him. He knew it was futile to fight it; the devil voice had already won.

'No thank you, Linda,' Ethan answered a few seconds later,

confidently, excitedly. 'I've already got an investment plan prepared. Actually, can I withdraw £5,000 back in cash?'

'Oh.' Linda slid her glasses back on and pursed her lips, clearly disappointed that Ethan had failed the temptation test. 'You'll have to wait until the cheque clears,' she said, tapping the keyboard before opening the deposit drawer beneath the counter and stowing the cheque inside. 'You currently have a little over £300 in your account. Do you want to withdraw that?'

'£300? Yes please, Linda,' replied Ethan, the ache morphing into a familiar flutter of excitement.

'As you wish, sir. Right then, your cheque has been deposited for you and here's your £300.' She counted out the notes. 'Don't spend it all at once!' she warned with a tight smile.

Ethan grinned broadly back. 'I'll try not to,' he lied.

CHAPTER FIVE

ALI

ALI MOVED his old laptop aside, leaned down and reached for the battered cardboard box under his bed. He took out a tatty photograph and unfolded it. Its creases scarred his own image and he stared into its memory, cocooned in time like a precious, protected, unearthed fossil. Christmas morning, 1991. The first Christmas after his parents' accident. He hadn't been a practising Christian, having been raised Muslim, but Bruce and Pam didn't care; neither were they really. They did care that he was treated as part of the family though – another son – and much to Ali's delight, there were presents under the tree for him too. He felt as though his eyes were popping out on stalks, like the cartoon characters he and Ethan watched on Saturday mornings. He had smiled so wide he felt his cheeks ache as an emotional Bruce crystallised their infectious joy on a disposable Kodak camera. Ethan always said that was the best Christmas ever. It was the last Christmas they celebrated before everything fell apart. Ali thought he could probably sketch his expression in the photo freehand, if he had been an artist, so imprinted on his brain it was. He would title the sketch *Purest Happiness* and sign his name to attest to its authenticity.

But that was then. He needed to think about now, about Ava. Ever since those first few tutoring sessions she stammered throughout, whilst desperately trying to remain professional, he knew they had connected on a deeper level. After three months of daily hour-long lessons, sometimes two, he finally felt as though they had gained each other's trust. He could tell by the way her blinking had slowed and her blushes had bloomed across her cheeks and down her bruised neck that her attraction to him was growing by the day.

He had initially stumbled across an online forum talking about English teaching sites during another long, boring, lonely shift in his uncle's clothing store. One of the threads discussed how online teachers were usually shy, introverted types looking for more than just a way to give back. The fact that the sites paid so little per hour also suggested that the tutors weren't in it for the money. Ali thought it was worth a try. He couldn't bear the loneliness and hopelessness much longer. He needed an escape.

Ramzi, his wayward older cousin, had taught him how to find and unlock concealed back doors behind paywalls years ago, and although Ali hadn't done it for a while, he managed to hack into the tutoring registration system quickly and easily enough. He created a basic profile and awarded himself plenty of free minutes. Within a week he met Ava. She was softly spoken and surprisingly sweet. And she lived in the UK city that housed his happiest memories. Ali considered it fate.

Prior to that, he and Ethan had found each other again online too. Finally setting eyes on his foster brother's familiar yet aged face, albeit through a cracked screen, had brought Ali immense joy and marked the second happiest day of his life, after that childhood Christmas. Ali looked at his laptop. It was his lifeline – first to Ethan and now to Ava – and as outdated as it now was, beggars couldn't be choosers.

He sighed as he gazed around the narrow, cell-like bedroom he'd slept in since he was ten, with its small, single-glazed, draughty window, single bed pushed against the wall and makeshift desk. An Islamic tapestry wall hanging gave the room its only colour and the remaining floor space was the size of a prayer mat. He hadn't spoken to Ethan in a couple of weeks, and he was craving the sound of his foster brother's voice and the sight of his face, always with a ready smile. But when they did talk again, Ali didn't want to hear any more about Eadie. Ethan had first told him about his new girlfriend in an excited babble during their last Skype call. Ali had listened with a sinking heart.

'She's a stunning free spirit, a sexy feminist!' stated Ethan, seemingly in awe of this woman who was no doubt about to trample all over his trusting heart, just as Ethan's mother had done to his father soon after Ali was fostered into their family. Pam finally admitted to having a long-term affair with Ken, their neighbour, a year after Ali arrived. She left them all, just like that, without an apology or backward glance. Her selfish, wicked choice had resulted in social services swooping in, taking one look at how broken Bruce was and yanking Ali away from his new home and family.

That day was forever seared onto Ali's brain. In broken English, he had begged and begged Bruce, and the social workers, to let him stay, tears coursing down his harrowed young face, but Bruce seemed vacant; unable to see or comprehend Ali's anguish because his own was so great. That was the day Ali realised certain types of women broke homes to satisfy their own selfish, lustful desires. Listening between the lines of Ethan's effusive descriptions, Eadie Lee sounded exactly the same type of woman as Pam Harrison.

'She's so gorgeous, bro, I'm going to buy you that plane ticket and you can come here and meet her. I just need to pay a few debts first.' Ali had thought Ethan's speech had seemed slurred, and that druggie son-of-a-bitch so-called friend-slash-wingman Ryder was loitering in the background, which immediately rang alarm bells; Ali knew how susceptible his foster brother was to any bad influence, especially when he was drunk. It sounded as though he was already as addicted to Eadie as he was to alcohol and gambling. Ali had tried his best not to scowl and worry throughout the call despite knowing all too well that after Ethan's giddy highs always came the devastating lows.

Now, he laid the photograph carefully back inside his box of memories, lingering over his beloved artefact for a moment before pushing the box back under his single bed. Every time he thought about the tragedy of his parents' deaths, then being cruelly wrenched away from Bruce and Pam and Ethan, he felt like screaming. He had lost two loving families within one year. Orphaned twice over. That was something he and Ava had in common – the aching desire for a real family. Despite willing it not to, Ali's memory dredged up the turn his life had taken after leaving Bruce and Pam. Nobody wanted to adopt a practically mute orphan of Saudi Arabian descent. Nobody wanted to foster him either, so he spent the next few months – the worst of his life – amongst volatile groups of other foster kids or shut inside boxy rooms during respite stays. Not necessarily alone depending on the perverted predilections of the foster parents. He still couldn't recall that time of his life without the contents of his stomach threatening to make a reappearance. Eventually, an estranged uncle on his father's side of the family was located and he was dispatched back 'home' to Saudi Arabia. But he wasn't any happier now than he was then. Daydreaming about returning to the UK, to the kind of life he had lived with his parents for a while, or with Bruce, Pam and Ethan during that halcyon year, was all that got him through.

So, this relationship between Ethan and Eadie needed to be nipped in the bud. Ali desperately wanted to help Ethan see that he should be with someone who truly deserved him, and to set him on the straight and narrow once and for all. No more rejection-sabotage cycle. Ethan needed an intervention. Although he had always been susceptible to temptations in all its forms, he didn't deserve another trauma at the hands of a harlot.

Despite promising him a plane ticket, Ali suspected that Ethan's financial situation was as dire as his own. The few debts he talked about probably ran into the tens of thousands and he doubted his recent game-show winnings would last very long. It wasn't his fault though; he was an addict, and Ali needed to overcome his own obstacles and get to Leeds as soon as possible to save him.

CHAPTER SIX

AVA

Ava flittered around her kitchen, unsettled and anxious. Rex was on his way home – more or less on time for once – yet she hadn't even started making his tea or ironed his shirt for the next day. How was she supposed to concentrate on the mundane when her world had been thrown completely off-kilter that very afternoon? She berated herself again for her stupidity; leaving the house was often a mistake.

She tugged on her bottom lip repeatedly, staring at nothing, as she replayed the scene for what felt like the thousandth time. She had sensed him before she had seen him. The atmosphere had somehow shifted, a whisper on the wind sharing a warning. A family of three, picture perfect, oblivious to everything beyond their own bubble. Two parents swinging a child between them, all three laughing the laugh of the privileged, the lucky, the smug. It should have been her. It should have been them – her and him. She heard a guttural sob, a weird, wounded sound, and was shocked to realise it was coming from her own mouth. A mouth that had kissed him many, many times, everywhere. A mouth that had readily agreed to everything he had falsely proposed.

'Are you okay, dear?' an old woman with tight grey curls had asked, stretching her walking stick towards Ava, presumably as a substitute comforting arm, wary of getting too close to the emotional woman in her way on the town-centre pavement.

Ava didn't acknowledge the enquiry and the old woman tutted and muttered and tottered off, jabbing her walking stick onto the ground. Ava followed in her wake, for just a few steps, then concealed herself against the outer wall of a corner building, an ideal vantage-point to watch surreptitiously from.

Her heart had beat a hard, fast, loud rhythm as she followed the family's progress across the pedestrianised town square. She watched as the child broke free of her mother and father's hands to bounce forward, like Tigger, entranced by the flutter of a butterfly. Ava watched as the little girl's parents smiled indulgently, as entranced by their daughter as she was by the pretty insect. They all looked so disgustingly happy, so diametrically opposite to Ava that she shook fiercely with the injustice of it, the karmic unfairness of it. Where was her happy ending? Where was her compensation for all the suffering she had endured?

He had turned his head in her direction but looked right through her, as if she was invisible, irrelevant, before turning his attention back to his adorable daughter. That moment had hurt Ava more than Rex's most severe beating.

She forced herself to look away, to spin around and lean against the wall, head back and eyes screwed tight against the saccharine scene she had just witnessed, fists clenched tightly at her sides.

'Don't think about it, don't think about it...' she chanted to herself, as if that would stop the memories coming, but came they did, in unfiltered Technicolour.

She had been in her third year at the University of Leeds when she met Professor Blake Harding. He swooped her up, literally, to save her from falling down the steps in her drunken haste to leave the club it had been a mistake to go to. Despite her shock at being manhandled, she felt small and safe in his strong arms right there outside Majestyk.

'Nearly a goner,' he had said with a laugh, his too-close smile making his kind brown eyes crinkle in the corners.

Gently, he set her down and steadied her on the pavement before stepping back, one palm outstretched in the universal gesture of peace. He ran his other hand through his wavy brown hair.

'I'm Blake,' he said, moving his palm to his chest. She felt his embarrassment, his worry that he had stepped out of line, and softened her expression in accordance with his rueful one.

'Ava,' she said, mirroring his gesture, offering him a smile.

Their mutual attraction crackled between them, and Ava's romantic heart knew then and there that he was special. She had always believed in love at first sight, and now it was happening.

Spontaneously, crazily, on an alcopop high, she had launched herself at him, the way you see at airports or YouTube videos of returning soldiers, kissing him with wild, reckless abandon. Taken aback at first, he soon returned her passion without hesitation, his fingers twisted into her long tendrils of hair, his mouth suctioned on hers.

When they finally parted lips, he boldly asked her, 'Your place or mine?'

'Yours,' she said, giggling, all thoughts of her friends in the club overridden by her instant lust for the gorgeous stranger she already felt she could trust implicitly.

Blake took her hand, flagged down a taxi and took her to his house; a grown-up semi near Roundhay Park.

Lying together after their slow and sensual sex, he had gazed at her appreciatively. 'You're the most beautiful creature I have ever laid eyes on,' he had declared, softly stroking her face. That was the way she remembered it, anyway.

In the weeks that followed they saw each other as much as his teaching schedule would allow. Already deeply infatuated, Ava was more than happy to bunk off lectures in favour of one-to-one tuition of a different kind in Professor Harding's bed, or on his sofa, or in the shower, but the fact that she couldn't see him as much as she wanted to only added to the thrill of their illicit relationship. At his request, being newly employed at the university, she told absolutely nobody about their love affair, naively believing he wanted to keep her all to himself rather than acknowledging he had crossed a professional boundary. However, after a few months of what she considered sheer bliss, there came a fly in the ointment, or rather, a bun in the oven.

'I'm late,' Ava told him one evening.

'Late?' he said, regarding her with confusion at first.

'Late,' Ava repeated, pressing her lips together and nodding, waiting to see how he would react. Hoping it would be the way she wanted him to react. Nearly a minute passed before he spoke.

'Right.' Blake rubbed his forehead. 'Have you taken a test?'

'Not yet, but I think I am.' She grabbed his hand and pressed it to her flat belly, smiling beatifically at him. He yanked it back as though scalded, and Ava's smile disappeared.

'What's wrong?' she asked, her voice small.

'It'd be quicker to answer what's right,' he said with a weary sigh.

'What do you mean? Aren't you happy? I'm happy!'

Blake closed his eyes and shook his head. 'I thought you were on the pill.'

Ava shrugged. 'I wasn't well a few weeks ago. It can't have worked properly.'

'Well, you need to take care of it if you are... pregnant.' He moved his hand to the side as though pushing the problem away.

'How can you say that?' she cried, her face pinched with pain at the coldness of his tone. 'You don't mean that!'

His eyes flashed with anger, and he jabbed his finger in front of her face. 'Yes, Ava, I fucking do mean that.'

She grabbed for his hand again, wanting to hold it, to anchor herself to him. He moved back, away from her. Dance steps gone wrong.

'But I want to have your baby,' she whispered. 'If I am pregnant.'

He gaped at her, incredulous. 'Have you done this on purpose? To trap me?'

'No! I promise I haven't, but we can make the best of it, can't we? We could live together.' She chewed her bottom lip. 'Maybe even get married.' She gestured at the house around them, a ready-made family home.

Blake chuckled cruelly, shaking his head. 'I don't think my wife would be too happy about that...'

And now, just this afternoon, she had seen him with his wife – no doubt another beautiful creature in his eyes – and the child they had created together. Why hadn't she been good enough, interesting enough, sexy enough for him to leave his wife for, even when she believed she was carrying his baby?

It turned out she hadn't been pregnant, after all, but he cut her off regardless. Severed her from his life like a diseased limb threatening to infect his whole body. Heartbroken, Ava had dropped out of university and gone back home, never daring to look for him on social media – he was one of the reasons she had steered clear of creating her own genuine profiles all these years. She couldn't have coped bearing witness to his life flourishing as her own faded further away from the one she had imagined for herself.

The key in the door roused her and she snapped into action as though a Stepford switch had been flicked. Rex always went straight upstairs to change out of his work suit, so she had a few minutes. Grabbing her compact mirror with shaking hands, she slicked on lip balm and swiped her fingertips underneath her eyes to erase the mascara smears. Next, she filled the kettle and hurriedly set two places at the island, not that she was the slightest bit hungry. Finally, she took the easy cook pasta, sauce and side salad out of the fridge and set them on the worktop just as Rex entered the kitchen. He wore jeans and a new blue cashmere jumper that matched his eyes. She was frequently surprised anew by his handsomeness – a beautiful outer package camouflaging the wretchedness within.

He didn't bother to greet her, instead pointedly surveying what he clearly assessed as her paltry attempts at an evening meal if his distasteful expression was anything to go by.

'I'm sorry,' she began, 'I felt poorly in town earlier, I only managed a quick shop in the express branch.'

He placed both hands on the edge of the island as he stared at her. His silences were always unnerving and usually a precursor to the opposite of silence.

'How was your day?' she attempted, brushing her hair back from her face with shaking fingers, jutting her chin out a fraction in a show of bravery she didn't feel, as she placed a pan of water on the induction hob and turned on the heat.

'All right, until now.' He didn't even blink.

'I'm sorry,' she repeated, pressing her lips together to prevent the pathetic excuses that threatened to dribble from her mouth.

He moved around the island and yanked her towards him. He gazed down at her, tenderly tracing her cheek with his thumb. Ava blinked rapidly, holding her breath. Suddenly, he grabbed her face in a pincer grasp, smiling tightly as the pan of water began to roil. 'You're still no nearer to winning Wife of the Year are you, Ava?' he asked through gritted teeth. 'If you think I'm eating whatever shit you're about to make, you are sorely mistaken. You can forget your fucking poor excuse for a meal because I'm going out to Barry's leaving do.' He punctuated his last three words with sharp squeezes of his fingers, clearly enjoying the fear and discomfort in her watery eyes.

Rex shoved her away from him and she banged her hip against the corner of the counter, the hand used to steady herself mere centimetres from the bubbling pan. Blinking back tears, Ava turned off the hob and the water quickly settled; she wished her inner turbulence would calm so easily. She listened to his heavy footsteps along the stone hallway floor as he headed out, not bothering to throw her any further scraps about where exactly he was going or who he was going with. She doubted he even knew anyone called Barry, but there was a way to find out.

As soon as his car had disappeared and the electric gates had closed, she raced to her office and logged onto Facebook. Her social media skills were strictly limited to light stalking using the anonymous account she had set up. She wasn't capable of checking Rex's private messages without knowing his password and he never left his phone unlocked or unattended so she couldn't check that either. She only used her desktop computer, and she always remembered to delete her history. She quickly searched for Rex's curated personal profile and found nothing new, so she clicked on the link to his dealership's page and scrolled through the posts. It was densely populated with close-up shots of very expensive car exteriors and interiors, so she had to scroll for a minute or two until she found a staff photo in honour of the dealership being nominated for an award. Many names were tagged, and surprisingly, Barry was one of them. She clicked on his profile and found a picture from earlier today of a bottle of champagne and a card with a brief caption thanking his workmates for his leaving gift.

Ava sat back. He was telling the truth this time then. She knew that although he hated most of his colleagues, who he assessed as slimy, stereotypical car salesmen, either of the upstart or tired old granddad variety, he hated the thought of his place in the hierarchy being usurped more. Losing even an iota of the power he needed to function, as essential as the air he breathed, was unthinkable for him. He had always implied he was of a far superior sales calibre than any of his team – anyone at all, in fact – and that he 'granted wishes' in his high-spec showroom, rather than smothered customers with prepared patter. He was a role model, the template on which they could all mould themselves, and he never missed an opportunity to show off his superiority, not even on a local night out.

He was excellent at his job though, she would give him that, especially with ladies of a certain age and status (and often men to Rex's disgust) who loved his good looks, charm offensive and disarming smile. She should know; she had fallen for that smile once too. More fool her and her bad judge of character.

Ava sighed, half relieved, half frustrated that she hadn't found any hard evidence of wrongdoing. Not that she was one to talk with the secret feelings she nurtured for Ali.

CHAPTER SEVEN

ALI

ALI SCOWLED at the text from Ramzi. He had been detained with suppliers, so he said, and needed Ali to work late and lock up. Ali fumed; this was becoming an almost daily occurrence. He gazed around the drab clothing shop that Ramzi and his father Ibrahim – Ali's uncle – owned and felt as though the shelves of traditional items such as hijabs, khimars, niqabs, burkas and abayas, and racks of long-sleeved shirts and blouses were equivalent to gates and bars penning him in. He wondered why his cousin insisted on keeping up the pretence of liaising with 'suppliers' when they barely sold any stock and hadn't bought any new clothing lines in years.

Ali had worked in the small shop since he was fourteen, more than half his life. Ramzi had made it clear to him that it was his duty, his debt to repay to Ibrahim for taking him in when he had returned to Saudi Arabia. It was also a noose around his neck, getting tighter and tighter with each passing day. Ibrahim, a widower, was now too old and ill to help out, and Ramzi seemed to have a packed calendar of personal and business meetings that Ali was never invited to attend. So he spent his days alone, except for the very occasional customer, knowing he was being used to babysit a shop that was probably a front for something illegal.

The only positive aspect of 'working' in the shop was all the time Ali had to pursue his own interests during his designated break times. They were supposed to be prayer breaks but Ali had long since begun to find certain aspects of Sharia law problematic, especially the value of prayers when none of his were ever answered. Instead, he chose to daydream, to continue his self-directed studies, or to speak to Ethan and Ava online.

During the rare evenings he didn't have to work late, Ali returned to his uncle's home, ate the meal that his female cousins and Ramzi's wife cooked for them all then retreated to his bedroom at sunset, choosing to remain there all night, re-reading his father's battered old medical textbooks that had survived all the same traumas he had. Despite now being thirty-five, it was still his dream to become a doctor one day, like his father. He knew how to save a life and how to take a life, in theory but not in practice. Although Sharia law dictated what one ought, in conscience, to do or to refrain from doing and thinking, Ali worked hard on preserving his own freedom of thought. He found it impossible to believe that Ibrahim and Ramzi had the same blood flowing through their veins as him and his father and often fantasised about taking Ramzi's life in various grotesque ways. He would enjoy spilling some of his polluted blood.

Occasionally, Ramzi visited Ali in his bedroom when he needed his help, paying no mind to the late hour. Just like last night. Barging in, he sat down on the end of his cousin's single bed and leant back against the wall, making himself comfortable.

'Will you do something for me?' He tapped his fingers on his widely parted knees, staring intently at Ali. It was always framed as a request, but Ali knew better than to refuse his moody, hot-tempered, dangerous relative.

Ali hitched his shoulders, carefully closing the medical textbook he had been reading for the hundredth time, using the sepia-tinted photo of himself and Ethan on Christmas day as his bookmark. Ramzi seemed even more wired than usual.

As a teenager, Ali had looked up to Ramzi, who was six years his senior, as a mentor of sorts, wanting to believe that his dubious tutelage was to benefit the failing family business, after scaring Ali into thinking they were about to lose the roof over their heads at any moment. Ramzi taught Ali how to hack and forced him to break into other shops to steal stock, occasionally dabbling in dealings the dark web had to offer, becoming more and more power hungry as the years went by. Ibrahim, unable to control his headstrong son as his health declined further, had taken his anger and despair out on Ali instead. The effect Ramzi had on everyone was toxic.

'I need you to deliver something for me.' Ramzi sniffed. 'To Bedram.'

Ali's lips parted. So that explained his fizzing aura; he should have guessed that Ramzi was caught in Bedram's web by now. Ali shook his head, disgusted. 'No, Ramzi, that I cannot do. I draw the line at becoming involved with him. I have heard rumours that he is involved in drug and child trafficking rings!'

Ramzi nodded, rubbing his bearded jaw. 'First of all, rumours are not proof. Second of all, I thought you might say that so I have brought something to persuade you.' He shoved his hand in his pocket and half brought out a wad of notes. Ali raised his brows, amazed. But he knew his cousin well enough by now; if he was offering this kind of rare reward, the risk was far too high.

'I said no.'

Ramzi scowled and stood, swiping Ali's textbook from his hands in one smooth movement.

'Maybe I can persuade you another way,' he said as he began slowly tearing the front cover off.

Ali looked on in horror, a strangled sound escaping from his lips. He made a grab for the book, but Ramzi held it aloft, laughing in the face of Ali's anguish. As he waved the book, taunting his cousin, the photograph dropped to the floor. They locked eyes for a split second then Ali bent down to snatch it up, but Ramzi shoved him back onto the bed. He threw the damaged textbook on the floor and plucked the photograph up, regarding it with a sneer.

'Look what it is, the precious memory of your time back in England.' He flicked the picture with his fingers. 'Do you still think you are ever going back there?' His laugh was callous. 'I have told you – get that idea out of your head. Your life is here now, working for me!'

He spat on the picture then ripped it right down the middle before throwing the two halves in the air. They landed on the bed and Ali scrambled for them. Ramzi hunched down towards Ali, grabbing his T-shirt in his fist, their faces two inches apart.

'You will deliver the package to Bedram by next week or I will damage more than a book and a photograph.' He slapped Ali hard across the face before wrenching the door open and striding out, shouting obscenities in his wake, not caring that his father, wife and sisters were all sleeping.

Ignoring his smarting cheek, Ali used his thin blanket to wipe Ramzi's spit from the torn pieces of the photograph then held them together, his tears blurring the image. Pressing them both against his chest, sorrow filled his entire being.

43

CHAPTER EIGHT

AVA

AFTER TOSSING and turning all night, Ava's ears pricked up at the sound of Rex's key in the door. It was 5am and he was just getting home from Barry's leaving do, apparently. Where had he been until this time? He was due at work at 9am. She heard his steps on the oak staircase and tensed, feigning sleep, waiting for him to enter the bedroom. Instead, he continued along the landing. A moment later he turned the shower on.

When the shower had stopped, Ava held her breath in the dark, listening to her husband padding back towards their bedroom. He used his phone torch to help navigate his way to their expensive superking bed, slid under the duvet as stealthily as an experienced thief, plugged his charger in and pushed his phone protectively underneath his pillow as he always did, guarding his secrets. Ava lay as still as a corpse in the morgue, aware of the physical and emotional space between them. She waited for his breathing to slow and become even and peaceful before finally allowing the tears to flow freely yet silently.

Ava's memory clicked its fingers and cruelly replayed a scene from their wedding day. She could vividly recall Rex's solemn expression as she stepped towards him down the West

Room's makeshift aisle in Leeds Civic Hall. Walking alone, her eyes were puffy, and her bottom lip had wobbled behind her veil while she desperately tried not to embarrass him by sobbing hysterically. He didn't like it when she cried in public. She had been hyper aware of the absence of her father by her side. Just when she had needed him the most, he had left her too.

Following her father's death six months earlier, Ava had clung onto Rex like a life raft. Yet she sensed he would rather float cowardly away from her, from their two-dimensional relationship, until she was a mere memory on the horizon of his life. She knew some people pushed those closest to them away whilst grieving, masochistically determined to cope with their rearranged reality alone, but not her – she wasn't strong enough for that.

As her groom's handsomely packaged form swam into focus through her watery vision, like a magic eye pattern revealing itself to her, she saw that his shoulders were stiff and he turned and lowered his head, as if in prayer. Was he nervous too? As she reached him, his head swung up suddenly, like a puppet being controlled by strings, without even acknowledging her. But she could see he was frowning. The frown remained, underscoring his insincere and hesitant tone throughout their vows. She saw it, she felt it, she heard it all, but she ignored it, choosing to convince herself it was because he hated public declarations of any kind. She received a chaste kiss on the cheek to cement their union. But he was so strong, so striking, so utterly anchored in her present that Ava, smitten and grateful, and determined not to lose two men she loved in the same year, had donned her blinkers and forcefully nudged the tight knot of foreboding down between her constant anxiety and raw, recent, endlessly replaying grief.

There had been no honeymoon either, no Maldives luxury or even English quaintness, revelling in their newly married joy.

The marriage had not been consummated for four days. In hindsight, Ava recognised Rex's reluctance, dressed up as concern over his car sales career aspirations and their then dire financial situation while she wrestled with tying up the frayed ends of her father's substantial estate, and wondered why she hadn't realised it sooner. It was true what they said: love really was blind. But she was heartbroken at the injustice of it. She loved him, despite everything, and she wished so desperately that he had shown her genuine affection throughout their marriage, instead of disdain and torment. She hated him for it, for the horrible things he had done and for the horrible man that he was. Most of all though, she hated herself for being consciously ignorant to his true self earlier in their relationship. Oh yes, she was culpable too, and in her darkest moments she often wondered if she had somehow helped create the monster she now considered him to be.

Ava, however, had reverted to everything she despised in a woman as her default reaction: needy, irrational and terrified of being alone, like a lone buoy in the ocean. Embarrassed to broach the topic with Rex's devoted mother, she struggled to understand the stranger she had married. The needier she got, the more Rex distanced himself from her, physically and emotionally, his own internal conflict flashing brightly, like an angry beacon, disguised in excuses and refusals. She knew she wasn't as interesting as she looked; she was underwhelming beneath the beautiful exterior because her outer shell had always been enough to get her what she wanted, initially at least. She was a prettily wrapped empty box, a university dropout, delivering disappointment before being quickly discarded. Keeping what she wanted had always been a problem.

She continued to weep for the years of heartbreak and heartache she had endured. First, the tragic death of her mum and the quicker than expected death of her dad, then Rex's refusal to entertain the idea of having children, or get a dog, which should have been a vibrant red flag in itself because what kind of person doesn't want a dog? Not the kind of person she ever thought she would end up married to. The discussions – if they could be called that – had caused ongoing difficulties until, finally, their marriage had warped into something every woman feared. How could she have let it all happen? Why didn't he love her like he was supposed to? Where had she gone so wrong?

The only thing that kept her going now was the thought of Ali. She frequently fantasised about him coming to Leeds, about funding his stay and sneaking out to be with him as often as she could. She was sure her dad would be happy she wanted to use some of her inheritance selfishly for a change, instead of Rex manipulating what she spent it on.

That thought alone was enough to stall her tears and bolster her mood. She slipped out of bed and while she washed and dressed quietly so as not to disturb Rex, she indulged in her usual daydream: Ali holding her, and kissing her, and helping her to escape her marriage. She felt sure that one day he would give her the courage she needed to leave Rex and they could be together properly.

CHAPTER NINE

ALI

July 2018

AVA LOOKED ESPECIALLY sad during their session today. Ali could see it in her eyes, although she put on a brave face. She always put on a brave face, even if that meant covering a black eye or another bruise. He wondered whether something terrible had happened to make her that way. Something bigger than just an unhappy, abusive marriage. He hadn't ever asked her those kinds of probing questions though. Just like he wasn't about to share the sorry story of his own life so far. Delicate details were only meant to be shared privately, with people you loved and trusted wholeheartedly. The only person in the world Ali trusted enough to hear his sordid history was Ethan. He was desperate to unburden himself to his foster brother, to explain what he had gone through since leaving the Harrisons' family home, to vent about the respite placements, to confess to the criminal acts that Ramzi had blackmailed him into doing when he was younger – and then older – but those types of talks were not for Skype screens, especially not with the likes of Ryder hovering in the background.

'Do you think you'll ever come to Leeds, when you finally visit the UK?' Ava asked, bringing Ali's focus back. She was getting more specific with her questions after enquiring about his 'life plan', as she put it, in previous sessions. He had told her of his dream to become a doctor one day and relayed his sadness that it was extremely unlikely to happen as he was tied to working in the family clothing business.

'I hope so,' said Ali. 'If I ever pass my IELTS exam and save enough money for the flight, I will certainly visit. I want very much to study in the UK one day before I get too old. But what is that saying? You are never old enough?'

Ava laughed. 'I think you mean "you are never too old" – and it's true! I'm going to help you get the qualification you need to study wherever you want. Leeds has a great university; I studied there myself for a while.'

'For a while?' he questioned. 'You did not complete your studies?'

Ava cast her gaze downwards, a blush of embarrassment, or maybe shame, colouring her usually pale complexion. After a moment she shook her head, pressing her lips together.

Sensing her discomfort, Ali was unsure whether to ask why not but Ava quickly posed another question of her own.

'Would you visit me if you were here, Ali? Hypothetically.'

Her boldness took him by surprise. He considered his response for a few seconds, shifting on his uncomfortable stool in the shop's empty storeroom.

'Yes. I think I would like that very much,' he confirmed, smiling.

She beamed back at him, tears shining in her eyes.

CHAPTER TEN

AVA

AVA WOKE IN A PANIC. She had been dreaming about her mum, her brain yet again attempting to fill in a few of the gaping blanks that remained, torturing her with questions she'd never have the answers to. How long did she suffer? Did she think of Ava in her dying moments? Would she still be alive if Kathleen had found her even minutes earlier?

Today was the anniversary of her death. Thirty years ago, Ava's world had exploded, and the aftershocks steadily dismantled the remaining debris of her life. Now, Ava automatically began the CBT techniques she had learned to steady her breathing, imagining the horrific images from her nightmare trapped within tightly knotted balloons being carried away on the breeze. Although she felt the hot tears streak down the side of her face, she forced herself to count the blessings she had. It didn't take long; there was only one as far as she was concerned. Ali.

Sitting up and swinging her long, skinny legs out of bed, she smeared her tears away with the heels of her hands, picked up her phone and checked the screen. Her throat swelled with more latent tears as she saw there was no message from Rex; he hadn't even said goodbye before he left for work this morning let alone remembered it was the anniversary of her mum's murder.

Her memory brandished a dog-eared scene of the day her dad had finally told her the truth about her mum's death, before the morphine rendered him practically comatose. Whenever she thought of it now, it was as if she was watching herself from afar sitting by his bedside, trying – and failing – to remain steadfastly strong. Even now, she winced at how unconvincing she had been.

'I need to tell you...' he had rasped, eyes closed against the pain, 'about your mum.'

Her eyes had widened, surprised at the mention of her from his dry lips, not daring to speak herself in case she interrupted whatever he was about to impart.

'He killed her,' he managed eventually, just as Ava feared she couldn't hold her breath for even a split second longer.

Ava's hand went to her mouth as a strange sound emerged. A funny feeling began fluttering inside her as though her thoughts had crawled rapidly around her brain, scuttling in the corners and foraging in the darkness for even a modicum of understanding. They found none. Someone killing her mum just wasn't possible. He must be delirious.

'What? Who, Dad?' she whispered, facing the craziness head-on, conscious of the time limit he was under.

More minutes passed and she briefly wondered if he had been talking in his sleep, not to her.

'Her fancy man...' he clarified, yellowish eyes springing open and locking onto hers ghoulishly as she stared dumbly back, trembling. It reminded her of a scene that had always terrified her in *An American Werewolf in London*. When she finally formed the thoughts required to ask him further questions, his eyes had already closed again, like a skeletal robot powering down, and he had fallen back into a deep sleep. She tried anyway.

'No, Dad, you're lying! Please tell me it's not true. You said she fell. This is cruel – it's the drugs talking!'

Ava shuddered now at the recollection, as she always did. She had stayed by his bedside alone for hours, chewing locks of her own hair, after trying to shake him awake again but failing miserably. Rex had been at work as usual. Staring at her father's gnarly knuckles, she remembered how he used to crack them before beginning his Sunday crossword, always reading out the clues to her younger self, pen poised over the paper. His now concave chest used to be her comfort, her castle wall, in the absence of her mum, absorbing all her upset over childish playground spats or teenaged broken hearts.

She stayed until the palliative nurses arrived for their final scheduled visit of the day, all the while trying to convince herself she had either misheard, or that her cancer-riddled dad was confusing nonsense with facts. If what he said was true, he had kept the truth from her for twenty-seven years, making her believe her recurring nightmares of blood-soaked quarry tiles and ripped stockings were fictitious imaginings rather than a repressed memory.

For the briefest, flickering, shameful moment she had wished him already dead for keeping the truth from her. And now her dad really had gone and all she was left with was tainted memories of her parents and their marriage which wasn't the ideal partnership she used to dream of emulating with her own husband. Instead, her whole life was infected with infidelity.

With a heavy heart, Ava left the comfort of her bed and got herself ready for her tutoring sessions. There was no question of cancelling them; she had reservations, students relying on her. And the alternative was rattling around in her soulless house alone all day, succumbing to the juggernaut of painful memories and flashbacks with no respite. No, she was determined to protect the tiny bit of joy she had in her life, and that meant powering through her grief, as she had been doing for years.

She thought back to her conversation with Ali yesterday, when he'd confirmed he would want to see her if he came to the UK. Although each time they spoke she willed their final seconds to suspend, they soon ran out and his face was nothing more than an imprint in her vision. She always closed her eyes against it, the space where he should be increasingly painful to bear.

Once showered, dressed and presentable, she scurried to her office, the need to see and speak to Ali again like a vice she couldn't kick. Her descent into dangerous territory had long since picked up speed, like one of Rex's fancy cars careering out of control. She felt constantly panicky, restless, susceptible to temptation. She hadn't felt dangerous emotions like these since being with Blake.

Fingers dancing over the keyboard, Ava quickly logged on to the tutoring site, navigated to the dashboard and stared in shock at the screen as she read the message from a moderator. A first and final warning that her and Ali's conversations were becoming too personal. It was against the rules for a tutor to disclose sensitive or personal information about themselves or respond to the same from a student. She'd naively never considered their sessions would be that closely monitored. Her cheeks flamed with fear and shame; they'd been caught out.

'Did you get the message too, from the moderator?' she asked, breathless with panic as soon as she saw Ali's face once her first session of the day was complete. She'd had to compartmentalise in order to get through it, all the while counting the minutes until she could see and speak to Ali.

'Yes,' he answered solemnly. 'But what else can we do but

comply? The moderators have warned us. They will not allow you to remain as my tutor if we break their rules again.'

She spoke quickly, damning the consequences. 'So, let's make this session count; it might be our last. I want to keep talking to you, Ali. I need to keep seeing you.'

'I cannot bear the thought of not speaking with you, *habibti*. I need to see you too,' he echoed.

Ava had an idea. It was the ultimate lightbulb moment, a metaphorical light shining brightly with hope and potential happiness. Having woken up suffocated in a fog of memories about her mum, she knew if she didn't say exactly what was on her mind before the fear took over, she would regret it forever. You only got one life.

'Quickly, tell me your number and I'll tell you mine and we'll talk on the phone every day instead.'

A pained expression crossed his face. 'I cannot afford the charges. The tutoring subscription is a much lower rate.'

'I'll call you. Tell me your number then log off and I will ring you straight away, okay?'

'But you are risking your job by asking me this now, while we are still online. Am I worth it, *habibti*?'

'Yes. You're worth it,' she replied straight away, gazing at him through the screen. A moment later, he relented. He voiced his number as she tapped the digits into her phone then, with a brief wave, he logged off.

She rang him immediately, hope fizzing inside her deliciously. Sod the tutoring. She didn't need it, not really; it had been a hobby to keep her occupied while she was lonely. Something she started after her mother-in-law randomly mentioned one of her writing group friends had taken it up 'on the side'. But Ava wasn't lonely anymore.

After seeing the moderator's warning, she instantly realised that seeing Ali on the tutoring site wasn't enough anyway. She was eager for his sweet, reassuring whisperings which made her feel intelligent and attractive again. Dare she say it: he made her feel *desired*. A montage of memories played in her mind of the little things she had told him, such as snippets of conversations she'd had with her other students, or the time she saw a man with his docile cat draped across his shoulder like a stole, or the friendly robin she often said hello to when she walked along the footpath behind her house. It had been wonderful to be able to share those moments of joy with someone again, because she certainly couldn't share them with her husband, and she didn't ever want it to stop.

'Come here,' she said urgently, swept away on a wave of heightened emotion. 'Come to Leeds. I'll pay for your flight. I'll pay for a hotel. We can be together properly, in person. Can you get some time off work? Will your uncle allow it?'

He was quiet for a few agonising moments. 'Are you sure that is what you want, Ava?'

She nodded fiercely against the phone. 'I'm sure. Surer than I've been about anything in a long, long, time. Say you'll at least think about it, promise me that,' she begged, eyes wide, cheeks flushed, imploring him to tell her what she wanted to hear.

'I already think about it every day, *habibti*,' Ali cooed soothingly. 'I think about you every day and I want nothing more than to visit you, but I cannot allow you to pay for me. My foster brother lives in the UK and he said he will help me financially, but he has many troubles. I am worried for him, and I am worried for you. I cannot bear being so far away from you both.'

'Where does your foster brother live?' she asked, feasting on another morsel that could potentially bring them closer emotionally as well as geographically.

'He lives in Leeds, the same as you.'

'But why didn't you say?' She laughed out loud at the

serendipity of it – finally feeling as though karma was on her side. 'Your foster brother lives here, I live here, you want to be here – just say yes, Ali. I'll make all the arrangements. Let me help you in return for helping me. You've been paying the tutoring site all this time. Just say yes.'

'But what about your husband, *habibti*? Can you do this without him knowing anything about it?' asked Ali.

'I don't know yet,' she whispered. Her eyes filled with tears, and she shook her head as they fell, not bothering to wipe them away. 'I don't know yet,' she repeated, taking a fortifying breath, 'but let me worry about that. All I do know is that I need you here and your foster brother needs you here, and nothing would make me happier than if you said yes.' The picture of her new life with Ali was being painted in her mind's eye as they spoke, finally giving her hope for the future.

'In that case, yes,' he said after an agonising pause. 'I will come.'

CHAPTER ELEVEN

REX

'HI, IT'S ME,' shouted Ava from the hallway, sounding surprisingly chipper for once. He tutted to himself. Of course it was her; who else would be letting themselves into their house? Everything she did fucking irritated him.

'Hey,' he called back regardless in his usual monotone, slipping his phone into his pocket, the pleasurable feeling from receiving Poppy's latest photo quickly diminishing. He wished he could set the sexy image as his screensaver. Rex forced a tight smile as Ava appeared through the kitchen archway. He didn't move from his stool to kiss her hello.

'Everything okay?' she asked as she placed shopping bags on the kitchen island. Was he imagining it or was there a slightly defiant look on her pale face?

'Fine. You?' he enquired, not even attempting to sound interested.

Ava nodded before beginning to unpack the groceries methodically, one item at a time, onto the clear, spotless island counter. She seemed different, somehow.

He observed her actions for a few seconds, getting increasingly incensed.

'What are you doing? Just put them straight in the fridge,' instructed Rex, interrupting his wife's infuriating routine. Christ, how many times did she need telling?

Ava looked at the collection in front of her as though surprised to see them there, her eyebrows raised and her mouth half open.

'For fuck's sake, Ava, I shouldn't have to oversee everything!' he shouted, his stool scraping the floor as he stood up. 'I do enough of that at work. What's wrong with you? Just unpack the shopping properly, like I showed you!'

'I'm sorry,' whispered Ava, forcing a smile. 'You're right – it's quicker your way.' She tucked her long straggly hair behind both ears in that prim way she always did before collecting up a few of the items and making her way towards the fridge.

He glanced at her, pleased with her compliance but still a long way off calm.

'I'm going out,' he said, tucking his stool neatly under the breakfast bar, exactly as he liked it. The brand new modern kitchen had been installed when they bought the house, before they even moved in. He remembered thinking it was the type of kitchen that would impress others. Impressing others was important to him; fancy cars, big houses, expensive watches and beautiful women – he almost had a full set.

'Now?' questioned Ava, spinning round on the spot, arms still laden. 'But I've brought you in something to eat. It's from that organic place you like.'

Rex shot her an incredulous look.

'Sorry, should I wait for your permission to leave my own house on my one day off to visit my mother?' His words dripped with disdain.

'No, of course not,' she replied, pulling the fridge open, sounding much breezier than she had for a while. He fleetingly wondered what had happened to put her in such an amiable mood then realised he didn't care. 'Say hello to your mum for me. Do you want me to cook this food for when you get back... how long will you be?'

He strode towards her purposefully, clenching his fists. 'As long as I fucking well want,' he hissed at her neck.

———

'Hello, Mum,' he shouted, crossing the threshold of the double-fronted Georgian house – his childhood home.

'Hello, my darling boy,' said Barbara, entering the hallway to greet him, arms outstretched to cradle her son's face in her hands. 'Let me look at you.'

He indulged her, putting the small gift bag he was holding down on the half-moon console table, placing his hands over hers and meeting her eyes.

'You look tired,' she announced. 'Busy at work?'

'Always, Mum, always,' he said. 'Here, this is for you.' He retrieved the gift bag and handed it to her.

She peeked inside, a childlike gesture she always adopted whenever he brought one of his presents.

'What's the occasion this time?' she asked, eyebrows raised.

'Do I need an occasion to treat my own mother?' he asked, giving her a peck on her cheek. 'Anyway, it's just a little something I thought you'd like, for your writing group meetings.'

Barbara delved inside the gift bag and produced a leather notebook, embossed with her initials. Her eyes glistened with gratitude.

'What have I done to deserve such a thoughtful son?' she asked.

'Raised me properly?' he answered with a grin. 'I know you've got your fancy Filofax, but a writer can never have too many notebooks, can they? You could even use it to keep track of which room you're going to decorate next, God knows you need a schedule,' he added playfully.

She smiled back at him then down at her notebook, stroking the cover affectionately.

'I did raise you properly, despite everything,' she said, a note of sadness in her voice.

'Yes, despite everything, especially he who shall not be named or referred to,' Rex muttered his usual refrain.

They moved through the light, bright hallway into Barbara's open-plan farmhouse-style kitchen. The French doors framed a pretty cottage garden featuring Barbara's beloved wooden-framed greenhouse centre stage. Rex always loved coming home and felt proud that his own house was now on par with his mother's.

'So, how are things with you really?' Barbara asked, once they were seated at the table with a cafetière of fresh coffee settling, her new notebook by her elbow.

He scanned her face, brows knitted together.

'What do you mean, Mum?'

'Between you and Ava. Last time you were both here I sensed tension and I haven't seen her for a while. Is everything all right?' She put her hand over his. Her wedding ring glinted in the sunlight. She still wore it despite being very single.

'I never could hide anything from you, could I?' he said, patting her hand before reaching to plunge the coffee.

'No,' she said, studying his face and leaning back in her chair. 'Where is she today?'

'She's doing that online tutoring thing,' he said, not knowing if it was true or not. He had no idea what his wife did with her time when she was alone in the house but as long as she completed her chores satisfactorily, he didn't care.

'Is she still doing that? Knowing Ava and her fads, I thought she would have given up on that by now, like she did with learning French and making candles. They fell by the wayside after just a few weeks.'

'Apparently not. She says it keeps her busy. She told me to say hello,' he said.

'Not too busy to take care of her husband, I hope? You've stuck by her through all her troubles and that's the sign of a good man. That's more than your father did. He casually announced he didn't want to be married to me anymore and left, just like that. Off to his fancy woman. I would have done anything to make him stay. I hope Ava realises how lucky she is to have you.'

Rex sighed at the familiar story of his father's abandonment, as well as at the state of his own frustrating marriage.

'I'm not sure she does actually, Mum. Things have been strained for a while, if I'm honest.'

Barbara clucked her tongue.

'I thought as much. She rarely comes with you on these visits and the few times I have seen her so far this year she looked... well, vacant, for want of a better word. The lights are on but nobody's home, as they say. I know she's been through a lot but goodness me, haven't we all?' Barbara shook her head. 'She ought to be grateful, having a man who grinds himself to the bone even though she's got all that money just sitting in the bank. I know how driven you are and you're more than capable of climbing the ranks, Rex, but I know you've got loftier ambitions than just Sales Manager.'

Rex nodded along, enjoying his mother's unconditional devotion.

'I don't think she realises how hard I do work, Mum. You know how much I want my own dealership one day, but that could take years without a financial leg-up.'

'I know you'll make it happen, son. That's one good quality you got from your father – you're a grafter. But why doesn't she help you? I know you've got a lovely home now but surely there's enough left over to invest in a business?'

He clenched his teeth. His mother could see it too – his own fucking wife didn't believe in him enough to help him work towards his dream business, despite having the means to do so. It was a sore point that had become infected.

'Anything above a certain amount needs to go through the accountant and I know he'll advise Ava that it's too big a risk. But all new businesses are a risk! I've got my credit card, but the limit's only a few thousand. Even if I managed to bank a few commissions from car sales, I can't raise enough capital without Ava's investment too.'

'You're not struggling for money, are you?' asked Barbara, a horrified expression on her face.

He barked a laugh and placed his hand over hers. 'No, of course not, Mum.' His smile faded. 'As long as I'm married to Ava, things are very comfortable. If I left her, I would get nothing, perhaps not even half of the house if she chose to contest my right to it. And if she left me, it would probably be the same. Her accountant would see to that.'

He regretted saying it as soon as the words left his mouth. His mum responded exactly as he knew she would.

'Are things that bad?' Barbara was stricken, her hand clutching the silk scarf draped around her neck.

'No, Mum, I was talking hypothetically,' he soothed, backtracking slightly. She had never recovered from his dad leaving her and he knew she considered men who walked out of their marriage without good reason the lowest of the low. 'Don't worry, I can still afford to keep you in the manner to which you've become accustomed. I wouldn't let you lose this house, would I?'

'Well, that's a relief.' She visibly relaxed. 'Remember, you're not your father, Rex, and I do appreciate how much you still help me out financially. Ava might have her problems, but you've seen first-hand the damage an absent husband and father causes, not that you're a father yet but it's my greatest wish to become a grandmother one day soon. It might be just what you and Ava need–'

'For fuck's sake, Mum, one thing at a time,' he interrupted, banging his hand down on the table in exasperation.

Barbara shrank back in her chair, and Rex felt immediate guilt about his outburst. He knew how much she hated to hear him swear, to see flashes of temper. The women in his life certainly knew how to wind him up though. The grandchild topic seemed to be coming up more and more frequently lately and he didn't have the heart to tell her that the last woman he wanted a baby with was his wife. She would be so disappointed with him if she knew about Poppy before he had found a way of ending things in his favour with Ava.

'I'm sorry, Mum,' he said, reaching over to place his hand over hers again. 'I didn't mean to get angry. I've just got a lot on my plate right now, what with one thing and another.'

She eyed him warily for a moment but didn't press the issue.

'All right,' she said, seemingly placated. 'But you need to stay in your marriage and work things out. Don't follow in your father's footsteps. Make her see that investing in you financially as well as emotionally is a safe bet. She'll come around. Do you want me to have a little word with her?'

Rex forced a smile. He didn't want his mother meddling in his affairs – metaphorically or literally.

'No, Mum, leave it with me. Thank you for your advice though, as always. Shall I pour?' he asked, gesturing to the cafetière.

She smiled, appearing to be satisfied with his response, and started twittering on about one of her writing group cronies. Rex pretended to listen while he sipped his coffee and considered his options. If he wanted his mother's blessing for a sumptuous future with Poppy, he was going to have to find a way of removing Ava from his life whilst keeping hold of his fair share of her money. Ava needed to disappear from his life sooner rather than later.

CHAPTER TWELVE

AVA

Ali opened the hotel door mid-knock. He must have been waiting right behind it. Ava's heart hammered so loudly she felt sure he could hear it. There he stood. Setting eyes on him in the flesh two weeks after their first illicit phone call was surreal. He was tall and lean and had the longest, darkest eyelashes she had ever seen. He was even more beautiful in three dimensions, this stranger who wasn't a stranger.

'Hello, *habibti*,' he said, shyly, a smile playing on his lips.

'Hello, Ali.' Suddenly shy herself, she waited for him to invite her in. Time suspended as they just stared at each other. She could feel the chemistry zapping between them as though it was a tangible force. She had only ever felt this way once before, and it wasn't when she met her husband.

When she and Rex had met, at a Halloween house party in 2014, she had been so drunk she could barely see straight. The party was being hosted by an old university friend and Ava had been propelled to go by the slim possibility of seeing Blake there, the desire to torture herself further still in full force despite ten years having passed since their breakup, and her subsequent breakdown. Whatever they had been, and done, had been so insignificant to him that he hadn't even bothered to tell her he was already married when they were together. He had tricked her and used her then abandoned her to an abyss of sadness and loneliness. It was this state of mind that had caused her to drink more heavily than she might have done otherwise, drowning her sorrows because Blake hadn't been there, and she had stumbled against Rex after emerging from the toilet, ending up clumsily contorted on the floor, almost dragging him down with her. He was the only one not wearing a costume. She had profusely apologised, and he had been so gentlemanly, helping her up and making sure she was okay.

It was she who had suggested marriage to Rex mere weeks before her dad's death the following March, out of sheer desperation to cling onto something, someone solid, who could steady her like he had at that house party. He hadn't actually said the word 'yes' in response to her casual proposal of sorts, but the mention of their engagement to his mother seemed to seal the deal, and within seven months they had exchanged vows.

It had been the worst decision of her life.

Right now, however, gazing at Ali's handsome face, she felt happy and hopeful and determined to rediscover the Ava she had lost a long time ago.

Ali grinned down at her, his brown-black eyes twinkling mischievously. She forced herself to continue to maintain eye contact, trying to appear less nervous than she felt. He gestured for her to enter and moved aside fractionally to accommodate her slim frame. Just being near him was intoxicating; she already wanted him desperately.

'It's nice to finally meet you,' she said earnestly after he had closed the door, shaking his hand, feeling a jolt of electricity as their palms touched. He didn't have manicured fingernails like Rex, he wasn't wearing designer clothes, and he wasn't clean-shaven. They could not have been more opposite, but he was insanely attractive to her. His black hair curled down to the collar of his black shirt and contrasted beautifully against his brown skin. His stubble appeared like pinpricks along his strong jawline. His full lips covered imperfect white teeth, canines slightly protruding. His strong eyebrows framed curious, intelligent eyes. All in all, he was even more gorgeous in real life, yet she didn't feel as inadequate in his presence as she had worried she might.

'Ah, yes, the traditional handshake greeting,' he said, with a chuckle. 'I was hoping for something a little less formal.'

Ava's cheeks bloomed. 'So was I,' she said, biting her bottom lip between her teeth.

He leaned towards her slowly, eyes locked on hers, his pace dictated by her reaction. She welcomed his brief, tentative kiss, their lips barely touching. He pulled back and she kept her eyes closed, enjoying the sensation of the butterflies inside her. Then he pressed his mouth against hers again, pushing her gently back against the wall, and she deepened the kiss, dropping her bag and snaking her arms around his shoulders, her hands up into his messy hair. All thoughts of Rex and Blake and her tragedies gone, just like that, as though Ali possessed the magic ability to erase all her pain. She felt light-headed and breathless and reckless and, above all, grateful, for being able to make their relationship a reality. All that mattered was the here and now.

'Are you sure you want this, *habibti*?' he asked, his mouth near her ear. She simply took his face in her hands and covered it with kisses before burrowing into the warmth of his neck and inhaling the unique, unfamiliar scent of him. She had waited so long for it.

'I want it and I want you,' she replied, no hint of hesitancy in her voice.

'Are you sure about me being here, about paying for me to

stay in this hotel room?' he asked as he tucked a lock of her hair behind her ear and stroked her cheek.

'I'm sure,' she said, against his lips, 'I'm sure, I'm sure, I'm sure...'

———

Afterwards, they lay together, tangled in sheets, sated and still. Ava's eyes were closed but her other senses were in overdrive. The feel of Ali's thumb circling her shoulder, the sound of his heartbeat against her ear, the taste of his kiss still on her lips. She felt dangerously ecstatic.

'I don't think I've felt this happy since I was a little girl,' she whispered.

'You had a happy childhood, *habibti*?' he asked after a pause.

'Until I was five it was perfect.'

'What happened when you were five?' he asked. 'I want to know. I want to know everything about you.'

She blinked, suddenly overcome with emotion. As well as it being such a harrowing topic for her, the very fact that he wanted to hear about her past instantly brought tears.

Picking up on her distress, he tried to tilt her face upwards to him, but she resisted, tucking her head further down, trying to conceal her sorrow. Years of conditioning by Rex had taught her that men hated to see women blubbering.

'What is this?' he asked, his tone soft. 'I am sorry, *habibti*, I did not mean to upset you. Please, talk to me. Tell me what is wrong.'

It had been a long time since anyone asked her to share her feelings. She trusted him, she really did. She extricated herself from him and sat up, pulling her legs to her chest, tucking herself into a ball with the sheet around her. Ali sat up too and stroked her naked back gently.

'What happened when you were five?' he repeated.

Ava sniffed, composed herself, comforted by the feel of his fingers slowly trailing lines up and down her skin. It echoed of her mum rubbing her back after a bad dream.

'It was an ordinary Friday,' she began, 'and I was having tea at my Auntie Kathleen's next door. She wasn't my auntie, but I used to call her that. I went there every week. She didn't have any children of her own, so she used to spoil me – we'd bake or craft or play in the local park, and I loved it. I loved her. But now I know the real reason why I was there all the memories are tainted.'

'What real reason?'

Ava swallowed and held her legs even tighter.

'Kathleen used to look after me while my mum spent the afternoon with her secret boyfriend.' She shook her head as if to prevent the fact taking hold and settling in her brain. 'This particular day, just as we'd gone through the adjoining gate and back into my garden, Kathleen sent me back to her house to fetch something we'd made that afternoon; I forget what it was.' She shrugged. 'Anyway, when I got back to my house, I saw... my mum was lying on the floor...' Ava took a shuddering breath. 'Kathleen didn't realise I was there until it was too late.' She squeezed her eyes shut, tears dripping thick and fast. 'Mum was on the floor in just her underwear. Her eyes were wide open and glassy, just staring at nothing. I could still smell her perfume.' Ava let out a sob, her body juddering with the force of it as Ali gripped her to him.

'I am so sorry, *habibti*,' he said gently.

'Dad never really got over it. He went from being a confident, outgoing man to a virtual robot, working all the time. He expanded his business, became even more successful, but he seemed to withdraw into himself at home. He never talked about her, and I spent more and more time at Kathleen's. A few months later, he sold our house but had to accept a knock-down price because dead bodies put buyers off, apparently.' She huffed out a mirthless laugh. 'We moved away, and I lost Kathleen too.'

Ali manoeuvred himself behind her shaking body and wrapped his arms around her, kissing her neck.

'Eventually, Dad and I grew close again but a part of him always seemed so... hollow. He told me the truth about Mum on his deathbed,' she stuttered, gasping. 'That her lover killed her. I think I know why he finally told me – to help me understand why he was how he was for the remainder of my childhood – but I wish he never had. Some secrets are best left buried.' She hung her head and fresh tears soaked into the bedsheets like invisible inkblots.

'Was this killer punished for his crime?' asked Ali.

'Eventually.' Ava nodded. 'He disappeared straight after. Laid low. Kathleen never met him, but she knew his first name and had seen him leaving through the garden, so she gave the police a brief description. There would have been ample evidence at the scene to prove it was him, but it was 1988 and DNA had only just started being used in criminal cases. Luckily, I suppose, the guilt got to him, and he handed himself in. Confessed. Apparently, he strangled her, and she hit her head as she fell. He was given a life sentence. He died in prison a few years ago.'

'Getting answers must have brought you closure, yes?' he said. She leant her head back against his, so grateful for his presence.

'It did. But what messes with my mind the most, more than the murder even, is that my mum and dad seemed so happy, always cuddling and kissing at home. I suppose appearances can be deceptive, especially to a child. Nobody knows what goes on in a marriage but despite the image Rex projects, I can't believe anyone would think that we seem happy. I wish I had a Kathleen to confide in. She was a good friend to my mum, even though helping facilitate her affair resulted in the worst outcome possible.'

Ali squeezed her tightly.

'You have me to confide in now, *habibti*,' he whispered. 'I will be your Kathleen.' Despite her sadness, Ava smiled, comforted immensely by his promise. She closed her eyes, feeling safe for the first time in a long time, within his warm embrace.

CHAPTER THIRTEEN

POPPY

GAZING out of the plush hotel room at the expansive view of the city, Poppy again justified their actions of the past nine months by reassuring herself that childhood sweethearts reuniting was a valid reason for wrecking a marriage. Not that the marriage had taken much wrecking.

Poppy thought back to when she first met Rex as a fourteen-year-old all those years ago. He was the clever, curtain-haired, eighteen-year-old heartthrob, with a dark psyche, who lived a few streets away. Their trysts were mostly conducted in the small front porch of her parents' bungalow after midnight when he would knock gently on her front bedroom window on his way home from wherever it was that he went to. He was usually pissed off about something or other. Poppy didn't care; his lips, tongue and fingers were something else. His kisses... well, they were memorable. She would write poems about him, daydream about him and, more recently, Facebook-stalk him. He was the one that got away when her family had moved house, tearing them apart in the process. Except she had managed to hook him back in and this time she was determined not to let him go.

With youth no longer on her side, and his suggestions about

losing the teenage puppy fat she carried back then ringing in her ears, her plan had been simple: become his perfect woman emotionally and physically. It was as straightforward as that. Her transformation had begun over a year ago. Having found, and stalked him online after yet another brutal break-up, a strange sensation had slithered through her, and she knew she had to do whatever it took to make him hers. So, she had found and appointed a personal trainer that very day and now, after showing utter dedication to improving her fitness and physical form, she was two stone lighter. A few personal shopping experiences and a hair and beauty makeover had created the most incredible version of herself, and the tasteful Botox and filler enhancements to her face and lips, as well as laser body hair removal, finished everything off nicely. She knew a man like him would appreciate the outer packaging, being clearly obsessed with appearances himself. And it was a kick in the balls to the losers who had gone before, the men who had made sly digs about portion sizes and self-control, men who were not worthy of her anyway. Men who were now suddenly happy to compliment her selfies and suggest a get-together for 'old times' sake'.

It hadn't been easy though. Undoing all the damage she had done to her body through comfort eating, laziness, fast-food Fridays and a sloth-esque lifestyle had been hard to do. For motivation, Poppy had created not a *shrine* exactly, more of a motivational mood board, which worked wonders. She moved it around the house: in front of the cross trainer in the spare room, in front of the fridge to resist temptation, beside the full-length mirror in the bedroom, and next to her on the sofa in the evenings to avoid snacking. As Rex gazed out, unseeing, from the many posed pictures she had printed off Facebook (there were no pictures of or with his wife), she dreamed about the perfect life they would have when she made him hers again.

When her transformation was complete, she had private messaged him the prettily filtered selfie and waited, biting her extra-plumped bottom lip. His complimentary reply arrived three minutes later. Her eyes flashed with victory, and she flushed with pleasure.

The messages had soon picked up pace after that, reminiscences of their teenage years and patchy shared history, embroidered together even more tightly by Poppy's rose-tinted memory-slash-imagination. She delighted in their interactions and enjoyed how they made her feel. They reaffirmed how right they were for each other even after all this time.

Now, she quickly rechecked her carefully applied make-up in the large gold-framed mirror and smoothed down the new lingerie she had bought specially – a beautiful teal chiffon overlay accentuated the lacy turquoise underwear, including stockings and suspenders, underneath. Her body looked amazing thanks to the three spinning classes she had taken last week on top of teaching her own daily Bodyfit classes. Her fake tan created a perfectly bronzed canvas, which contrasted beautifully against the turquoise, and her hair and nails were immaculate.

Next, Poppy stepped onto her scales, the ones she always brought with her, and let out a little squeak as the numbers settled and flashed. Another pound off! She had never looked or felt better and yet again she thanked her past self for deciding on her successful course of action – boot camps, gym classes, healthy eating, achieving her Bodyfit instructor's certificate, and superficial cosmetic procedures.

The Rex Project was finally coming to fruition.

No, Poppy felt absolutely no shame about the fact that he was someone else's husband. All she knew was that his marriage had been a miserable mistake from day one but Rex, being the good man he was, had tried to do all he could to make it work.

However, she felt nothing but twisted jealousy – he had been hers first and she was going to take him back with absolutely no regard for any collateral damage. Mrs Rex Bateman had a definite ring to it, and Poppy was determined to become her.

The nostalgic, gentle knock at the door brought her sharply back to the present and her heart started hammering excitedly. Rex – her Rex now – was here.

CHAPTER FOURTEEN

ALI

ALI WOKE, disoriented for a few seconds before being infused with joy as he remembered where he was. The lovely hotel room was at least three times the size of his basic bedroom in his uncle's house, and he could still barely believe his sumptuous surroundings. He pressed his face into the soft feather-filled pillow, stretching out his arms as wide as they would go. His fingertips only just reached the edges of the mattress, and he felt cosily cocooned in the clean, warm bedding.

He reached for his phone on the bedside table. There was a message from Ava:

> Meet me this afternoon? I'll text you the address. xxx

Ali replied immediately, agreeing to her request. He already knew Ethan had an audition lined up today so he couldn't surprise him with a visit as soon as he had hoped. During their last call just before Ali left for the UK, Ethan had seemed buoyant and optimistic, hoping to stay on a roll after his game show win a few weeks before. Despite being desperate to tell him, Ali hadn't revealed he would soon be on his way to Leeds, wanting the moment they reunited in the flesh to be perfect. Until then, he was happy to revel in the lap of hotel luxury, grateful for Ava's generosity.

A couple of hours later, he walked into the local coffee shop, searching for and finally seeing Ava's pale face, anxiously looking out for him. She was sitting at a table at the back in the corner, petite body twisted round to face the door. She was wearing a jumper tucked into a long, flowing skirt, swathes of material draping to the floor.

He had been surprised when the address Ava sent turned out to be so public given their clandestine situation and her controlling husband, but she had already admitted she considered him worth the risk. She was much more fragile than he had anticipated though, given what she had confided in him about her tragic history so far. They had made love again after her tearful account of her mother's murder, and then she had left him alone in the huge, comfortable bed with a satisfied smile on his face. Although he too had risked a lot by sneakily leaving his uncle's house and Ramzi in the lurch, it had been worth it so far. He refused to be used anymore – now he was in control of his own destiny.

Registering Ava's anxious expression as he made his way towards her, he suddenly felt panicked – had nerves overridden her desire for him and now she was going to withdraw her offer of financing his stay? However, the instant he sat down, she visibly relaxed and he knew she would have paid double the travel and hotel price to have him with her.

'Thank you for coming,' she said softly, leaning towards him, her hands clasped in her lap. 'Despite me paying for... the hotel, you know... it wasn't a demand. I don't expect...' She pressed her lips together and shook her head. 'I don't want you to think I've bought, well, extras. Just you being here is enough.' She cleared her throat, a flush creeping up her neck.

Ali chuckled, understanding her meaning.

'I do not think you have bought *me, habibti*,' he confirmed. 'But please know that I am happy with what has transpired between us so far.'

'Me too,' she agreed, meeting his eyes, the flush reaching her cheeks.

They spent over an hour in the coffee shop. Ali encouraged conspiratorial whispers and edged his knees and fingers towards her, lengthening his gazes and secret smiles, which both spoke of later possibilities. Every now and again her hand travelled towards him, but she looked around nervously and withdrew it again. Careful not to show any physical affection towards each other, to any observer they would have appeared nothing more than good friends.

However, once their second cups were empty, she quietly suggested going to her house, her invitation seemingly pre-planned and weighted with expectation. Her slender fingers worried at her bag strap as she waited for his response, her wedding ring clearly visible.

He was surprised by the offer but agreed, only posing one question.

'What about your husband?'

She cast her eyes downward.

'Don't talk about him, please,' she whispered. 'Just know that we won't be interrupted.'

Ava drove them to her home, which was even more impressive than he expected. In her oversized, open-plan kitchen, suddenly shy, she had bustled about, making drinks they didn't need whilst he leaned against the wall, arms folded, smiling at her patiently. She *was* attractive; petite, tousled long blonde hair, a naiveness about her that projected innocence and trust, yet a weariness too, thanks to her tragedy-tinged life. Something he empathised with after his childhood heartbreak of losing loved ones himself.

Watching her, he reflected again on the risk she was taking by inviting him to her marital home and smiled because he knew that meant she trusted him completely. Perhaps she was too trusting, and too generous, but he wasn't going to refuse her kindnesses, not when he had dreamed of a life like this for so long.

He stepped behind her and placed his hand gently on her waist. She turned instantly, pupils dilating as he pulled her into his arms. She met his kiss eagerly and he knew she would do whatever he asked her to do. But first, he wanted a distraction from the frustration of wanting something else that he could not yet have.

CHAPTER FIFTEEN

REX

REX HAD BEEN CAJOLED into socialising with his work mates, or his minions as he liked to think of them. He was in a bustling pub in Leeds city centre, downing his second bottle of lager, embroiled in shop floor small talk and hating every second of it. He had finally agreed to join the pub and club crawl for two reasons: to shut them all up and to avoid a Saturday night in with Ava because, unusually, Poppy was away that weekend visiting her parents. Anything was better than a night in at home – even this – but he wasn't happy.

Outwardly, he gave none of this away. His handsome face, all well-defined jaw, symmetrical features and perfect smile, was convincingly arranged into an amused expression as Ian – boring bastard at work but life of the party outside the dealership it seemed – was doing his third Basil Fawlty-esque impression of recent tyre-kicker timewasters as everyone guffawed with hilarity around him. Rex despised these people. Rex despised everyone with no self-control or self-awareness. Didn't they realise how inferior they were?

His gaze wandered, flitting over similar groups of rowdy work outings, lingering longer than it should over brightly coloured clusters of too-young girls all dolled up waiting for everyone to notice them, and skimming past a few couples probably on 'date night' as that now seemed to be a thing. He had nipped that in the bud when Ava first broached the topic; he definitely did not want a standing arrangement to spend a strained evening in public with his wife.

A curvaceous woman standing with her back against the bar caught his eye. She faced the packed pub, staring brazenly at him through the narrow gap in the crowd. She was striking – black shiny bob, porcelain skin and the most invitingly plump cleavage he had ever seen. She was a bit plumper in general than he preferred but he appraised her favourably anyway. She looked vaguely familiar – a minor celebrity maybe – but he couldn't immediately place where he might have seen her before. She seemed to incline towards him ever so slightly and surveyed him openly with narrowed, black-rimmed eyes, like an unpredictable cat awoken from its slumber. He was captivated. Their gazes locked, then she crooked her index finger and beckoned him over! Rex could hardly believe the audacity of the woman. He raised his eyebrows then looked away before looking back a second later. She did it again, clearly expecting him to comply.

Despite her cheek, he felt compelled to go over.

'My round... same again?' he asked nobody in particular as a rousing cheer propelled him to the bar, his underlings whooping like teenagers at a rave. As he shouldered his way confidently through the throng, he watched her watching him, no doubt drinking in his strong frame and model good looks, all thanks to genetics, a good skincare regime and a three-times-a-week weights session. He knew he was a ten and she clearly knew it too, although it didn't seem to faze her; her eye contact game was strong.

'You are fucking gorgeous,' she stated emphatically, over the music, as he positioned himself next to her, completely throwing him off-guard. They were never this forward! Most women became simpering and tongue-tied in his presence, like Ava had been when they first met.

She didn't turn around, instead choosing to leave her elbows on the bar with her chest pushed out and directly in his eyeline. He struggled to suppress the desire to lean down and bite into her gorgeous white flesh right above her low-cut neckline. Everything about her outward appearance was immaculate and he could barely take his eyes off her juicy red lips. Such a shame she was a bit of a fatty, but he could overlook that he supposed.

He smiled faux modestly while he caught the barman's eye and ordered another round of drinks for his already inebriated, lightweight group before finally turning his tall frame towards her and fixing her with his gaze.

She looked up at him, her false lashes and perfectly flicked liquid eyeliner framing the most vivid green eyes he had ever seen.

'Rex.' He offered her his hand to shake. She ignored it and smiled seductively, not breaking the invisible thread of zingy electricity that was passing between them.

'Want to get out of here?' she enquired, seemingly certain of his response. 'My place is ten minutes away.'

Rex again drank in the utterly sensational package of her while thoughts of logistics and taxis and time frames raced through his head, as well as the feasibility of extracting himself from his work night out without arousing unwanted, rowdy attention to himself. He did not for any of that split second entertain a thought of his wife but the thought of cheating on Poppy gave him pause. This would be the last time, he promised himself. After this, he would be a one-woman man.

'Why not?' he answered. 'Wait for me out front.'

He swiftly deposited the round of drinks onto a table beside his minions and simply walked outside to meet her, offering them no explanation at all. He would lie tomorrow, if necessary, invent a plausible reason for his early departure. Outside the pub, beneath the light drizzle, he saw the object of this night's affection climbing extremely gracefully (for someone of her size) into the first taxi in the rank. Hurrying to it, he climbed in beside her.

Ten silent but sexually charged minutes later, they arrived at her flat. Once inside, she walked through to a spacious, vintage-styled, open-plan kitchen and living area with exposed brick walls, shedding her jewelled clutch bag and long, dangly earrings along the way. He followed behind, appreciating the view.

'I'm Eadie by the way,' she said. 'Drink or something else?' She spun around to face him, walking backwards slowly, encouraging him with a wink.

'Something else,' Rex said as he strode towards her, grabbed her arm and lunged for her mouth. She laughed and ducked and twisted back away from him, eyes flashing playfully in the dim light.

His eyes flashed too, but with fury. He countered by grabbing her again and slapping her across her face in frustration, not very hard but enough to make it clear he didn't appreciate her silly games. Time slowed as he waited for her reaction; screaming, crying, recriminations usually followed the first slap and he honestly didn't want the hassle, but what was her problem? She had come onto him. She had brought him to her home. She had offered herself up to him on a plate, and now she was playing hard to get? Fucking women.

Her palm cradled her cheek and her gorgeous green eyes bored into him, wide and shocked and glittering with something he couldn't identify.

'Do that again, but harder,' she commanded, breathing heavily.

CHAPTER SIXTEEN

AVA

FEELING brave and reckless but most of all desperate for him, Ava had invited Ali to a local coffee shop, knowing full well Rex was out for the night. He had informed her earlier, during his daily check-in phone call, that he would be crashing at Jason's because it was likely to be a 'messy' one, whatever that meant. She had made the right noises, careful not to sound too disappointed because he hated her being all whiny, while her heart soared with joy and possibility. It was karma delivering good fortune, she thought, to make up for all the nights she had spent alone, and lonely, in this big house while her husband was out with God knows who doing God knows what. Finally, it was her turn to feel free.

Her and Ali's very first meeting the day before had been even more magical than she had dared to hope it would be, and she felt closer to him than she had ever felt to anyone since Blake, but she wanted a taster of what their future might hold, to experience 'real life' situations with him. Simply enjoying a couple of coffees in public together exceeded her expectations and she shyly invited him to come home with her. He had accepted her invitation and as they moved around each other in her big, expansive kitchen, everything felt even more perfect than she could have imagined.

As she bustled about nervously, hyper aware of the presence of the first house guest that wasn't Rex's mother, Ava felt him behind her. As soon as Ali placed his hand on her waist, she felt possessed, wanting to demonstrate her true self in a way she never had with Rex, and she shocked herself by moving his hand down her body, making it clear what she wanted.

He obliged and soon his fingers were touching her, playing with her, as she slipped her own around his neck, grabbing his hair, gasping with pleasure in between kisses so frantic and deep she thought she might faint. She moaned into him as a delicious cascade of exquisiteness pulsed through her, cheeks flushed and eyes shut tight against all else except the feeling of it, the feeling of him. He pulled down her skirt and knickers and pushed her back against the island, kissing the length of her legs as she stepped out of the puddle of clothes now on the floor. He rose again to pull her top over her head and unhook her bra before standing back to look at her. She reached for him, embarrassed to be so vividly naked before him in daylight, the purplish evidence of Rex's violence visible on her body, but he shook his head with a smile and remained where he was, looking her over, drinking her in whilst undoing his jeans.

'You are beautiful,' he whispered, undressing himself before stepping towards her again. She welcomed his advances, so incredibly turned on and wildly eager to feel his body against hers again. She led him across to the unused dining table, pushed him down onto one of the expensive wooden chairs – Rex's choice – and knelt before him, taking him in her mouth as he threw his head back in ecstasy.

She revelled in him watching her, sucking and licking, maintaining eye contact seductively, before he pulled her up to him to kiss her passionately again. She straddled him, slowly lowering herself onto him, losing herself in the pleasurable sensations...

———

This morning, she had woken to kisses on her eyelids and felt herself float gently towards consciousness as she giggled with pleasure. Never once had Rex ever woken her with eyelid kisses, or any kisses at all, in their whole marriage.

'I have a favour to ask of you.' She heard Ali's voice and opened one eye, delighting in the sight of him, propped up on one elbow looking down at her.

'I think you've had enough favours,' she responded. She wriggled happily beneath him as he tickled her, relishing the feeling of his toasty bed-warm skin against hers, and the sound of his laugh near her ear. It reminded her of Blake, in the early days of their torrid affair. She had never felt the same happiness since, until right this minute. It was only going to get better too.

'I very much enjoyed your favours,' he joked, 'but I must ask you another. Will you meet my brother Ethan?'

Her eyes widened at the invitation. Being asked something so momentous was a bit of a shock. She already knew how important Ethan was to Ali, but she didn't imagine they'd be at the meeting family stage so soon. Then again, they were naked in bed together for the second time since meeting in person just two days ago.

She turned away from him so he wouldn't see the disappointment in her eyes. 'I don't think I can,' she said. 'I'm so sorry.'

'I know it would be a risk, but maybe you could come to the restaurant just for–'

'You want me to go to a restaurant?' she interrupted, aghast. Despite desperately wanting to agree, she knew she would never be able to do something like that without rousing suspicion. Rex may work late a lot, but if she wasn't here when he got home one evening, without good reason, there'd be hell to pay.

'Ali, I can't. A quiet coffee shop is one thing, but a busy restaurant is quite another. What if Rex found out?'

Ali folded her hands in his. 'But you must, *habibti*. Ethan has a girlfriend now and I want to show you off too, soon. It will be a double date! You say your husband is out most nights – like last night – so if he is out, will you come? Say you will at least think about it. You deserve some fun, some lightness in your life. Is that not why I am here, after all? You have already given so much to me, let me give something back to you.'

She freed her hands and hugged the sheet around her, panic bubbling in her stomach. 'But I've already taken a huge risk asking you to come here yesterday, asking you to stay the night, letting you be here now, this morning, in our bedroom. What if he comes home and finds you?'

'Does he usually arrive home after being out at night?'

'Not if he's told me he's staying somewhere, but what if he decides to come home first today?' She was instantly wild-eyed and alarmed. 'No, no, you have to go. You don't know what he's like.'

'*Habibti*, I do know what he is like,' said Ali, putting his hands gently on her shoulders. 'I have seen your bruises. I have watched you cry. I know I am asking a lot, but I want very badly for you to meet Ethan. Will you please consider it, for me?'

She stared at him, chewing her bottom lip, chin showing a hint of a wobble, her brain frantically running through the possible lies she could tell so that she could spend more precious time with Ali. Could she get away with it? Did she want to try?

'Okay, I'll think about it,' she whispered, acquiescing.

He nodded and smiled. 'Thank you. It is important to me. I

will be very grateful.' He traced a finger down her arm, and she trembled against his touch. 'Shall I show you how grateful, or must I go now?'

'You're a bad influence,' she said, pulling him towards her, panic temporarily allayed.

CHAPTER SEVENTEEN

EADIE

Rex was fastening his belt when Eadie woke up.

'Rushing off so soon?' When she got what she needed, she wanted it again, and last night had been exactly what she needed after fielding Ethan's many petty jealousies over the past few weeks. She was fine with jealousy if it led to intense passion (in fact, she often encouraged it), but Ethan remained completely respectful, although not quite vanilla, where sex was concerned. Rex could certainly not be described as respectful, but he had fulfilled her twisted needs in other ways, as she thought she had fulfilled his.

'Yeah, I need to get to work.' He slipped his fancy watch onto his wrist. 'I used your shower.'

'You should have woken me. I would have joined you,' she said, checking her phone as she always did first thing. Going by the flurry of comments and direct messages, last night's selfie had caused quite the commotion. She didn't need the validation, but she liked it. In amongst the influx of adoration was a scathing message from Ethan who, annoyed at being rejected last night, had headed straight for the casino. A blurry selfie had followed the message, of Ethan with his arm thrown around a glamorous croupier. A pathetic attempt to make her jealous, she presumed. She yawned, deleted the message and placed the phone face down on her bedside table.

She rose from the bed and walked towards Rex, naked. He watched her, his gaze gravitating towards the marks he had created on her skin. She couldn't tell if his expression conveyed pride or regret. She stood before him, hands on hips.

He jutted his arm out and grabbed her face, squeezing his fingers closer together until her full lips puckered. She stared back at him defiantly, not even attempting to break free of his grasp.

'Whatever this kinky little rendezvous was, there won't be a next time,' he told her. Eadie raised her micro-bladed brows. 'I'm in love with someone else.'

Eadie shrugged, still in his vice-like grip, and he shoved her backwards onto the bed. Her flesh bounced and wobbled. She ran her tongue around the inside of her cheeks.

'Sure.' She laughed, already knowing exactly how to rile him.

He stared down at her with a look of pure disgust.

'Fuck it,' he said, undoing his belt again.

CHAPTER EIGHTEEN

ETHAN

ETHAN STUMBLED GROGGILY from the casino like a wounded soldier, holding his head and blinking against the city's early morning Sunday sunrise, feeling utter despair at the thought of a new day. And the subsequent days to come. He hated himself in this moment, hated his own inability to harness his impulses and consider the consequences before making mindless decisions that would ruin his life, and potentially his dad's life. If only his audition hadn't been such a shitshow yesterday, he wouldn't have felt the need to get wasted. It was Ryder's fault too, for dragging him out in the first place. Like all seasoned addicts, Ethan was adept at blaming others for his actions, but despite his current brain fog, he knew Ryder was fighting his own battles and encouraged Ethan's drinking and gambling habits because they dovetailed nicely with his own.

Ethan checked his wallet and pockets, knowing he would only find loose change but praying it would be enough for the bus home. His dad would be worried. As his phone had died around 1am, just after his last scathing message to Eadie, Ethan hadn't let Bruce know that he was staying out. His dad never slept well, and he would already be up now, performing his set morning routine, making his toast and tea before settling in his armchair to watch his game shows on Challenge TV. His day was structured around them and had been for years now, his most recent crutch to lean on between breakdowns which, mercifully, seemed to happen less often these days. Ethan had no deliberate intention of making anything worse for his dad, but he was now worried about affording his lion's share of the bills over the coming months after another blackjack disaster last night. He remembered that bespectacled bank cashier warning him not to spend all his game-show winnings at once and bitterly wished he had listened to her. Now there'd be no treating Ali to a plane ticket, or whisking Eadie away on an exotic holiday, or helping his dad out with the mounting red bills.

Walking along the street he had grown up on, hands shoved in his pockets and head down beneath the soft morning light, Ethan averted his eyes as he passed number 37 – the house his mum had lived in with Ken since she left his dad, abandoned him and Ali and wrecked all their lives over twenty-five years ago. Ethan had refused to speak to her since and was sure the fact that she still lived so close by was the main reason for his dad's ongoing mental health issues. He saw her and Ken occasionally, from a distance. She used to attempt a wave but now she looked away, rightly embarrassed of the heartbreak she had caused two children and one man with her selfish actions.

'Sorry, Dad, I've had a nightmare of a night,' Ethan called as he opened the front door, attempting to explain his whereabouts before he had even entered the house. He could hear the game-show noises of the TV and smell burnt toast and breathed a sigh of relief; all was normal. In the living room, Bruce was sitting in the same chair he had been sitting in since Ethan was a child.

The same framed photos Pam had left were displayed on the same mantelpiece (one of Ethan and Ali on Christmas morning taking pride of place) surrounding the same gas fire in the same bay-windowed room that Ethan and his foster brothers and sisters had blown out birthday candles and opened Christmas presents and eaten Sunday dinners in.

'You okay, Dad?' Ethan asked.

Bruce hesitated, as he always did before answering, as though his brain needed a few seconds to deliver his thoughts, like the rolling marble in the games of *Mousetrap* they all used to play.

'I was worried,' he stated simply, eyes fixed firmly on the TV.

'My phone battery died, and Ryder's did too. It was a bit of a late one. Do you fancy a cuppa?' Ethan asked in an attempt to appease his father.

'If your mother could see you now.' Bruce shook his head.

Instant fury fired inside Ethan. Why couldn't his dad just forget about her?

'Well, she could, if she wanted to – she still lives on the same street as us, Dad! But she left us, and she's never looked back, so it's well and truly out of sight, out of mind, isn't it?'

Ethan shook with anger, but Bruce, who refused to engage in confrontations of any kind, didn't even turn his head towards him. Ethan felt instant regret that he had lost his cool. He was meant to be the man of the house now. Since the trauma, and scandal, of his parents' divorce, Ethan had watched his dad wither and shrivel into a husk of the strong, active, charming man he had been while Ethan was young, never managing to overcome the mental deterioration he suffered after his wife's betrayal. Bruce's anxiety had twisted darkly into manic depression and as Ethan reached his mid-teenage years, he felt the pressure to keep things afloat. He had been acutely aware of the acrimonious divorce and its financial repercussions thanks to the bills his dad left around the house, unpaid and ignored.

'I'm sorry, Dad. I didn't mean to shout.' Ethan pinched the bridge of his nose. 'It's been a rough night, that's all. How about that cup of tea now?' he asked.

'Go on then,' Bruce replied after a pause.

In the kitchen, Ethan filled the kettle and flicked it on, then retrieved the spare charger out of the bits and bobs drawer and plugged his phone in to charge. Within a minute the expected missed calls and texts flashed up from his dad but amongst them were missed calls and a text from Ali too. He read it:

> We need to talk, my brother. It is important.

Ethan rubbed his face with his hands. He was dog tired, but his curiosity was piqued. He calculated the time difference – Saudi Arabia was three hours ahead. Sod the long-distance expense. He could do with a quick mental diversion and as he'd lost practically all his money, a few more quid wouldn't make things much worse.

'All right, bro?' he said as Ali picked up. 'I've just seen your message. What's up?'

'Ethan!' Ali answered cheerfully. 'I was about to call you again. Guess where I am?'

'I dunno. Where?' Ethan put the phone on speaker to free both hands as he retrieved a teaspoon from the drawer and set about making himself and his dad a cup of tea each. His head was absolutely banging and all he wanted was to sleep it off as soon as he'd got Bruce settled for the day. He was aiming to get Ali off the phone sharpish.

'I am here, Ethan,' said Ali, a note of glee in his voice.

'Yeah, mate, you're here for me. I know that. I appreciate that, but honestly, I'm whacked–'

'No, you misunderstand. I am here – outside.'

With that the doorbell sounded.

'Ethan, who's that?' shouted Bruce above his TV show, unaccustomed to the sound of the doorbell as there were so few visitors to the house.

Ethan span on his heel, all the conflicting audio doing nothing for his hangover. He peeped out into the hallway and saw a blurry figure beyond the frosted front-door glass. Ali? How did he even get here? Ethan remembered how gutted he had been when he told him he might not be able to keep his promise to stump up for a plane ticket after all. It had made him feel even guiltier than he already felt. In a bizarre turn of events, was Ali here to confront him about letting him down? He hoped he wasn't in for an in-person lecture about Ryder or Eadie. As fond as he was of his foster brother, he couldn't handle anything heavy right now.

'Ethan, who's at the door?' asked Bruce again, his voice pitching at his routine being rudely interrupted.

'It's okay, Dad, I'll get it,' shouted Ethan as he passed the living-room doorway, spotting Bruce pushing himself out of his chair, his spindly arms struggling under the strain. He twisted the latch and Ali, in the flesh, grinned widely at him. Ethan ended their call and pocketed his phone, agog at the surprise visitor standing on the doorstep.

'Ali?' Bruce's voice sounded behind Ethan, and he turned to see his dad, teary eyed, hovering in the hallway. 'Is it really you, son?'

'It's me, it's really me, Bruce.' Ali looked like he was

bubbling up too, glancing between his old foster father and brother.

'Come in, come on in! Ethan, let the boy in!' exclaimed Bruce, more animated than Ethan had seen him in years.

An hour later, the three men were reacquainted. Ethan was amazed at the effect Ali had on Bruce; it seemed he was the key to unlocking the few happy memories his dad had about the brief time they were a proper family. They reminisced about the one Christmas they shared, and Ali was delighted to discover his favourite picture was still on the mantelpiece.

To be honest, it was a bit of a headfuck for Ethan, as well as a welcome distraction from yet another disastrous night at the casino. Despite his raging hangover and empty bank account, it was one of the nicest mornings he had experienced in ages.

With a slightly lighter heart, Ethan went to make everyone another cuppa, relishing the sound of his dad and Ali laughing next door.

Just as he was adding the milk, Ali appeared in the kitchen and slapped him on the back affectionately. Ethan shook his head, smiling again at the incredible situation.

'It's good to see you. Dad is absolutely made up.'

'That makes me very happy, Ethan. He is such a good man. He says he wants us all to watch your game show together,' Ali said.

'Not again.' Ethan mock sighed. 'He's seen it, like, ten times.'

'He is a proud father. Anyway, how are you – genuinely?'

'You know me, bro, I'm all right. I'm always all right. So, how did you manage to get the money together, then, to come over?'

'I was lucky enough to find a very generous benefactor,' said Ali without further elaboration.

'Look, man, I'm so sorry about letting you down with that. My winnings just didn't stretch–'

'No apology necessary,' Ali interrupted, his palm facing Ethan. 'I understand. I am just glad to be here now. I found my way and now I can help you find yours.'

Ethan watched Ali cross his arms and smile sadly, the ghost of the child evident in the man before him. He knew Ali could see right through him. He remained silent as he stirred the drinks, knowing exactly what was coming.

'How is your relationship with Eadie?' asked Ali.

Ethan winced. The warm, fuzzy feeling oozed out of him, and he felt instantly defensive. He regretted what he'd told Ali during their last Skype call about the pictures of guys he'd seen on Eadie's Instagram account, knowing it hadn't painted Eadie in a good light.

'Yeah, good, good,' he lied, handing Ali his coffee.

'Is everything all right between you two now?' asked Ali, referring to that previous conversation.

'Yeah, all sorted, I think. It's her job, mate. I was overreacting, so she tells me.' Ethan smiled ruefully and rubbed the back of his neck.

Ali nodded.

'If you say so.'

'Anyway, come on, let's get back to Dad. Watch my game show, which I'll cringe through. I bet he'll have fished out even more old photos by now too.'

Ethan lifted the two remaining mugs and moved to leave the kitchen, but Ali put a hand on his arm.

'I am staying around for a while, Ethan. I propose we go out for a meal – the three of us, maybe next week? I would very much like to meet the famous Eadie.'

Ethan searched his foster brother's face for any trace of sarcasm or disingenuity but found none.

'Yeah? That'd be awesome, bro,' he said, internally squirming at the thought of the unpleasant, jealousy-fuelled texts he had sent her recently. Surely the offer of a night out would get him back into her good books.

Ali smiled.

'That is good. I shall make the arrangements.'

CHAPTER NINETEEN

ALI

THE FOLLOWING FRIDAY, Ali waited nervously and impatiently for the first glimpse of Ethan and Eadie. He had arrived at the newly opened Italian restaurant and taken his seat, becoming more anxious and furious as the minutes ticked by. He wished he couldn't believe Ethan would be late to meet him on their first official reunion outing after all these years, but he knew his foster brother's foibles by now. Yes, they had spoken almost weekly over the past fifteen months, due to Ali's dogged commitment to their calls, but apart from last Sunday at Bruce's house, they hadn't seen each other properly in over twenty-five years!

After nearly thirty fraught minutes, Ali finally spotted them and he huffed a sigh of relief. Ethan pushed the door open then twisted back, holding it wide for Eadie, arcing his arm in front of her with a gentlemanly flourish as though presenting royalty or a celebrity. Ali thought he looked like her staff member rather than her boyfriend and curled his lip in disgust, his enthusiasm and excitement at seeing Ethan again instantly dampened.

Eadie waited for Ethan as he bustled behind her, removing her garishly patterned coat. She took it from him and draped it over a porcelain arm whilst surveying the interior of the restaurant coolly. Ali couldn't deny she was striking; he could certainly see why his foster brother was so infatuated, having seen pictures of the less glamorous women he had settled for previously.

As they approached, Ali appraised Eadie more closely: her black, glossy bob shone under the restaurant's spotlights, her make-up was applied with an artist's skill, and she certainly knew how to dress to accentuate and flatter her curves. Ali could appreciate the exterior even if he suspected her heart was hollow.

Ali stood, preparing to greet them and at that moment he and Eadie made eye contact, his blazing, hers superior, already, the beginnings of a small smile evident. He swore he felt the physical manifestation of trouble emanating from her but silently vowed to remain civil tonight, for Ethan's sake. Once he and his foster brother had reconnected properly, alone, they would talk privately and he would make Ethan see that she was just another addiction, something he needed to withdraw his fragile self from before things really got out of hand.

Ethan bounded over to Ali like a loyal Labrador, enveloping his foster brother in a heartfelt bear hug. Ali laughed at his exuberance, relishing it, reciprocating the embrace wholeheartedly. Eadie looked on, her expression blank.

'It's so amazing to see you again,' Ethan told Ali, fluidly removing himself then sliding his arm around Eadie's shoulders. 'But, without further ado, allow me to introduce my beautiful girlfriend. This is Eadie.' He was looking at her as though she was the most perfect creation on Earth and Ali's heart sank – Ethan was clearly smitten. And already tipsy.

'It is a pleasure to meet you, Eadie,' said Ali, his pronunciation almost perfect. 'Ethan has spoken about you very much these past few weeks.'

'My two favourite people in the world are finally in the same room!' Ethan enthused, squeezing Eadie's shoulder and clutching Ali by the arm affectionately. Ali registered that Eadie had not yet uttered a single syllable.

The atmosphere remained awkward, not that Ethan seemed to notice whilst reminiscing with Ali and regaling Eadie with tales of their brief brotherhood as children, artfully skimming over the difficult reality. Ali watched him carefully, smiling in the right places. He also observed how Eadie appeared to enjoy how unsettling he found her presence, whilst heartily enjoying her meal. Ali thought she should exercise better portion control. Ethan, a fan of wearing his heart on his sleeve, spoke fondly of Ali's shy arrival at Bruce and Pam's house (as it then was), and about how he had known they would have a special bond forever. Throughout their two courses, ignorant to the tension between his foster brother and girlfriend, he regularly repeated his disbelief about finally having the two of them in the same place together, looking the happiest Ali had seen him in months.

Ali inwardly recalled some of their long-distance calls over the months – Ethan manic or sobbing or, worst of all, begging – and would have found it hard to reconcile the worst of him with the confident, charming, together showman he was observing now, had he not known the truth. The reality was that this was all an act, an act for Eadie and an act for himself, and sooner or later his mask would fall and splinter into nothingness alongside his recent winnings. Yet Ali vowed he would be there for him, as always.

'Anyway, you never did say who your mysterious benefactor was,' said Ethan, wobbling his head and voice on the word 'benefactor'. 'Do they live here too?'

Ali moved his empty plate forward slightly and leaned on the table.

'It is interesting that you should ask because she is joining us here, tonight.'

'She? Woohoo!' whooped Ethan, excitedly flicking his hand in a faux gangster move, inviting amused glances to their table. 'You don't waste any time, do you? Tell me more!'

Eadie grimaced as though Ethan disgusted her. She took a sip of her drink as though to cleanse her palate of his distastefulness but remained silent.

Ali found Ethan's enthusiasm infectious and smiled along with him, enjoying being the centre of his attention, albeit for a few moments.

'You will meet her, soon enough.'

'I'm so happy for you, bro. I've never heard you even mention a woman since we got back in touch so I'm glad you've found someone. I can't wait to meet her!'

As their plates were cleared away and Ethan excused himself from the table to visit 'the little boys' room', Ali felt the already tense atmosphere between him and Eadie shift perceptibly as Eadie finally stared openly at him, like a hungry feral cat waiting to pounce. He forced himself to stare back.

'Let's play a game, Ali,' she said, leaning further towards him slowly, her beautiful green eyes fixed on him. 'Let's play two truths and a lie. Do you know that game?'

Ali frowned and twisted his glass on the tabletop.

'I do not wish to play a game with you,' he stated before knocking back the last of his drink.

'I'll make three statements and you decide which one is the lie,' continued Eadie, ignoring him.

'No,' hissed Ali, firmly placing his glass back down.

'One. I love Ethan. Two. You love Ethan. Three. You hate me. Which is the lie?'

Ali was unable to prevent the shock from registering on his face – she was challenging him!

'I thought so.' She smiled smugly. 'But guess what?' she continued, undeterred by his silence, licking her red lips and sliding a beautifully manicured hand onto his thigh underneath the table, 'I don't give a fuck.' She enunciated the 'fuck' with a suggestive smile and slid her hand upwards, clearly enjoying the power she had over him in that moment, literally holding him in the palm of her hand.

Ali flinched away from her, as though stung by a scorpion, and stood up with a start, sending his chair clattering over. A waiter rushed over just as Ethan returned to the table.

'Everything okay?' Ethan asked, concerned, looking from a flushed, flustered Ali to a calm and collected Eadie. 'What happened?'

Eadie shrugged one shoulder nonchalantly, her expression one of boredom, as Ali looked at Ethan whilst the waiter righted the chair before scooting away again.

'The chair, it slipped,' explained Ali, forcing a smile and an open-palmed hand raise, 'I am fine. Perhaps a bit embarrassed, that is all.'

Except he wasn't just a bit embarrassed, he was seething with anger. A quick glance at the smirk that had snuck onto Eadie's face, however, confirmed she was thoroughly entertained with it all.

At that moment his phone vibrated with a message, and he pulled it from his pocket.

'Is that Mrs Lover Lover?' Ethan butchered Shaggy's 90s song lyric, practically swinging off Ali's shoulders, craning to get a better look like a child needing a screentime fix.

'Excuse me for a few moments, please,' said Ali, still smarting after Eadie's shocking behaviour. He strode quickly towards the front of the restaurant, out the door and into the delicious fresh summer air, sweet and pure after the suffocating atmosphere inside. He looked around for Ava – her text had said she was almost there.

While he waited, he glanced back into the restaurant and could see Ethan snuffling into Eadie's neck like a pig in a trough while she studied the dessert menu, her generous appetite clearly still not satisfied. How dare she proposition him that way! And disrespect his brother like that? No, he wouldn't allow it. As much as he wanted to enjoy Ethan's company, he did not want to be around that wily witch for longer than absolutely necessary. Ali took a deep breath and composed himself. He was rattled but tonight had already served its purpose in proving to him that his instinct about Eadie was correct.

Seeing Ethan had reinforced his determination to save him from himself – he desperately needed help. He needed someone who really cared about him to set him on the straight and narrow. So did poor Bruce. His foster father had put a brave face on things last weekend, but Ali could see he was in a bad way. Ethan had shielded them both from so much, shouldered so many burdens alone.

'Hello,' whispered Ava, standing in front of him, ankles together, arms by her side, eyes wide, like a little girl looking up innocently at a stranger. He jumped slightly. He hadn't even seen or heard her approach, so consuming were his thoughts. Quickly recovering, he greeted her.

'Hello, *habibti*. I am so glad–'

'Can we go inside, please?' she interrupted, glancing about. 'Quickly.'

'Yes, of course,' he said, pushing open the door.

Inside the restaurant, Ali guided the way back to Eadie and Ethan. Ava followed closely behind, keeping her head down, as though a timid guest reliant on her escort to navigate her to her destination. In every respect, she was the polar opposite to Eadie.

At the table, Eadie and Ethan's gazes fell upon her.

'This is Ava,' announced Ali, standing by the table like a dignitary facilitating a mediation. 'Ava, this is my foster brother Ethan. And this is Eadie.' Ali noticed that Ava visibly squirmed under their curious scrutiny.

Ethan leapt up like a Jack-in-the-box, thrusting his hand out to shake Ava's, his smile wide and genuine, his stance a bit shaky. Noticing the wobble, Ali's forehead creased out of concern. Ava limply returned the handshake before twisting her arms in on themselves then clasping her hands tightly together. Her body language could not have been more obvious; it screamed its despair.

'This is my girlfriend Eadie,' said Ethan proprietarily, up-levelling Ali's introduction. He beamed down at Eadie whilst using the edge of the table to steady himself. Eadie raised an eyebrow but did not offer a greeting.

'Hello,' said Ava, not making eye contact and shaking her head so her long, blonde waves fell further forward; a curtain of hair to peek out from.

Ali willed Eadie to say something bitchy. To give him a reason to whisk Ava out of there and prove to Ethan that she was bad news.

Instead, she rose from the table and spoke one word to Ava: 'Loo?'

If Ava had looked like a rabbit in the headlights before, she looked like a wild deer staring down the barrel of a gun now. Her eyes, what Ali could see of them, widened into saucers as she looked at him for guidance whilst Eadie's red heels click-clacked towards the toilets.

'It is okay, *habibti* – go,' Ali reassured her gently, briefly touching her arm. He was ecstatic at the thought of speaking to Ethan alone, if only for a few minutes.

'She won't bite,' called Ethan as Ava turned to follow Eadie. He laughed. 'Well, not straight away.'

Once both women were gone, Ali and Ethan settled themselves back down at the table and Ethan caught the attention of a passing waiter.

'What does Ava drink?' he asked Ali.

Ali chuckled in response and shook his head. 'I do not know, actually.'

'You don't know, bro?' Ethan laughed with him, putting a hand on his shoulder. 'Why not? She's not a pay-by-the-night kind of lady is she, you old dog?'

'Old dog? What is this expression?' asked Ali, palms up to accompany his innocent shrug. This, and the waiter's obvious bemusement at their conversation as he waited for their order, only made Ethan laugh harder.

Ali whipped out his phone and took a selfie of them both. In that moment, he felt fit to burst with happiness.

CHAPTER TWENTY

AVA

'ARE YOU ALI'S GIRLFRIEND THEN?' Eadie came straight out with it as she plonked her clutch bag down on a copper shelf. 'He didn't actually say, did he?'

Ava let go of the restaurant's heavy toilet door and stepped towards Eadie, one arm across her body protectively, the other holding her small black bag against her side. She looked at Eadie's reflection in one of the oval mirrors above the row of three industrial-style sinks. Large filament light bulbs dangled from the ceiling by thick black wires, and the bottle-green metro-tiled walls gave the space an underground feel. She was unaccustomed to visiting public toilets, let alone with another woman, and she felt incredibly anxious, more so than usual. She knew Eadie could tell. Eadie looked like she could eat her alive and spit her remains down the drains if she so desired.

Eadie retrieved a lip gloss from her clutch bag but paused its trajectory to her mouth as she looked back at Ava for an answer to her question. Ava thought she looked sensational and felt half the woman in comparison, both physically and mentally.

'No, it's... we're friends... Ali and I. It's... we're... friendly.' Her words came awkwardly, and she was instantly worried that she'd said too much, given herself away. In her mind's eye, Ava saw flashes of their steamy scenes in Ali's hotel and her kitchen and blushed. She was terrified of anything getting back to Rex, despite there being no way he could know where she was or who she was with, having been relieved to hear him complaining about attending a 'mind-numbing corporate thing' tonight. Still, she was trying to tread very carefully indeed.

Eadie snorted.

'Right.' She reapplied red gloss that didn't really need reapplying, brushed her ring fingers under her jewel-green eyes, checked her shiny white teeth, then took out her phone, held it aloft and, Ava presumed, took a few pictures. Having never taken a selfie, Ava watched in fascination as Eadie fractionally changed her expression and the angle of her face with every shot. She felt as though she were an extra on a film set watching the star in action.

'Want a photo?' Eadie asked, one corner of her mouth turned up.

'Sorry.' Ava cast her eyes downward, embarrassed at being caught.

'Don't be. I like it. Most people stare. They always did – I mean, look at me...' She swept her hand down her voluptuous body. 'But since I won that gameshow it's a new level of crazy.' Eadie crossed her eyes and wiggled her head, to depict said craziness. 'Did you see it?'

Ava shook her head.

'I don't really watch television.'

'At all?' asked Eadie as her phone buzzed.

Ava shook her head once more as her eyes rose to a safe spot on the wall.

'Not really.'

Eadie looked at her phone and whistled through her red lips.

'My Instagram's exploded since the show. Nearly a million followers now. Are you on Instagram?' asked Eadie next, using her thumb to efficiently tap her phone's screen, obvious muscle memory at play.

Ava coughed and stood up a little straighter, not wanting to stutter an answer again. She chanced a glance up at the other woman.

'No, I'm not on any social media.'

'Interesting.' Eadie stopped tapping and stared at Ava. 'In my experience, the only people who don't have any social media accounts are people with secrets.' She tilted her head to the side. 'What's your secret, Ava?'

Ava stiffened automatically, clutching her arm even more awkwardly to her body. 'I... I...'

Eadie flashed a smile.

'I'm only messing with you,' she said, turning her attention back to her phone, her thumb deftly swiping. It kept buzzing as she did so. Ava was astounded at her obvious popularity. 'If you and Ali are together though, I'd get on Instagram, quick smart. That one needs keeping tabs on.'

'Tabs?' said Ava, confused. 'What do you mean?'

Seconds later, Eadie held her phone out and Ava stepped tentatively forward to look at the screen. She glanced quizzically up at Eadie, frowning, then back at the roll of photo after photo of Ali and Ethan, faces close and smiles wide.

'Well, what's wrong with that?' she asked after a moment. 'They are related,' she said, still confused.

'Hmm, tenuously,' quipped Eadie. 'Yet from this feed it looks like they've spent many a happy time together, doesn't it?' Eadie asked. 'Let me see...' she said, turning the phone back towards her and scrolling through it, 'this feed goes back at least a year with new posts every couple of days.'

Ava's stomach was beginning to do that painful spasm it did

when Rex made it clear she'd said or done something to displease him. Despite only having just met Eadie, she knew she was one of those confident, unapologetic women she wished she could emulate. It didn't feel as though whatever she was about to tell her came with the intention to stir up trouble unnecessarily, but she knew instinctively she was about to learn something about Ali that she did not want to know.

Ava hitched her shoulders.

'Is that strange?' she asked. Even with her limited understanding of Instagram, she knew from her Facebook stalking of a certain person that people posted pictures of themselves, with and without and others, online frequently.

'The frequency of posts? No. The strange thing is that they haven't seen each other in over twenty-five years.'

Eadie slid her phone back in her clutch bag and faced the mirror again. She pulled down her dress, smoothing the fabric over her generous hips and thighs.

'So, you know what that means, don't you?' she prompted, looking pointedly at a bewildered Ava.

Ava's mind tried desperately to make the connection between the images she had just seen and what Eadie was insinuating but she just couldn't get there. She stared blankly at the other woman.

Eadie rolled her eyes and spelled it out for her.

'All those pictures have been photoshopped to include Ethan. And Ali's profile is so obscure that he doesn't want just anyone to find him. I only found it because I'm practically a private detective where Instagram's concerned.'

'Photoshopped?' repeated Ava. 'But why would he do that?'

'That's not for me to say. I have my suspicions. But I will say this: watch out for that one.' And with that she sashayed out of the restaurant toilets, leaving Ava's head reeling.

CHAPTER TWENTY-ONE

ALI

ALI SCOWLED at the memory of Eadie's return from the restaurant toilets last Friday. The look she gave him as she sat down, through narrowed eyes, as though piercing his very soul, had made him shudder. Ava had followed behind, looking even more timid than before. Eadie's inflated ego didn't leave any air for anyone else, so they just withered in her presence. The cosy atmosphere Ali had fostered between himself and Ethan in her absence instantly evaporated, and Ali was left feeling dejected and irritated once more. As soon as puddings had been eaten, Ethan had checked his phone and announced that it was past their bedtime, raising a small smile from Eadie's glossy mouth. Ali, suspecting that Eadie had covertly messaged Ethan with instructions to leave, cringed with disgust at the implication. He couldn't think of a worse prospect than getting naked with that fleshy witch.

However, despite the outrageous conflict between himself and Eadie at the restaurant, Ali was optimistic. Overall, things were going even better than he had expected: Ava had been extremely welcoming, his reunion with Ethan and Bruce had been emotional and wonderful, snippets of the restaurant double date had been successful, and he and Ethan now had a whole evening together, just the two of them. Ethan had made noises about inviting Ryder, but Ali had managed to scupper that by suggesting a trip to the cinema; correctly assuming that Ryder couldn't sit still for two minutes let alone two hours.

Steering his focus away from Eadie, Ali opened Instagram and looked at the latest post on his feed yet again. It was the only un-doctored one on there, from that same night in the restaurant, when it had been just him and Ethan for a few minutes. He gazed at their happy faces, their shining eyes, and felt the bond between them emanating from the photograph. Yes, Ethan had been quite drunk by then, but they were celebrating – brothers finally reunited.

Putting down his phone, Ali pulled a photo from his wallet and grasped it in both hands. The vintage picture was faded and one of its corners was peeling, but Ali could see his mother's serene smile and his father's stern expression as clearly as if they were standing right in front of him.

'I think you would be proud of me,' he whispered to his father's image. 'I am making good progress now. I know I have not lived the life you hoped for me so far, Baba, but once I am settled here in Leeds I hope to follow in your footsteps and become a GP. I know it will be hard to achieve but you always told me that all you wanted for me was to be happy. I think I can be, living here and pursuing a career as a doctor, just like you. Please give me your blessing, both of you. I promise I will make you even prouder.'

He closed his eyes and tried to conjure up their voices, trying to imagine what they would say in response, but it was too difficult to remember how they sounded after so long.

Opening his eyes, he replaced the photo and checked the time. He was meeting Ethan soon; he needed to get ready.

———

Hours later, they were in Ethan's local pub dissecting the latest Marvel film they'd just been to see. Ethan was three pints down to Ali's one and was enthusiastically extolling the virtues of *Iron Man*, punctuating his points with playful punches to Ali's left knee. If Ali had felt extreme happiness the other night in the restaurant, he now felt as though he had died and gone to heaven. He could barely believe he was in a country that allowed such freedoms. It gave him so much hope for the future. Despite his fears, Ali felt the time was right to bring up what he had wanted to bring up for a long time.

Ethan finished his sentence and downed the dregs of his pint.

'Another?' he asked, signalling to Ali's half-empty glass as he stood up.

'Yes, but in a moment, Ethan. Can we please discuss something important first?'

Ethan looked over at the bar with a longing Ali recognised but acquiesced to the request and lowered himself back onto the bar stool.

'Yeah, bro, sure. What do you want to talk about?'

Ali rubbed his hands along his thighs and stretched his back and neck upwards, glancing around, mentally preparing himself. He had rehearsed this so many times but now he wished they were somewhere more private. Perhaps he could just test the waters rather than jump straight in at the deep end. He took a deep breath and... heard a shout.

'Ethan! Ethan, mate!'

'Ryder!' Ethan jumped up at the sound of Ryder's voice, a Pavlovian response.

Ali looked at the two men in astonishment as they morphed immediately into lad mode. His chance to speak to Ethan was instantly lost in a blur of guffawing and back-slapping, like they were the long-lost brothers finding each other again after years of separation. Why did people keep coming between them – first Eadie and now Ryder! Ali clenched his jaw and looked away. The pub was practically empty, but the space was filled with Ryder's noise.

'All right, mate?' Ryder threw the words in Ali's direction but didn't wait for a response. 'Same again?' he asked Ethan, his hand on his shoulder. He finally looked down at Ali. 'Sorry, mate, I can only shout my bro here – bit skint right now but I owe him one.'

'You're buying me a pint back? Fucking hell, Ryder. Wonders will never cease!' Ethan laughed.

'Course I am. I'm proud of you being a big shot off the telly, aren't I? I know that audition went tits-up but it's about time you got yourself another well-paid game-show gig. Especially after that huge blackjack fail at the casino. Maybe this pint should be to commiserate you being a loser instead!' Ryder cackled.

'Oi, you cheeky fucker.' Ethan pretended to sucker punch Ryder in jest, showing no sign of being embarrassed by his so-called friend's public mockery.

Observing the exchange, Ali was instantly wounded by the fact that Ethan had not confided in him about how badly his recent audition had gone, nor that he had suffered another big gambling loss. But an even greater injury was that Ethan showed no signs of formally introducing him to Ryder. His supposed best friend and his brother? He knew Ryder knew about him. He'd seen him hovering in the background of their Skype calls enough times, vying for Ethan's attention.

Ryder and Ethan moved to the bar together and Ali shook his head in disgust. He sat, fuming, for a few seconds before grabbing his coat and bolting for the exit.

'Ali, wait!'

Ali heard Ethan's shout as he pushed open the pub door and stepped out into the drizzle. He felt the mist on his skin and yanked his coat on, pulling the collar up before setting off. Although unsure of his direction, he needed to walk off his rising anger.

'Where are you going?' Ethan shouted, jogging to catch up with Ali's long strides.

'I am clearly in the way between you and Ryder, so I am leaving you alone.'

Ethan sighed. 'Come on, bro, we're not kids anymore, you can't sulk and storm off because my mate's turned up.'

This wasn't like Ethan. After just five minutes in Ryder's company, he was different. Distant. Irritated.

'Oh, so now I am your bro again? Why did you not say so inside?'

'What?' Ethan shook his head, arms outstretched, as though waiting to catch Ali's drift.

Ali stopped and turned to face Ethan. He was wound tight, ready to spiral out of control. 'To Ryder. You did not introduce me. Am I not important enough to you?'

'What the fuck are you talking about being important for, Ali? It's not a best friend competition!' Ethan ran a hand through his hair in exasperation and looked back at the pub.

Ali shoved his hands in his pockets. The drizzle had morphed into splats of rain. He was concerned that Ethan was outside without his coat on, but he desperately wanted him to want to go with him, wherever it was he was going, to choose his company over Ryder's.

Ethan gestured up to the sky and stated the obvious.

'Look, it's raining, I'm going to go—'

'Yes, go!' Ali raged suddenly, hands jerking out, fingers outstretched as taut as his nerves. 'Go back to your *mate*. Why not invite Eadie and she will join you? Perhaps she will put her filthy hands on Ryder too.'

He stared into Ethan's face and watched his expression change as he processed Ali's words. Finally, he would understand that Ali was trying to protect him from people who treated him badly. Finally, he would see that only Ali had his best interests at heart.

'What do you mean by that?' asked Ethan, cocking his head, a frown creasing his brow.

'What do you think I mean?' retorted Ali, glowering.

Ethan held Ali's gaze as a raindrop dripped off his hair and down the bridge of his nose. He swiped it away.

'That's fucked up,' he said, grimacing. 'And you're fucked up.' He turned and walked back to the pub and back to Ryder, leaving Ali standing alone.

CHAPTER TWENTY-TWO

AVA

August 2018

EVER SINCE SHE had risked meeting Ali at the restaurant, the same scenes had been haunting Ava's dreams: a faceless intruder drilling directly into her brain, splintering her skull as he stole her memories and then sold them to a sour, scowling Rex. The torrid evidence presented to him was enough for him to do much worse than he ever had before. Each time she had woken to the sound of screaming, which turned out to be her own, before she ran to the bathroom and vomited, thankful for Rex's frequent, recurring absences.

Even though she had only been at the restaurant for an hour, she had come home and thrown up out of pure relief that Rex had not been waiting for her in the dark hallway, primed and ready to punish her. Deservedly this time. She had checked every room just to be sure, then showered, scouring the smell of Ali and her infidelity off her skin while praying to keep getting away with it.

But the paranoia was now taking firm hold, attaching itself to her like a barnacle.

In the kitchen, Ava threw two paracetamols in her mouth and glugged down a glass of cold water. She wiped the escaped drops from her chin then rinsed, dried and put away the glass in the correct cupboard. The stress of it all was beginning to burrow inside her, like a tapeworm, and settle itself in her stomach, rendering her constantly nauseous. She cringed when she thought about all the careless, out of character decisions and actions she had taken recently. She felt adrift, not least because of her lack of schedule. She hadn't tutored since the moderator's warning over her and Ali's conversations, initially too caught up in making the arrangements for Ali's visit, and then because she felt embarrassed, like a naughty schoolgirl who had been exposed and chastised. Despite evidence to the contrary in her life, she didn't actively court conflict or negative attention.

Yet the previous three weeks had been the happiest Ava could remember since her fling with Blake. Except there was no need to think about him ever again; he and Ali didn't even compare. She felt as though she had been living in a delicious daydream. Nothing had been able to burst her bubble during that time, not even Rex, who had been more distant than ever on the rare occasions he had been at home, preferring to lose hours in his games room like a teenage boy. She was grateful for the fragile, lonely peace, always preferable to the alternative of his intimidating presence.

Thinking again about that night at the restaurant, and the relief she felt afterwards, a shocking thought suddenly occurred to her. She crossed the room and opened the tall storage cupboard door. Rex hated anything fussy on any of the walls, so the calendar was hung inside. Not that they really needed one. Rex would never forget his mother's birthday and there was nothing else to write on it apart from their own birthdays. They didn't celebrate their wedding anniversary, and the only other anniversaries that were important to Ava weren't the type to be written on calendars.

Ava didn't check the calendar for something she had to remember; she checked it for something she had forgotten. With her finger, she counted the days. Then she counted them again.

Trembling, she grabbed her car keys and left the house.

Returning half an hour later, she rushed inside and straight up to the bathroom, ever wary of being caught by a stealthy Rex inexplicably returning home hours early, even though he never did. He didn't spend any more time with her than was absolutely necessary, but she lived in fear of him switching his routine to catch her out. His lack of love merged with a damaged ego would be a destructive combination.

Three minutes later two blue lines confirmed both her worst fear and her dream come true.

Sitting on the bathroom floor, fluctuating between extreme joy and abject terror, she tried to imagine the cluster of multiplying cells inside her, transforming over time into a living, breathing illegitimate child. Well, that explains the sickness, she thought. A carousel of thoughts chugged steadily round her head: Was not using birth control with Ali a reckless but conscious choice? Why did my mum and dad never get the chance to be grandparents? How will Ali react to the news he's going to be a father? Should I be worried about Eadie's cryptic warning about him? And the most pressing thought of all: How can I escape my abusive marriage without my controlling husband finding out I'm pregnant with another man's child?

CHAPTER TWENTY-THREE

REX

REX FIDDLED with his wedding ring. It wasn't on his finger – he had taken it off soon after his and Ava's wedding and lied that he'd lost it. Ava had fruitlessly searched for it several times, to no avail, obviously, and she'd given up making noises about replacing it long ago. She had bought him a nice TAG Heuer watch soon after though – the Carrera Porsche Special Edition Chronograph with the stitched black leather strap – so he had benefited well from his untruth. And now he was going to trade in that platinum wedding ring to buy a solitaire diamond for Poppy. The irony made him smile wryly as he chucked the ring up in the air and deftly opened his desk drawer for it to land into, sliding it shut as it did.

He leaned back in his chair and the smile soon disappeared from his mouth. He stared out at the showroom with glazed eyes, his thoughts all-consuming. Life was getting increasingly complicated, and he needed to simplify, streamline. Stop fucking random women, propose to Poppy, and end his marriage. In that order. He felt more guilt than he thought he would after having surprisingly hot sex with that curvy bird – Eadie, was it? – but it was like a sick compulsion or something, a need within him. Poppy deserved better. She deserved a one-woman man and if he didn't lock her in soon, he might miss out. He knew she was devoted but he couldn't expect her to wait for him forever. It was time to fast-forward.

Jason appeared at the door of his office.

'All right, boss? You okay to look over this paperwork for Mr and Mrs Flashbastard outside?'

Rex smirked at Jason's usual refrain for any customer who was considering spending over £200,000 on a luxury car without needing a finance plan.

'Sure, bring it here.' Rex glanced outside and caught Mrs Flashbastard's eye. She smiled, crossed her shapely legs and tucked her highlighted hair behind a bejewelled ear. He knew this was a slam dunk – she was at least twenty years younger than her husband and he was clearly used to glamorous, high-maintenance toys. He'd buy the car just to prove he could. Rex congratulated himself on his excellent psychoanalysis of the buyers and began to check the trade-in details Jason had brought in.

'I meant to say, I saw your missus last week,' Jason said, leaning over Rex's shoulder, tie held back to stop it hanging in the way. He didn't wear a designer tie pin like his boss.

Rex felt like he'd been given an electric shock to his groin.

'My wife?' he clarified.

'Yeah, it's Ava, right? I'm sure it was her, but I haven't seen her for a while, not since that messy Christmas do that year. She left before the messy bit though. Do you remember–'

'Where did you see her?' interrupted Rex, trying to sound as casual as possible, fingertips pressed down firmly on the Vanquish's paperwork.

He knew Jason must have heard the edge in his voice because his star minion stood up and backed away from Rex slightly, scratching his face.

'Erm... that new Italian restaurant in the city centre everyone raves about.'

'Right.' Rex's mind was scrabbling. What the fuck was Ava doing out by herself in an Italian restaurant? He frowned. The idea of her eating out alone was as ridiculous as the idea of him becoming celibate. Unless she hadn't been alone.

'Who was she with?' he asked.

'Erm... a couple of guys and a girl,' Jason answered, rubbing a hand along his jaw. 'A really hot girl, actually, I think she's one of those influencers – Ellie something...' He trailed off, a flush creeping up his neck. 'Anyway, I'll leave you with that paperwork and come back in a bit. Better go smarm the Flashbastards some more.' He laughed nervously as he took a step towards the door.

'Wait.' Rex was aghast at Ava's blatant disrespect. He would not fucking tolerate it. Yes, he wanted rid of her, to wrench himself free from their agonising bear trap of a marriage, but he would be the one to decide how and when, not her.

Jason stopped, rooted to the spot.

'Get dolly bird on reception to get your customers fresh drinks, then come straight back here and tell me everything you saw and heard in that restaurant that pertains to my wife.'

Jason nodded. As if he had any other choice.

CHAPTER TWENTY-FOUR

POPPY

POPPY ENJOYED the sensation of the blade against her cheek. The beautician softly sloughed off the dead layer of skin as Poppy daydreamed about her next Rex fix. She had sent him a WhatsApp message of her naked breasts just before her appointment, to tide him over, and was now imagining his response at work when he received it. She hoped he would send evidence of his reaction back; she loved seeing how much she turned him on.

In the meantime, she was grateful to be able to indulge in a bit of necessary maintenance. She had already taught her morning Bodyfit class as well as worked off another five hundred calories on the cross trainer, performed a full body scrub in the shower, recited her affirmation mantras in front of the mirror and written in her manifestation journal, and now she was treating herself to a dermaplaning facial. Rex enjoyed perfection, so perfection was exactly what he was going to get.

Things were ramping up a notch; he was staying over more often, and she hoped it wouldn't be much longer before he left his wife for her. Everything was going nicely to plan. She thought back to their last encounter two evenings ago.

'Favourite childhood memory?' Poppy had asked him as they lay naked in bed, toned legs entwined, in her small but pristine terraced house. She was always eager to know as much as possible about him, taking pleasure in filling in all the gaps in their history in an effort to further strengthen their future, as though one without the other made them nothing more than a sordid affair, and she no more than a mistress.

Rex hadn't opened his eyes, but he had smiled lazily in that way he did that made her stomach flutter. She ran a finger down his bare chest, waiting for another nugget of his past to store away as evidence that they were meant to be.

'You,' he said simply, perhaps predictably, reaching down and caressing her thigh, sneaking a quick glance at her.

'You are so sweet but I'm serious,' she said, pouting. 'We were teenagers when we met and I want to know your favourite childhood memory, not your favourite teenage memory.'

'I don't really have one. I was glad to get childhood over with to be honest,' he said, untangling his legs from hers.

'What? Why?' asked Poppy, registering the change in his body language and desperate to know the answer.

'I don't really want to talk about it.' He got out of the bed, picked his discarded pants up off the floor and stepped into them. Appearing to have second thoughts he stood, hands on hips, looking down at her, a frown appearing on his face.

She was used to seeing him angry or stressed – something she often helped him alleviate – but she didn't often see him look sad. Her heart swelled with love and concern. Kneeling up in the bed, confident enough to not need to cover herself, she waited patiently for him to say whatever he was struggling to say, praying that he wasn't about to think better of it, put the rest of his clothes on and leave.

'My dad left us when I was five. It tainted everything for a long time,' he said, short and to the point.

Poppy gasped.

'How come you never told me that when we were younger?' she asked, placing her palm across her heart.

'As I recall, we didn't do much talking back then,' he said, a wry smile appearing on his lips. It disappeared as he continued. 'He left my mother and me for another woman. They weren't happily married, so my mum has told me since, but she struggled to get past the betrayal because she still loved him. She's never had another relationship since, not one. I help her out financially, and I suppose emotionally, now. She's only got me, and her writing group friends.'

Poppy had never heard him speak so openly and she could feel their emotional connection strengthening with every word. She wanted him to get back into bed, to comfort him, but she was also afraid to interrupt him. The thought of five-year-old Rex, abandoned by his father, growing up to be the man of the house, was enough to bring tears to her eyes. No wonder he had been such a troubled teenager, carrying such a weight of responsibility on his shoulders. And when she thought back to their naughty nocturnal meetings, she remembered that sharing secrets was never her priority either.

'Speaking of which, I need to pop in to see Mum on my way home, so I'd better get going.' He began looking around for the rest of his clothes.

'Wait,' said Poppy, reaching out an arm and wiggling her fingers to entice him to her. 'Come here to me, baby.'

He crossed over to the bed and kissed her hand, concern marring his handsome features.

'If I were to leave my wife for another woman, I'd be no better than my dad, would I? And I can't afford to be fleeced by whatever flash divorce solicitor Ava appoints – I'd end up skinter than I am now while still having to pay my mother's mortgage, as well as trying to finance my own dealership and any life we hope to build. It's fucking frustrating!'

She finally understood his hesitancy all these months, although she didn't like it. She thought fast, always mindful of not pushing him for decisions or making stroppy demands. He was the type of man that needed to be handled carefully. She knew he had a temper, especially when he felt under pressure, and she didn't want to bring it out of him, to jeopardise her top spot in his affections.

'You don't have to make any promises to me,' she lied. 'You're not your father, Rex.'

He sighed heavily, stretching his neck back.

'That's what my mum always says. I just need to get all my ducks in a row first.'

She rose up, wrapping her arms around him, tilting her chin towards him.

'I love you and you love me and that's enough for now. Whenever you're ready for us to be together properly, I'll be waiting.'

'What did I ever do to deserve you, Miss James?' he asked, leaning down to meet her mouth.

'Absolutely nothing, Mr Bateman. I'm the karma for all your unhappiness,' she said, pulling him back to bed.

Now, as she emerged fresh faced from the treatment room and headed to the reception desk to make her next appointment, she was surprised to see a face she recognised in the waiting area. It was Eadie Lee – Instagram influencer and one of her beauty idols. Despite being twice her size, Poppy thought she was even more stunning in the flesh than she was online. Her skin was an exquisite porcelain canvas. Her style was edgy yet feminine. Poppy knew she wouldn't be able to resist fangirling. She signalled to the receptionist that she would be there in a moment and tentatively approached Eadie who was engrossed in her phone.

'Hello!' Poppy half waved and half crouched in front of Eadie. 'I'm sorry to bother you but I just wanted to say I adore watching your make-up tutorials on YouTube. I'm such a fan! Your easy eyeliner technique is just legendary.'

Eadie lowered her phone, her striking green eyes regarding Poppy.

'Thanks.'

'You should bring out your own make-up range one day!'

'That's the plan,' stated Eadie.

'Oh wow! Well, you're looking at a guaranteed customer here!' Poppy pointed to herself and giggled.

'Thanks,' repeated Eadie.

Poppy cast around for something else to say, eager to keep the stilted conversation going.

'Goodness, that's a beautiful ring,' she said, pointing at the huge rock on Eadie's left hand. 'Are you engaged?'

Eadie emitted an incredulous laugh.

'God, no! It was a present from me to me.' She extended her arm and indulgently admired the radiant cut diamond. Poppy felt vindicated; she knew they'd get on!

'A present to yourself?' she asked, amazed. Poppy invested a lot of money in her appearance, but she'd never thought to buy herself expensive jewellery before.

'Yeah,' confirmed Eadie. 'Dual purpose too. It's obviously gorgeous but it doesn't hurt to let men – or women – think that I'm already taken. It makes the interesting ones work harder.' She winked. 'I used to send smaller gifts to myself, but I thought I'd level up now I can afford it.'

'What kind of gifts?' asked Poppy, entranced by the notion.

Eadie cocked her head. 'Flowers, underwear, the usual. Always perfectly timed so the right person would see the surprise delivery at the most opportune moment.' She made air quotes when she said the word 'surprise' and the ring sparkled in the low afternoon light streaming through the salon window.

'And does that work?' Poppy's mind was blown.

'What do you think?' Eadie smirked, standing as the receptionist called her name. Poppy moved aside to let her pass, processing the genius tactic Eadie had just shared, then she smiled gleefully to herself. She felt sure that with a little bit of creative thinking of her own, she would become the next Mrs Rex Bateman sooner rather than later.

CHAPTER TWENTY-FIVE

REX

REX TURNED off the car's engine and looked up at his property. The automatic outside light had sprung on as soon as the electric gate had opened but the house itself was shrouded in darkness. It was a modern, detached, handsome house, with a double garage, wide gravel driveway, and six-foot walls that gave him the privacy he desired. Accessed by a shared private road, it was tucked away in one of the most prestigious areas in Leeds. It was the kind of house that befitted him perfectly.

He imagined Ava inside, squirrelled away in her fucking office no doubt, although the fact that someone with such a menial job even had an office was laughable. Why she persisted with online teaching he couldn't even fathom. It wasn't as if she needed the money; she was loaded. And so, by the laws of marriage, was he. He just had to stick it out a little while longer. Except now she had embarrassed him publicly, and his fucking minion Jason of all people had borne witness to it.

As instructed, Jason had returned to Rex's office after their initial conversation and spilled more beans about Ava's little Italian adventure. Rex had watched him carefully throughout and deduced that the lad didn't seem to be lying, nor had a motive for doing so. Rex knew the older sales guys were a bit wary of him after that one night out when things had got a bit out of hand, and he had manipulated that wariness ever since. Nobody would ever dare wind him up for a joke.

Rex picked up his phone from its dock and navigated to Poppy's most recent picture message. He was met with a close-up of pert, naked breasts and Poppy's parted, full lips just visible at the top of the photo. His dick instantly hardened. He wanted nothing more than to start the car, wheelspin it out of his driveway, and put his foot down to get to her. The thought of her soft, sweet, supple skin against his mouth was almost too much to resist. But resist he must because he had a problem to deal with. He undid his trousers, pulled down his Calvin Kleins, and snapped a reciprocal treat for Poppy. She knew not to contact him after 7.30pm if he was at home, so he sent his message safe in the knowledge he wouldn't be interrupted again that night. The impending radio silence added to his already dark mood though. Fucking Ava ruined all his fun. Even his penis had already deflated.

He tidied himself up and finally got out of the car, psyching himself up for what was to come. He remembered snippets of Jason's surveillance-style observations of Ava and her three supposed friends enjoying their cosy get-together: 'Couple of tall, dark fellas, one looked a bit foreign...' 'Tasty glamour-puss friend...' 'Shared pudding with the foreign guy...' Where the fuck had she managed to find three friends, including some foreigner? he wondered. What the hell did she really get up to on a day-to-day basis? What lies had she been twisting around her tongue? He'd rip it out of her mouth with his bare hands if she didn't tell him the truth tonight.

Rex quietly entered the silent house and locked the door behind him. He could see a slit of light at the end of the hallway signalling Ava was indeed in her office, but a second later she opened the door and turned the light out. She must have heard him come in. He was annoyed; he had wanted the element of surprise.

'Hi, are you hungry?' Ava asked, pulling her long sleeves over her palms in that way she did, and biting her thumbnail while she waited for him to answer. Kisses hello had never been their thing.

He stared at her, standing at the end of the long corridor, and gritted his teeth. The spotlights in the ceiling shone on her golden hair. Objectively she was beautiful, but she was so damned mousy and pathetic, and that made her unattractive to him. The childish way she was standing was anything but endearing. He thought for a moment about how to begin to say what he needed to say and felt his heart speed up with the thrill of it.

'Yes, I'm hungry,' he said after a minute, shaking his car keys in his hand casually, pretending to think. 'I've got a hankering for Italian, actually.'

She was wearing one of her shapeless jumpers, the front tucked into a long, pleated, floral print skirt that skimmed the floor. The clothes drowned her small frame. That was something else that infuriated him: she didn't care what the latest fashion trends were, she dressed as if she was a fucking pensioner. She dropped one hand to her side and plucked at the skirt, folding her other arm across her body protectively.

He didn't think she had caught on yet, but she always seemed to sense trouble the way a dog did when its master was displeased.

'In fact,' continued Rex, suddenly jaunty, half turning his body back towards the door, shiny brogues skidding on their heels, 'why don't we go out to eat for a change? I heard that new Italian restaurant in the city centre is a hit.'

He paused, mid-skit, eyebrows raised, keys pointed outside

towards the car. He watched the penny visibly drop behind her eyes. As soon as it landed her lip started to wobble. Her face immediately creased, and her hands shot to her mouth, as though forming a barrier to anything incriminating that she might say.

But it was too late; she knew he knew.

He carefully placed his car keys in the artisan bowl on the console table next to the front door, took off his designer suit jacket and hung it on the oak newel post at the bottom of the stairs. He wouldn't normally disrespect his clothes by not hanging them up properly, but it would only be for a little while. He could hear her softly whimpering already. He hated that sound and he grimaced against it. It'd stop soon enough.

Removing his cufflinks then rolling his shirt sleeves up, he walked slowly towards his wife, halting right in front of her. Her eyes were wide and leaking, and her nose had already started to run onto the cuffs of her jumper. She snivelled every single time and he found it an extremely unattractive quality. Poppy would never allow herself to get in such a sorry state in any situation, but Poppy was ten times the woman anyway, and that's why she was more deserving of him.

He wiped all thoughts of Poppy from his mind as he appraised Ava. He sighed and put his hands in his pockets, forcing himself to look relaxed. The spotlight made her tears glisten quite prettily. He spoke calmly.

'I'm giving you the chance to tell me the truth. I know what I've heard but you're entitled to explain yourself. If you lie to me, I'll know. Do you understand?'

Ava maintained her whimpering but gave one nod of her head.

'Good. Now, I'm going to ask you two questions and I want two honest answers. One: why were you in that restaurant? Two: who were you with?' He counted the questions with his thumb and index finger and stared at her, letting the silence fill the space. He had read about the technique in a book called *Using Silence to Get What You Want* by an inspirational guru he admired. It was a successful technique he liked to use in many areas of his life.

Ava's body was trembling, and she stared at the expensive limestone flooring rather than at her husband. She sniffed, wiped her nose on her sleeve and took a deep breath. She wrapped her arms around her torso and shook her hair out of her eyes.

'I was with Eadie,' she whispered.

Rex wasn't expecting that. Eadie? The name was familiar. Surely not the same Eadie he had fucked a couple of weeks ago? It wasn't that common a name and now that he thought about it, Jason had described the other woman he had seen as a chubby celeb type. He blinked away flashes of memory, and desire, as he recalled their energetic trysts, and her predilections as depraved as his.

Rex raised an eyebrow and turned his fingers so they were pointing at her, like a child's imitation of a gun.

'I... erm... we met online... on Facebook. We're friends.'

'Friends?' Rex repeated her last word, as per the guru's guidelines, belying his fresh inner turmoil. His brain was buzzing. Since when did Ava have a Facebook account? She didn't even have an iPhone. Did Eadie contact her because of him? Did Ava know about him and Eadie, or him and Poppy? Did she know about them both, and the others? Christ, what if she divorced him for adultery and he lost his share of the money, and the house, and the chance of a future with Poppy? He needed to figure it out, but he forced himself to stay quiet; allow his silence to loosen her tongue a bit more.

'I'm sorry I didn't tell you about Facebook,' she said, reaching out to him but thinking better of it. She folded her fingers back into her sleeve-covered palm. 'I know we agreed it wasn't good for me, but I get so lonely, Rex. You're hardly ever here and you know how much I've struggled since Dad...' Her face crumpled and the tears came again.

He regarded her with curiosity. Was she playing him, or was this genuine? Pretending he had cared about her ex-lover – that professor – contacting her through Facebook had been an effective ploy to get her to stay offline. She had been all too willing to agree, wanting to please Rex, as well as diminishing all possibility of ever running into the bloke virtually. She was still messed up about him even now. Rex had played it to his own advantage perfectly, regularly extolling the negatives of social media to his increasingly isolated wife, while he used Facebook like a hook-up app.

'How many times have you met up with her, this Eadie?' he asked, dropping his finger gun and crossing his arms.

'Just the once, I swear. At that restaurant.' Her hands were out of her sleeves now, palms up, demonstrating her innocence. 'It was meant to be just us, but she brought her boyfriend and his brother. I stayed for less than an hour. That's it.' Her wide, watery eyes were pleading with him to believe her.

He considered her answer. It was plausible. He prided himself on being a reasonable man and could easily give her the benefit of the doubt, but what if Jason let it slip to the other sales guys about seeing the boss's missus out on a double date with another man, even though Rex had warned him not to? The imagined humiliation burned brightly within him already, like a fire he was unable to douse. And if that humiliation became a reality – it was unthinkable. He'd be a laughing stock and would lose the respect of his minions. No, he needed to test her, to find out what she really knew and what she had really done.

He forced a half smile, to give the impression of softening towards her.

'Facebook, eh?' He took out his phone and brought up the app. 'What account name did you use because as far as I know my wife isn't on Facebook.'

Panic crossed her face, and he knew she naively hadn't expected him to check. Her thumbnail returned to her mouth, and she looked back down at the floor, trembling.

He employed the silent technique again while he did an obvious search for her middle name with her mother's maiden name. Bingo. This was too easy. He looked back at her again expectantly for few seconds, and when she still didn't answer he held the screen in front of her face.

She nodded and the snivelling resumed more intensely.

Her profile didn't have a photo. He clicked on it and scrolled down. There was nothing in her feed and she didn't have a single friend.

'I'm going to find out the truth, Ava, you know I will. And when I do find out who you're fucking behind my back, I'm going to divorce you for adultery and my solicitor will have a fucking field day with your inheritance.'

'I'm not the one having an affair!' she shouted, surprising him.

Like an automatic pincer, he grabbed her hair, twisting it around his hand so she was forced to stand on her tiptoes, neck tipped backwards at an awkward angle. Seething, he stared down at her.

'Don't you dare accuse me of something you're guilty of. You were seen, out with your fucking foreign fancy piece. Are you trying to deliberately humiliate me?'

She shook her head frantically and he let go of her hair, pushing her roughly away from him.

He paced the length of the hallway, fingers to his temples to block out the sound of her stuttering attempts to placate him. He had her bang to rights and she knew it. But what did she know about him? She didn't know how to check up on him online, did she?

He brought himself to a stop in front of her again, lowered his hands to his sides and closed his eyes. He clenched his hands into fists, trying to regulate his breathing. He wanted the truth because the truth could be his get-out-of-jail-free card. If Ava was cheating on him, he could walk away with a clear conscience, with her money and probably the house, and with his mother's blessing. All complications erased.

He opened his eyes and stared at her.

'Right. Let's start again. What were you doing in that restaurant last week and who were you with?'

'I really was with Eadie, I promise,' she said, not blinking.

He nodded.

'Okay. Get her on the phone. I'll check myself.'

She opened and closed her mouth like a fish, seemingly unable to formulate a response.

'I... I don't...'

He knew it. She was lying to him. He didn't need to hear any more, his disgusted glare conveyed everything he wanted it to. Maybe using the name Eadie was a lucky guess or maybe Ava had seen her profile online. Whatever. She'd never say that name to him again.

'Rex... please... I'm sorry–'

He punched the apology back into her mouth.

CHAPTER TWENTY-SIX

AVA

A BEEP INTERRUPTED Ava's addled thoughts and she instinctively ducked down in her seat, wary of being seen. Covertly glancing around from behind her large, dark sunglasses, worn despite the overcast August day, she realised that the beep had come from a car horn further down the road and was nothing for her to worry about. She was so on edge yet wired, too. It had been a bad couple of days.

She still didn't know who had told Rex she had been at the restaurant, but she again chastised herself for taking such a huge risk anyway. Her desire to feel free and to spend more time with Ali had overridden everything, but it had been a terrible mistake. She thought about her conversation with Eadie in the toilets. Eadie's warning about Ali still seemed cryptic to her, but Ava had never been great at figuring out anyone's motives for anything. Maybe Eadie was jealous. Ava may be biased but Ali had a charm that Ethan didn't. He had charisma. Perhaps Eadie had noticed that too and wanted him for herself. Ava felt instantly territorial at the thought.

Sitting up again, as comfortably as her bruised ribs would allow, she started the car. She needed to get home and again attempt to erase the stubborn bloodstain still visible on the hallway floor before Rex's next inspection. The grout was tinged pink despite her scrubbing, and he had looked at it pointedly this morning. He didn't like to be reminded of the consequences of his temper.

As she drove, she cradled her belly and thought about the flat she had just viewed for the second time. It was small but stylish and, most of all, safe. The landlady, Debra, had confirmed it would be available to move into next month and Ava had reached into her bag and brought out the deposit in cash. She needed to do what she promised herself she was going to do this time.

Ava had first seen the flat advertised in the local post office months ago, after a particularly nasty incident with Rex, and it had taken her days to pluck up the courage to arrange to see it. After the first viewing, during which Debra had glanced at Ava's bruises before offering her a sympathetic smile, her resolve had wavered. She was afraid – afraid of Rex, afraid of the stigma of being an abused wife and, most of all, afraid of the seemingly insurmountable number of steps she needed to take in order to remove herself cleanly from her nightmare of a marriage. There was so much to be separated, not just their physical selves, beginning with the house that she had sunk a huge chunk of her inheritance into. The impressive home that had witnessed the absolute worst of times.

However, despite going as far as applying to rent the flat after the initial viewing, Ava had stupidly stalled the process as her marriage again retained a slightly firmer footing in the days that followed, foolishly convincing herself that things might improve somehow. Rex wasn't exactly apologetic, but he was calmer, as though depleted of his rage temporarily. And so, she slowly but surely talked herself out of leaving him. She couldn't access any substantial amounts of money – even the remainder of her inheritance – without him knowing about it and she couldn't just sell the house without his agreement. She had really backed herself into a corner and here she was, again, battered and bruised physically as well as emotionally because of her inability to escape. Well, she was braver now. She had a baby to consider. She was going to find a way.

Rex was working until at least 7pm and she suspected he may not be home until much later, as had been the norm for months, so she had plenty of time to surreptitiously start packing a few clothes and hiding them out of sight. She planned to just slip away one day, move into the new flat and begin divorce proceedings straight away. She meant it this time.

Arriving home, Ava parked, crossed the gravel driveway and unlocked the door to the soulless, loveless house she lived in. Retrieving a slim rectangular box from her bag, she went straight to the downstairs toilet, desperate to check.

With shaking hands, she retook the pregnancy test then placed it on the edge of the sink, rubbing her still aching abdomen. There had been spots of blood yesterday, and this morning, and she was worried.

She should have known things were too good to be true. All those secret months talking to Ali had bolstered her courage and confidence to ridiculous levels. All that smugness she had felt after he first arrived. She foolishly believed that having Ali here would somehow protect her from any consequences, somehow magically make it easy to walk away from Rex, to simplify her complicated feelings for her husband, but things were never that simple, were they? At least, not for her.

As she waited the required three minutes, Ava thought back to the terrible scene two nights ago. The worst one yet. Rex had somehow found out about her visit to the restaurant, and he had left her, broken and barely conscious, on the limestone floor of the hallway as he had stormed from the house, turning off the lights and locking the door behind him as she fell down her own black hole. She had regained consciousness in the dead of night and managed to sit up against the wall, trying to breathe through the pain. When she finally had enough strength to stand and turn on the hallway lamp, repeatedly blinking one unswollen eyelid until she could focus on her reflection in the mirror, she saw bloody tendrils of hair framing an unrecognisable face. Tenderly, she had run her tongue over her teeth one by one, and thanked God none were missing or loose. Her split lip and her ribs, however, were excruciatingly sore. It crossed her mind to call for an ambulance but if she did, she suspected it would be both the first and last time.

Instead, she had shuffled to her office. Taking short, sharp breaths, she located her phone, found the number she wanted and pressed the green dial icon.

As soon as she had heard Ali's voice, she began sobbing uncontrollably, ignoring the agony it prompted.

'*Habibti*, whatever is the matter? Are you hurt?' he had asked, voice still tinged with sleep yet instantly alert to her distress. 'Try to be calm, try to breathe...'

He had soothed her until she was able to speak, her words slightly distorted through her sore, swollen lip and aching jaw. He had listened without interruption, coaxing her story out of her whenever she stopped to cry again. Eventually, her pitiful recount had ended, and her sorrow had subsided enough to allow a chink of anger to seep in.

Ali had picked up on and bolstered that anger.

'Listen to me,' he had said, his beautiful accent urgent and stern. 'You must leave. You need to be safe. It is too dangerous. Let me help you.'

She had nodded into the phone with fervour, grateful for such simple instructions. Yes, she would leave her abusive husband. She would leave him immediately, for Ali. Wasn't that the plan anyway? She was determined to take action this time, especially now that she had Ali. Now that she finally had the true love she had been waiting so long for.

Clutching the phone with shaking hands, she begged, 'Please help me, Ali... I need you to help me... I'm pregnant.'

She heard him inhale sharply. She listened to silence for a few moments, trying to steady her breathing.

'Are you still there?' she asked.

'Yes, yes, I am here. You are sure?'

Anxiety had risen at his less than effusive reaction, sadly reminiscent of Blake's response to the same news years before, but she reminded herself that she had just assaulted him with a lot of information and chided herself for telling him something so important over the phone. She should have waited to tell him in person, but that was out of the question for a while. Rex obviously had eyes everywhere.

'I'm sorry, Ali,' she had said automatically and began to cry again. 'Aren't you pleased?'

'No, I am sorry, *habibti*. You have surprised me, that is all. You need to see a doctor. Go to the hospital and I will meet you there.'

Ava had shaken her head against the phone, wiping her tears away with the sleeve of her bloodstained jumper.

'We can't. He'll find out. If this is what happens after going to a restaurant with you, imagine what he'll do to me – and maybe you – if he finds out I'm carrying your baby.'

'Okay, okay, I will think... We will make a plan. You will be safe...'

They had ended the call a while later and Ava exhaled with relief whilst wincing against the pain in her split lip. She brought her fingers tenderly to her face and again checked the skin around her swollen eye; it was becoming tighter and even more painful, if that was possible. Shameful tears threatened to fall for what felt like the millionth time since Rex had promised to love and cherish her until death they did part. She thought bitterly that perhaps he had misinterpreted their vows and thought he got to choose when death came. She was terrified it would come sooner rather than later, just like it had for her mum. She knew what men were capable of, yet she kept putting herself in harm's way. It was escalating, masochistic behaviour and it had to stop.

Now, she reached for the pregnancy test balanced on the edge of the sink and cried fat, blobby tears of relief as it still showed positive. Despite the brutality she had endured at the hands of her husband, her lover's baby had survived.

CHAPTER TWENTY-SEVEN

ALI

THE PAST TWO weeks had been amongst the most horrific of his life. Worse than after his parents' accident. Worse than being sent away from Bruce and Pam and Ethan when he was a child. Almost as bad as the respite foster homes. Ali didn't think he could take much more. He paced the hotel room like a caged animal, stopping after every circuit to redial but Ethan wasn't answering his calls, not since Ali had suggested Eadie's filthy hands had been where they shouldn't after their night in the pub.

He knew he could win Ethan round if he could just speak to him, convince him that Eadie was bad news. They were brothers – maybe not by blood but their bond was the truest of any Ali had ever known in his entire sorry, lonely life. Yet now they had been reunited, things were not going to plan. All because of that witch of a woman!

And then Eadie had found him on Instagram. He checked the message again. Just one word: *Peekaboo*. He didn't understand what it meant at first, so he had Googled it and realised that she was playing with him! What if she was going to show Ethan his account with all its photoshopped images?

What if she already had? He had deleted it all immediately, sadly sacrificing his carefully curated grid rather than archiving it – better safe than sorry – but she could have taken a screenshot. He knew how these things worked. How her evil, calculating mind worked.

He just needed more time, but now he had another problem to deal with: Ava. Things were getting complicated there too. A few days ago, she had phoned him in the middle of the night, distraught.

He had gasped at her pregnancy revelation, stomach instantly roiling. He certainly wasn't against the idea of having children, but he hoped to adopt one day, or perhaps use a surrogate. He didn't want the added complication of Ava's inevitable expectations, or to be tied to her for life. However, as guilty as the thought made him feel, perhaps her husband had already solved the problem with his violent outburst. Surely the abuse she had tearfully described was too much trauma for a foetus to withstand.

His mind had frantically considered options. First and foremost, he needed confirmation: she needed to go to hospital. He offered to meet her there, but she was too scared for them to be seen in public again, anywhere. So they had spent hours on the phone, like they used to, which had suited him fine in theory. But in practice, without Ethan too, he remained isolated and alone. And he was still alone now, going out of his mind wondering what the hell was happening with Ava, with Ethan, with Eadie. How had it all gone so wrong so quickly?

A knock at the door jolted him out of his zigzagging thoughts. Could it be Ethan? Hope flared in him as he jigged this way and that, suddenly unsure how to play it. But if it was Ethan, he didn't want to keep him waiting. He crossed to the door, took a deep breath and opened it wide.

Eadie stared back at him.

Ali's jaw dropped. How had she found him? She really was a witch!

'Drink?' she asked, pushing and twisting past him, walking backwards slowly, clutching a bottle of alcohol in one hand and her phone in the other. She placed both down on the desk and looked at herself in the mirror. Hanging her black leather jacket on the back of the desk's chair, she smoothed down her hair with both palms, elbows out wide as she did so. She was wearing – barely – a corset top which supported her ample breasts as if by magic. It was the exact same shade of green as her eyes. It practically shone against her porcelain skin, cupping the extra layer of fat on her back snugly. Her black leather pencil skirt strained against her bulbous bottom and tapered down to her chunky knees. Red-soled green heels completed the outfit.

He sneered at her reflection, tired of being taunted. She looked like a whore. He would record her with his phone and get proof. It was right there, on the bedside table, and all he had to do was set it up without her seeing.

As though anticipating his plan, she turned and looked around the room, eyes dancing over the bed, then she turned her attention back to him. She closed the distance between them, and he caught the scent of her surprisingly subtle perfume. Begrudgingly, he acknowledged to himself it smelled good.

'Aren't you thirsty?' she asked.

He shook his head, glaring at her, fists clenched. What did Ethan see in this woman? She was bold and brash, and ruining everything for him.

'How long are you staying here?' she asked, gesturing around the room, seemingly unfazed by his repulsed expression. 'It must get lonely, in a hotel room all by yourself.'

Ali remained tight-lipped, stubbornly refusing to engage with her.

She reached up and drew a long, red fingernail down his cheek.

'It's okay if you don't want to talk to me, Ali. I'm into the strong silent type. There are other things I'd rather do anyway.'

She had bewitched him, that must be the only explanation. He should be forcing her out, not allowing her to speak to him this way. He took a deep breath and reminded himself that she was trespassing, she had no right to be there, this was his private room!

'Get out,' he said, finally. Even to his own ears, the command sounded weak.

She tutted and smiled playfully before turning back towards the desk.

Ali exhaled with relief. She was doing as she was told. However, instead of collecting her jacket, he watched her pick up her phone.

'How about a selfie?' she asked, raising her perfectly shaped eyebrows. 'I can post it on my Instagram as your account seems to have disappeared. Ethan will see how well we get along. He might even answer your calls if I put in a good word.' She sashayed back over to where he was standing, her breasts and stomach practically touching the fabric of his t-shirt.

'Why are you here?' he asked, through clenched teeth, staring her down. Her face was like an artist's canvas, so many colours and textures on display. Her eyelashes were extraordinarily long, and thick. They looked like shiny spider's legs. He had never particularly enjoyed looking at women who painted their faces and added so many extras to their appearance, but he couldn't deny she was flawless up close.

Eadie ignored his question.

'He's really mad at you, you know? For what you said about me on your boys' night out.' She said 'boys' night out' like it was something sordid. 'Why did you tell him about us?' she asked, pouting her plump lips into his face.

'Us? No, there is no such things as "us", and Ethan deserves the truth!' Ali raised his voice. 'You know what you were trying to accomplish in that restaurant.'

'What was I trying to accomplish?' she asked, cocking her head and throwing her phone down on the bed behind her. She stared at him as she slowly stroked his leg, her fingers rising upwards. He hardened despite himself as she caressed his crotch. She grinned as she felt it.

'I like Ethan,' she said. 'He's very generous in lots of ways. He treats me like the queen I am. I want to keep him around – for now.'

'For now?' Ali was outraged. He slapped her hand away. 'He is not a dog to give away when you grow tired of him!'

Eadie grinned.

'Yes, he is. He's a loyal little puppy with a jealous streak, and he loves his mistress. He's a lot of fun to be around, most of the time. When that changes, I'll rethink the relationship.'

'You don't love him like–' Ali stopped himself.

'Like what?' Eadie asked, smirking. 'Like you do?'

His nostrils flared.

'What do you want?'

'Finally, there's the question I was waiting for.' She reached round to the back of her corset. Not taking her eyes off him she unzipped it, letting it fall away to the floor.

Ali's breath hitched. Her green, lacy, strapless bra criss-crossed intricately at the front, spectacularly scaffolding her big, bouncy breasts. He wanted to feel disgusted, affronted, but something was stirring inside him. Inexplicably conflicted, he wanted her out of his sight before he did something he would regret, yet he still didn't move.

She reached for his belt and began to unbuckle it. He felt frozen in place, one part of his body becoming increasingly stiff.

'Why?' His voice cracked on the lone word.

'This is what I do,' she said, shrugging her ivory shoulders as she slid the leather belt out through the loops. 'Now pour me a drink.'

With a delayed flash of fury, he slapped her across her face in frustration, to make it clear he was not going to stand for this seduction attempt, no matter how eager a certain part of his anatomy seemed to be. Her palm instinctively cradled her cheek and her gorgeous green eyes bored into him, glittering with something he couldn't quite identify.

She smiled.

'Do that again, but harder.'

———

Ali woke to the sound of his phone buzzing. Disorientated for a moment, he struggled to surface, the alcohol he and Eadie had drunk last night muffling his memory. He was getting fragments... snapshots... then full Technicolour replay. He groaned with deep regret as he felt around on the bedside table for the vibrating device, half hoping and half dreading it was Ethan. Would Eadie have told him what they had done?

'Hello?' he questioned, glancing at the neon numbers on the hotel room's digital clock. It was just past 5am. He was in the bed alone but traces of Eadie's perfume lingered on the tangled sheets. The curtains were partially open, and he could see a panoramic slice of the city's lights through the tall picture window. He felt cold and small and revolted with himself.

He could hear sobbing. Was it Ethan? Was he distraught about Eadie's infidelity? Or had he finally seen through her wicked ways and was phoning Ali for comfort?

'I'm bleeding,' a choked voice stated.

'Ava, is that you?' he asked. 'What has happened? Has your husband hurt you again?'

A pause.

'No, no.'

He listened as she retched from crying so hard. He was confused. How could she be bleeding?

She came back on the line, breathing heavily.

'Ali...' she whispered.

'*Habibti*, tell me what is wrong,' he said, his tone firm.

Another pause.

'I think I'm losing the baby. I'm losing your baby...'

CHAPTER TWENTY-EIGHT

REX

PRACTICALLY DROOLING, Rex watched Poppy parade through the showroom's automatic doors and remove her Chanel sunglasses. She was greeted enthusiastically by his suited and smiling minion Jason, who simpered around her, whilst she slowly surveyed the space. The high-spec cars shone beautifully in the August sunlight, and Poppy seemed to glow alongside them. Her smile grew wide as she caught sight of him emerging from his office and she playfully bit down on the arm of her sunglasses as she turned her knockout body in his direction. She began to cross the floor, short skirt swinging around her tanned, shapely thighs, her patent pink heels clicking prettily on the tiles as Jason gaped behind her.

'Miss James, what a pleasure to see you again. I'll take over here, Jason,' Rex called to his underling as he shook Poppy's hand, squeezing it before letting go.

'Test drive, was it?' he asked, playing their pre-planned game. He collected a set of keys from the board as Jason goggled from afar, his tongue practically hanging out at the sight of the real-life goddess running her manicured fingers along the bonnet of the luxury car beside her.

Rex drove the Vanquish quickly and confidently out of the city centre, enjoying the masterful sensation of Poppy's hand rubbing against his erect penis as he did so. Today was their ten-month anniversary. Nearly a year filled with secret messages and romantic meetings and relived teenage trysts. He switched to sixth gear and smoothly manoeuvred the Porsche along familiar country roads on another of their 'sex drives' as he called them, pleased with himself for creating the clever pun. Poppy had brought a small bottle of champagne to celebrate. He already knew she was not wearing any underwear; she clearly wanted to treat him to full and unrestricted access this afternoon.

Once they had reached their familiar destination, their secret place beyond the city, Poppy straddled him mere seconds after he switched off the engine. Their sex was frantic, desperate. Vocalised memories of the sensations they felt when they were teenagers always intensified the experience for them both, the feelings of déjà vu and serendipity driving them both towards loud, fierce orgasms.

Panting, Rex enjoyed the sensation of Poppy covering his face in butterfly kisses.

'I love you,' she whispered. 'I can't wait for us to be together properly.'

She always got like this after they made love and Rex, as always, placated her gently whilst drinking in her adoration like a revitalising tonic.

'We *will* be together properly soon, just a while longer, baby. You know I can't risk leaving her just yet.' He banged his hand against the door in frustration.

Her eyes widened at his show of anger.

'How can you still be stressed?' She pouted, snuggling into his neck and nibbling his ear. 'I thought I relaxed you...'

'You do,' he said, sighing. 'It's just a fucking mess. Hey, you haven't had any weird messages on Facebook, have you?'

'Only from you.' She giggled. 'Why?'

'No reason, I'm probably overthinking it. This situation is driving me crazy.' He rubbed his forehead roughly.

'I know, I know,' she soothed, gently smoothing out his brow with her fingertips. 'But you drive *me* crazy – literally.' He looked at her trusting doe eyes and smiled. 'You're worth waiting for,' she said, kissing him again.

———

'I wish we had longer together.' Poppy pouted as Rex pulled up outside her house.

He reached over and placed a hand on her bare thigh, giving it a squeeze.

'Me too, but we've made the most of it, haven't we?' He grinned. 'I need to return this motor to the showroom as well as make sure my staff of reprobates haven't been slacking off while I've been out.'

'Walk me to the door before you go?' she asked.

'Your wish is my command, Miss James, but I can't let you tempt me inside this time, I really do need to get back.'

Rex exited the car and walked round to the passenger side to open the door for Poppy. As soon as he did, he noticed a large, boxed bouquet of flowers on the doorstep. Poppy unfolded herself gracefully from the low seat then followed his gaze and gasped, bringing her hands to her face.

'Oh, Rex! They're beautiful!' She looked up at him, eyes glistening, before rushing off down the path. Rex followed closely behind, blood already beginning to boil as Poppy giggled girlishly at the romantic gesture. She plucked the card from its pronged holder in the middle of the bouquet and slipped it out of its envelope, glancing coyly at Rex. A split second later, the smile had gone. She bit down on her glossy bottom lip.

'Oh, that's a surprise.'

'Who are they from?' asked Rex, unimpressed with this unexpected occurrence.

'Ben,' she said after a pause. 'One of my personal fitness clients. He hit his goal weight this week and wanted to say thank you. That's so kind of him.' She shrugged apologetically; her palm pressed to her chest.

'Right.' It took all the willpower Rex possessed not to rage with jealousy, rip the bouquet apart flower by flower and scrunch them under his heel. He'd never heard of this Ben bloke before, but he just knew he was a prick clearly trying to hit more than just a weight goal.

Poppy pressed her body against Rex's rigid frame.

'When will I next see you?' she asked, smiling up at him.

He gazed down at her perfect face while trying to suppress his anger – at himself, for not being the one to send her flowers today, at Ben, whoever the fuck he was, and at Ava for keeping him stuck in his marriage. If he didn't find a profitable way out soon, this Ben, or any other man who fancied their chances for that matter, could swoop in and steal Poppy from right under his nose. And he wasn't about to let that happen.

CHAPTER TWENTY-NINE

AVA

Despite being cocooned in her bed, Ava felt as though she had fallen into a prickly pit of hopelessness. The distinctive hospital smell still clung to her clothes and a wave of nausea carried her straight back to last night's trauma. Once home, she hadn't bothered to undress before she curled herself into a ball in bed, hands cradling her aching belly, grimacing against the pain making itself known, like a needy, screaming child. A cruel comparison, given the circumstances.

Now, fresh tears escaped from under her closed lids, and she turned her face into the pillow, again sobbing away her grief for the baby that had gone. It had taken mere hours to lose something she had waited her whole adult life for. She had never felt so desolate, not even after her parents' deaths, and given the choice, she would happily hack off one of her own limbs in exchange for her mother's comforting embrace right now. Yes, she had Ali, and he was being extremely supportive, but she was married to Rex. Yet Rex had beaten Ali's baby to its untimely death before it had even had a chance to live as a punishment for betraying him. How could she ever be free of someone who didn't want her but who didn't want anyone else to have her either?

Despite her grief and exhaustion, she found enough strength to leave the comfort of her bed and pad feebly along the landing to the bathroom. Steadying herself against the vanity unit, she breathed out slowly and caught sight of herself in the mirror above, startled by the reflection of the broken woman looking back at her. Straw-like, stringy hair frizzed around her pale, yellow-tinged face. Her eyes looked too wide for their dark sockets. Her cracked lips were colourless around the fading bruise. There had been questions at the hospital, from a kind nurse, but she had muttered a brief, vague story about being mugged and no, she didn't want to report it to the police thank you.

Stepping back, she stripped off her clothes to her underwear and stood, assessing her nearly naked body. She felt fatter than ever despite rarely eating proper meals. She noticed a few spots on her usually clear skin, angry psoriasis on her elbows, and her bloated stomach felt swollen and sore to the touch. Bitterly, she acknowledged that she looked more pregnant than before.

She went to the toilet and changed her sanitary pad, not daring to look in the bowl before returning to the bedroom, delicately pulling on clean pyjamas, taking two of the trazodone tablets the doctor had prescribed, and returning to her empty bed. Empty was still preferable to her husband's presence.

While she waited for the antidepressants to take effect, her phone buzzed from somewhere under the duvet and she felt around blindly for it. There was a message from Ali.

Telephone me when you are awake, habibti.
How are you feeling now? xx

With shaking fingers, she deleted the message then rang him back. Emotion overwhelmed her before she had even heard the sound of his voice.

'I wish you had allowed me to accompany you to the hospital.'

'If anyone had seen us... look what happened the last time...' More tears dripped down the sides of her face into her pillow. There seemed to be a bottomless well of them inside her.

'How can I help you?' he asked. It was a sweet symphony to her ears; someone cared about her. But there was nothing he could do now.

'It's too late, Ali, you can't help me anymore, you can't bring our baby back...' She allowed the grief to consume her once more, no longer hearing his soothing words. They had already had this conversation, as soon as Ava had returned home, but she hadn't cried like this then. She must have been in shock, creating a barbed wire barrier against the truth of it. There was no way they could continue seeing each other in person now. She felt the loss of him keenly already.

She heard the house phone ringing. Her body immediately tensed. Nobody called the house phone except Rex. If she didn't answer it, there would be consequences.

'I have to go, I'll be okay,' she said, her nerve endings fraying more with each shrill ring that echoed around the hallway. 'I'll call you again soon.'

'Okay, *habibti*. Ring me at any time.'

She ended the call, rose gingerly from the bed and headed out of the bedroom. Gritting her teeth against the agonising cramps, she descended the stairs as quickly as she could and picked up the handset on its ninth ring. Just in time.

'Hello?' she said breathlessly, as if she didn't know who might be on the other end.

'Were you still in bed?' he asked, without a greeting.

She closed her eyes against his hostility, trying to compose herself enough to hold a conversation.

'Ava! Are you even listening to me? What took you so long to answer the phone?' he asked.

She shook her head, trying to jostle her thoughts into some sort of order. Where had he been last night? Perhaps she should ask him that.

'I'm sorry,' she said instead. 'I was cleaning the bathroom and I spilt some bleach...'

'For fuck's sake,' he said. 'It better not have left a stain. Anyway, I'll be home late. Staff appraisals.'

'Again?' she dared, feeling a pathetic thrill of defiance.

'What do you mean by again?' He affected a high-pitched mimic on the last word. 'You know we have staff appraisals once a month. What's with all the questions?'

'No, I meant... you'll be home late again?' she asked, backtracking meekly.

'Yes, I'll be home late again. I work. I work fucking hard. I worked so late last night, schmoozing the fuckers from head office, that I had to crash at Danny's because his place was closest. I messaged you.'

'Danny who?' she asked, frowning into the phone.

'For fuck's sake, Ava, I don't have time for this. He's one of our service staff, Little Miss HR department,' he said sarcastically.

'I...' she began but fell silent as it became clear Rex was talking to someone else on the other end. She waited for him to finish, noticing how he spoke to his colleague with more respect than he ever spoke to her. She wondered if he was speaking to

Danny then admonished herself because she knew for a fact that Danny didn't exist.

He came back on the phone.

'I need to go. Get that bleach cleaned up and while you're at it, the hallway floor could do with another going over. Do it properly this time; the grout's still slightly discoloured from the mess you made last time.' The line went dead.

She listened to the silence for a few seconds before throwing the handset, with as much force as she could muster, against the wall.

———

By mid-afternoon Ava was standing in the queue in John Lewis, waiting to pay for a replacement phone. She knew what would happen if things weren't exactly as they should be when Rex got home. It had taken every ounce of effort she could summon but she had showered, dried her hair, camouflaged her bruises with make-up, and stuffed her knickers with another of the thick pads the hospital had given her. She was still bleeding but it wasn't as bad. The strong painkillers and antidepressant tablets had taken the edge off her physical agony, but her watery eyes told a different story.

'Next,' said the perky young cashier as Ava stared into space, her brain full and foggy while she performed her mundane, ordinary task.

'Next,' she said again, more loudly, as the old woman behind Ava gently nudged her.

'Oh, sorry,' Ava said to the old woman, before stepping forward to the counter. 'Sorry,' she repeated to the cashier, shaking her hair forward, not wanting to make eye contact. As she waited, she wondered what would happen if she just told the cashier what was happening to her. She may look like a respectable, middle-class, attractive, unassuming woman, but she wanted to scream the truth from the pit of her soul: 'My violent husband caused my miscarriage!' She wanted the perky young cashier, and the old woman, and the other shoppers in the vicinity to spring into action and make all the decisions for her. To coddle her, to efficiently sever her from her marriage, to expedite the brand-new life she desperately needed but didn't know how to find the strength to make happen for herself.

Instead, Ava said and did nothing. She paid with cash so that Rex wouldn't see the purchase on their joint bank statement, accepted the bag the smiling, oblivious cashier held out for her, walked away from the counter, and bumped straight into a fellow shopper.

'Sorry,' Ava said, for the third time. She glanced up and discovered she was face to face with Eadie.

'No harm done,' Eadie replied, although her expression didn't convey that she genuinely meant it. Ava wondered if *permanently pissed off* was her default expression. She wished she could be as assertive. She chanced a longer look at the woman in front of her, admiring her red-and-white polka-dot tunic, black leather leggings, and red silk bomber jacket. She looked like a sexy, stylish Minnie Mouse. Despite the humid August day, her hair and make-up were professional standard.

'Anyway...' said Eadie in response to Ava's stare, raising her perfect eyebrows and holding her bags out to indicate she had things to do and places to go.

'Wait,' said Ava, struck by a sudden bolt of bravery. She clutched the handle of her John Lewis bag in both hands. 'Can I ask you something?'

Eadie narrowed her eyes at Ava.

'Suppose.' She slid her own bags down her arm, freeing her hand to take her phone out of her jacket pocket. Ava watched her bring the screen to life as she checked the time. Behind several notifications on the screen, Eadie's screensaver was a photo of herself. 'I need to be somewhere in a bit though, so make it quick,' she said, still holding the phone, which buzzed as she spoke.

Ava looked around them. The old woman had disappeared, and the perky cashier was nowhere to be seen. The electrical section was empty except for a lone man who was practically leering at Eadie from behind a bank of TVs. Ava felt invisible in comparison, yet the last thing she wanted was to be noticed anyway. Eadie was either absolutely oblivious to him or choosing to ignore any attention she didn't personally orchestrate. Ava suspected it was the latter.

Given her recent trauma, Ava didn't want to get herself involved in any more mess, but the question had been playing on her mind and she needed to know if the faint but persistent niggling feeling she had was justified. Karma had made sure she and Eadie had met today, and she wasn't going to waste this opportunity.

'What did you mean at the restaurant when you said to watch out for Ali?'

Ava saw a juggernaut of thoughts dance behind Eadie's jewel-coloured eyes: surprise, irritation, curiosity, pity perhaps. Another buzz punctuated their conversation, but Eadie ignored it.

'I think you already know the answer to that,' she said, just as Ava was about to ask again.

'He loves me,' Ava declared, tears already formed and threatening to fall. She jutted her chin out in an effort to prevent it from happening, but they fell anyway. Ava swiped them from her pale cheeks quickly.

'Are you married?' Eadie asked as Ava's hand, with its gold band on her ring finger, returned to fiddle with her bag handle. 'Are you planning on leaving your husband for him?'

'What?' Ava breathed out the word, taken aback by both Eadie's boldness and insight.

'Is Ali your bit on the side?' Eadie rephrased the question. Her phone buzzed again.

Ava was too shocked by her forthrightness to answer. She glanced around the store, terrified that someone, anyone, could be within earshot of such an embarrassing question. Her stomach began to throb again, and she held her bag even tighter.

'Here's what I think,' said Eadie, cocking her head to one side. 'I think that Ali has got himself a very convenient and generous sugar mummy who is blind to the real reason he is here.'

'What real reason? What do you mean?' asked Ava. She had never heard the phrase 'sugar mummy' but she thought she understood its implication in context.

'He loves Ethan,' Eadie said flatly.

'I... I know that,' stuttered Ava. 'They're brothers... foster brothers. They've stayed in touch since childhood.'

Eadie snorted a laugh and Ava was offended by the harsh sound. She saw a brief flash of perfect, white teeth and discovered that even the hint of a smile elevated the other woman's already outrageous beauty to a whole new level.

'Let me spell it out for you,' said Eadie, her face slipping back to its mask-like state. 'Ali doesn't just love Ethan, he's IN love with him. You're his meal ticket, and a very tasty one at that, from what I can tell so far.'

Ava's vision blurred.

'But... that's not true... he told me...'

'Yeah, well, men fucking lie,' said Eadie, enunciating the words carefully. Her phone buzzed again. She glanced down at it and smiled at whatever message or notification had popped up.

Eadie looked back at Ava and tutted, rolling her heavily lined eyes.

'Look,' she said, appearing to momentarily soften, 'I don't give a shit about so-called sisterhood, but I hate to see people being taken for a mug, and you're clearly being taken for a mug. I'd dump him if I were you. You're welcome.'

With that, she left the department store, tapping away on her phone, as Ava started to tremble.

CHAPTER THIRTY

EADIE

EADIE CAREFULLY APPLIED her make-up using her illuminated magnifying mirror while she thought about how much she loved playing games with people. She had enjoyed telling Ava the truth about Ali when she saw her in John Lewis a few days ago. Pathetic women needed saving from themselves. Especially women who didn't have a clue about the secrets social media held or revealed. Eadie had done her a favour; now she could make an informed decision rather than continue feeling her way blindly through a sham of a relationship. Who the fuck did Ali think he was anyway, using Ava like that?

Acknowledging she was a hypocrite and not much better than Ali when it came to using people brought Eadie no shame, and her thoughts segued to their tawdry night together. She smiled to herself – by propositioning him at the hotel she had not only got herself two amazing orgasms, but she had taught Ali that women actually had the upper hand. Hopefully Ava would realise that eventually, too.

She had very much enjoyed playing with Ali. Despite his pretend protestations, he soon showed her what he was made of, surprisingly vigorously. His obvious passionate loathing of her certainly had its benefits; hate-driven sex was often the best sex. There was no man on earth she couldn't have if she wanted him, and those who persisted in fooling themselves about their attraction to her were usually the most satisfying between the sheets.

As for Rex, well, she didn't know where the hell things might go with him – if anywhere – but the games they had played together were the most fun of all. However, you could have too much of a good thing so she decided to nip that in the bud before it had time to bloom. She didn't like to encourage the sociopathic narcissists for too long.

She had enjoyed her dalliances with Ethan as well – he was kind and generous, and had an impressive dick, but it was about time for him to go. She normally liked being stuck in the middle of messed up situations, but she had to draw the line somewhere and a fucked up incestuous obsession was it.

'Hey, babe,' Ethan said, flopping down on her new suede chaise longue like a trespassing sloth. He frowned at his phone screen. 'It's official: I didn't get a call back after that shitshow of an audition, surprise fucking surprise. Can't seem to get a break lately. How can I get some of your success to rub off on me?'

Eadie looked at him lying on her chaise longue like he owned the place. She had treated herself to that, and all her new bedroom furniture, with some of her game-show winnings, planning on using them as extravagant props for the upcoming lingerie campaigns she had booked for a big brand she worked with. The four-poster bed especially lent itself to those types of photos well. Ethan, however, was making the whole room look a mess.

'I think Ali's getting the hint,' he continued. 'He's only messaged me, like, fifteen times today which is less than yesterday. I haven't replied – obviously.' He stretched his head back and ran his free hand through his curtain of hair in exasperation before looking back down at the phone. 'My dad keeps asking when we're going to see him again though and he'll be gutted when I tell him never.'

Eadie rolled her eyes. She was sick of hearing about this. She was sick of his maudlin attitude. At least when he was drunk, or gambling, he was fun. She looked at his reflection in her dressing-table mirror. He was in the same room as her and yet he wasn't even looking at her, wasn't even giving her the slightest bit of attention, despite the fact she was only wearing a purple lacy bra and thong. And she'd had her lips redone and her microblading topped up since she'd last seen him, and he hadn't even noticed. It wouldn't do. Well, she would make sure she had his attention and then she would get rid.

'Ali and I fucked,' she said, turning on her padded dressing-table stool to face him.

He was giving her his attention now.

'What?' he said, a strange, high-pitched laugh accompanying the question, phone flat and forgotten in his open palm.

'We fucked. In his hotel room. I went there to fuck him, and it happened. It was pretty great, actually, much better than I expected for a man who likes boys too.'

'What?' Ethan repeated. He stood up, slid his phone in his back pocket and took a step towards her. His face was already crumpling in confusion due to her cruelty. 'I don't believe you. Why would you even say that to me?'

She pouted and narrowed her eyes, already bored of the spectacle he was about to make. She wanted it over and done with. She wanted a shiny new toy with no weird baggage or desire to confide in her about feelings or family problems. She wanted something simple and straightforward, and kinky sex on tap.

'I don't lie, Ethan,' she said with a sigh. 'I tell it like it is.' She picked up her phone from the dressing table, unlocked it with her thumb and tapped the screen a couple of times. She found what she was looking for and held the phone out for Ethan to see.

'Here's the proof. Not about him liking boys – I can't prove that but I'm telling you it's true – but proof that we were in bed together. It's over between us – you and me. You need to leave.'

Ethan looked at the screen, at a picture of Eadie and Ali. Their faces were close together on a pillow, bare shoulders visible. Ali looked like he was asleep, but Eadie looked sexily dishevelled, and victorious. He immediately looked away.

'But why?' he asked.

'Because it's my flat and you're not welcome here anymore.' She put the phone back down and inspected her long, purple talons. She'd opted for the abstract nail art this time – a freebie from a new salon who wanted to work with her – and she was pleased with the results.

'No, why did you have sex with Ali?' he cried, his face a contorted mask of pain.

Eadie flipped her palms up.

'For fun, Ethan. To amuse myself. To get fucked,' she told him. 'For the same reasons anyone has sex with anyone.'

Ethan held his head in his hands. After a few seconds he wiped his running nose with his wrist. He looked like a lost little boy, and she felt nothing but annoyance.

'What about love?' he asked.

She frowned, confused.

'What about it?'

'You're the love of my life,' he said, his voice catching with emotion.

Eadie sighed at the ridiculous statement, thoroughly at the end of her patience.

'Get out,' she said, standing up too and walking out of the bedroom and down the stairs.

'Please, Eadie...' He followed her, palms together as if in prayer. 'I thought we had something special going on. I was planning on booking a surprise luxury holiday for us both, for fuck's sake! What did I do to make you treat me like this?'

'How were you planning on paying for a luxury holiday now that you've gambled away all your winnings?' She threw the question over her shoulder as she led him through the kitchen and headed to the door.

'Is that why you're breaking up with me – because I'm not rich enough anymore?'

She turned to face him, hands on hips.

'£125,000 doesn't make you rich, Ethan. But no, it's got absolutely nothing to do with money. I don't need your money, or any man's money for that matter. I make plenty of my own.'

'Then why?' he pleaded, his face gurning unattractively.

She shook her head to reiterate her desire to end the conversation. She had experienced many just like it and was loath to let this one continue any longer.

'Don't take it personally; it's not you, it's me.' She smiled sweetly and held the door to her flat wide open, gesturing for him to leave.

His expression hardened as he realised she was not going to budge. She wondered which insult he was going to throw at her, because they all did, when their ego had been sufficiently wounded. If she was the gambler, she'd bet all her game-show winnings on it being 'fat bitch'.

Ethan appeared to try to compose himself. He stared at her, and she gazed steadily back, conveying statue vibes – cold, stunning, and immoveable.

'You're nothing but a fat bitch,' he snarled in her face, before storming out.

Yes, thought Eadie, men were so fucking predictable. She swung the door closed and returned to her dressing table to finish doing her make-up. Then she was going to treat all her Instagram followers to a scantily clad selfie.

CHAPTER THIRTY-ONE

POPPY

Poppy admired herself in the full-length mirror. She had gone all out – black plunge basque, stockings, suspender belt, seven-inch stilettos, Hollywood wax and spray tan. Well, the wax and tan were frequent occurrences regardless, but the new lingerie had been carefully chosen for maximum impact.

She gazed around at the beautiful room. Recently built, the hotel had only opened a few weeks before and Rex knew how much she had been coveting a night here with him. The statement monochrome carpet popped against the yellow lacquered furniture, and the faux fur throws draped across the bed added an extra element of luxury. The fact that he had booked a stay to belatedly celebrate their ten-month anniversary in style set the perfect tone for their future together. Funnily enough, he informed her of this extra surprise the day after he saw that 'Ben' had sent her flowers. Poppy once again mentally thanked Eadie Lee for her superb advice that day in the beauty salon; it had certainly worked to Poppy's advantage so far, and she had a few more ideas up her sleeve to speed things up, if necessary.

Where was he though? She had already sent him two advance preview picture messages and weighed herself (two pounds under her ideal weight!) and now she was counting the minutes until she saw him. Surely he wasn't having second thoughts about spending the night with her here? Had things become even more difficult in his marriage? She honestly didn't think she could carry on sharing him for much longer – the thought of him still living in the same house as his wife made her want to scream.

Poppy idly wondered what Ava was doing now. Rex never really shared any details about her, except to say how flaky she was (no ambitions or respect for herself like Poppy had, apparently) and Poppy chose not to ask any questions outright. Out of sight, out of mind, most of the time. And as soon as he extricated himself from his wife, he'd be fully committed to her. Poppy prayed Ava would accept the divorce in a dignified manner, no matter how difficult it will be for her to lose a man like Rex, and that would be that. She just had to bide her time a little longer, and hopefully a few nudges would escalate things even further. If she ended up with a real engagement ring on her finger, she'd be forever indebted to Eadie Lee!

Poppy jumped when she finally heard a knock. Rushing across the room to open the door, she laughed with delight as a bunch of roses appeared through the gap, Rex's TAG Heuer watch visible beneath the stems. She took the flowers, nestling them in the crook of one arm as she welcomed him in with the other.

He dropped his overnight bag on the floor and circled his arms around her seductively dressed body, lifting her easily. Kicking the door shut behind him, he kissed her hungrily and she wrapped her stockinged legs around his waist, squashing the roses between them. He carried her over to the bed and placed her down on the fur throw before transferring the bouquet to the bedside table.

'Thank you for my flowers,' she said as he turned back to her and began unbuttoning his shirt. 'I like them better than the ones Ben sent me.' She giggled.

Grabbing the collar of his shirt, he pulled it over his head and threw it onto the nearby chair. He leaned down over her.

'You make me crazy, Miss James,' he uttered, drinking her in with hungry eyes. 'You look sensational.' He kissed her again.

Her body responded in kind, as it always did, a slideshow of their younger selves locked in a similar embrace flashing through her brain, as intoxicating now as it was then. Rex broke away first, fumbling in his trouser pocket. She assumed he was loosening himself and sat up to help him.

Poppy squealed loudly when he brought out the small red velvet box. She flapped her hands in front of her eyes, a giddy action to prevent the tears that had sprung automatically from falling, which did nothing to stop her body spasming with sobs.

Rex kneeled before her. He opened the hinged box and the square cluster of diamonds atop a platinum ring sparkled and shimmered like nothing she had ever seen before. She was captivated by it, and him.

'Marry me?' he asked earnestly.

Ten months she had waited... well, almost two decades in total, and now it was finally happening! Her Rex mood-board-of-sorts flashed into her mind – she had finally manifested what she had dreamed of for so long! Her joy was indescribable. At least now she wouldn't have to consider getting pregnant on purpose to force his hand.

Slipping the engagement ring onto her slender finger, Rex seemed as elated as she was. He was certainly excited. They were making love within seconds in their usual rough, passionate way, two honed, beautiful bodies working together like an oiled machine.

Poppy felt as though she had died and gone to karmic heaven; she had finally won her prize.

CHAPTER THIRTY-TWO

ALI

ALONE IN HIS HOTEL ROOM, Ali felt like a hotline to Ava's distressed calls, which had become more and more frequent as the days had passed. She was still so distraught over the miscarriage, but Ali was beginning to crumble under the weight of her emotional support expectations, as if he didn't have enough on his mind.

In between Ava's calls, he was panicking that Eadie was going to tell Ethan what they had done. She had sent him a picture she had taken while they were in bed together, afterwards, while Ali had been sleeping. She had played with his body and now she was playing with his mind. Why had he done it? Even now, nearly two weeks later, he still could not fathom how it had happened, how he had been so easily persuaded. She must have bewitched him somehow!

He detested himself and this limbo. Things were worse than ever; Eadie had ruined everything. If only he could find a way to make Ethan see that Eadie was bad for him. Wicked through and through. If only he had a way of getting Eadie out of their lives altogether.

A knock at the door made him freeze. There were only three

people it could possibly be. He prayed to not see a female on the other side.

Ali opened the door and stood there agog. It was Ethan! He could barely believe his eyes. A swell of happiness rose within him – he knew his foster brother would come around eventually. But his immediate joy quickly began to dissipate as he registered Ethan's sorry state. His eyes were bloodshot, his hair was unusually dishevelled, and the fumes coming off him tickled Ali's nostrils. He had clearly been drinking.

'Ethan, are you okay?' he asked, instantly worried. He briefly hoped Ethan had been drowning his sorrows after breaking up with Eadie, but that idea did not account for Ethan's disgusted expression, which was directed at him.

'Are you gonna let me in or what, *brother*?' Ethan slurred, pushing past Ali.

Ali didn't like the way he said the word brother, like it was a bad taste in his mouth. His stomach sank, a cold frond of fear slithering through his body.

Ethan came to a stop at the end of the bed and stared down at it. Ali closed the door, turned towards him and waited. He realised Ethan emanated the same sorrowful air as that terrible day Pam had left Bruce. Although he knew Ethan was prone to catastrophising, especially when he was on a losing streak, he looked like his world had been destroyed all over again.

Dread began to dance inside him. He suspected he knew exactly what was coming and there was nothing he could do to stop it now.

'Why did you do it?' Ethan asked, running his hand through his ragged hair. He began to cry openly, just like he had as a child. Another woman he loved had smashed his heart into pieces, but this time it was his own brother who had held the hammer.

Ali felt his own heart crack. He thought he might throw up

as he clumsily foraged for the best response. He could feign ignorance or deny it completely. Except it was obvious things were too far gone for that. Instead, he felt the best defence was attack.

'She came here! She seduced me! She blackmailed me, Ethan. She threatened to tell you terrible lies about me unless I had sex with her,' he cried.

'Fucking bullshit!' Ethan screamed, eyes wide, spittle flying from his mouth, fingers splayed by his sides.

Ali had never seen his mild-mannered foster brother behave this way. Never when he was drunk or had lost a bet, or when he was frustrated with the burden of looking after Bruce. Ali had brought this temper out of him, and he felt wretched, but Ethan needed to understand that Eadie was the one at fault in all this.

Ethan breathed like a boxer mid-fight.

'Was it here – in this bed? Hmm? Did you fuck the love of my life in this bed?'

'Love of your life?' echoed Ali, mirroring Ethan's fury. 'You have known her only five minutes! She is a devious devil who manipulates people both physically and emotionally. I told you she groped me in the restaurant, but you did not believe me. I tried to warn you!'

Ethan clapped both hands to his head and scrunched his hair in his fists.

Ali took a step towards him, hoping for a chance to calm him down, for the chance to comfort him, but Ethan looked up again and Ali stopped in his tracks.

'What about Ava?' he spat, his eyes now as wild as his hair. 'Why would you betray me and her? You came here to be with her, didn't you? How does she fit into all this?'

Ali remained silent. He clenched and unclenched his fists, trying to think of a way to answer such a complicated question.

He was backed into a corner. The only way to face it was head-on.

'I can explain–' He reached out for Ethan.

Ethan stepped back, out of Ali's reach, and crossed his arms, tapping his foot impatiently on the carpet.

'Go on then. Explain. Make it all make sense because I'm fucked if I know what's happening here.'

Ali opened his mouth, but despite willing them to, no words of explanation escaped his lips. He simply stared at Ethan, trying to telepathically convey his hope, his sorrow, his love.

'Oh, fuck.' Ethan's expression changed from one of confusion to one of clarity. 'Eadie was right, wasn't she?'

CHAPTER THIRTY-THREE

AVA

Ava wandered around the supermarket like the walking dead, looking for something for Rex's tea. The tediousness of the task seemed completely at odds with the tempest of emotions swirling around inside her. It had been two weeks since her miscarriage and she was still barely functioning.

As she stood in line waiting to pay for the food Rex had ordered her to get, she watched the checkout woman scan everyone's items. She seemed in as much of a miserable trance as Ava. What was she thinking about? The woman's large frame and particularly rotund stomach prevented her from getting comfortably close enough to the till, so she had to stretch slightly every time she pressed a button. Could she be pregnant or just fat? Ava thought unkindly. And if she is pregnant, why does she get to keep her baby and I didn't?

If Rex had been with her his lip would have curled in disgust at the woman's 'gross rubbery gunt' as he would have called it. One of his typical fatphobic comments. He abhorred people who didn't take care of their bodies, which was ironic as he didn't mind damaging hers. Ava craned her neck to see the cashier's name badge: *Genevieve*. A pretty name that didn't match her dead-behind-the-eyes expression.

As Ava emptied her basket of the sirloin steak – Rex didn't touch carbs, but he didn't mind swallowing animal flesh – and the few other groceries she had bought, she noticed the fundraising bucket for the homeless positioned at the end of the checkout. She felt the heat rise in her face and scolded herself for her seemingly constant self-pity. There were still people worse off than her, after all. She imagined what it must be like to sleep rough, to not feel the comfort of your own bed for weeks, months or years. A loveless bed in a lonely, childless home was still better than none at all.

After paying for the groceries, Ava headed for the exit.

'Ava! Ava, dear! Is that you?'

Ava turned towards the voice and saw a silver-haired woman waving at her, a kind smile on her familiar face. Ava gasped as she realised it was Kathleen, her old neighbour.

'Oh, it is you! I thought it was,' said Kathleen, clutching Ava's arm and regarding her tenderly. 'How wonderful to see you.'

Ava fought to remain dry-eyed as childhood memories instantly assaulted her and caused her heart to twist with pain and longing. A lumbering man knocked Ava's shopping bag as he passed and Kathleen guided her to the side of the exit, out of the way of the main thoroughfare.

'I haven't seen you since your wedding, gosh, what is it – three, four years now?' asked Kathleen.

'Nearly three,' confirmed Ava, the words sounding strangled to her own ears. She cleared her throat, composed herself. 'Thank you so much for coming, by the way; it was lovely to see you there. I'm sorry we didn't get a chance to catch up properly. I'm afraid I was still in a bit of a state after Dad...'

Kathleen nodded sympathetically as Ava's words trailed off.

'To be expected. I was so sorry to hear about your father.'

'Yes. Did I thank you for the card you sent?'

'You did, at the wedding. You looked so beautiful; your parents would have been so proud.' She pressed her thin lips together, clearly struggling to contain her emotions too. 'Ava, I've been meaning to—'

'I know about Mum. How... why she really died,' Ava interrupted.

Kathleen's face contorted and she pressed a pale, liver spotted hand to her chest. A few moments passed before she spoke again.

'I knew you'd find out eventually. I'm so sorry, Ava. I was just...' She shook her head, unable to get the words out, visibly distressed.

'Please don't get upset,' Ava said, gently placing her hand on Kathleen's arm. The older woman was the same age as her mum would have been now. 'It's okay. I understand.'

Kathleen teased a tissue from her sleeve and wiped her nose. She glanced around the supermarket.

'Look, this isn't the time or place to talk about this but come and see me soon. I still live in the same house, if you can bear to visit it again?' She shoved the now crumpled tissue back in place. 'Or perhaps I could come to you if you can't face the memories.'

Ava smiled.

'I'd love to come and visit you.'

'Good. We'll have a proper chat about everything, dear.' She nodded at Ava, her teary eyes full of affection. 'So, nearly three years married, eh? Any special plans for your anniversary?'

Caught off guard by the question, Ava shook her head, twisted her lips.

'I'm not sure yet. Rex might have to work late so we'll see nearer the time.'

'And no pitter patter of tiny feet on the horizon yet?'

Ava recoiled as though she'd been slapped. She gaped at the older woman, aghast.

'Oh, I'm so sorry,' Kathleen said, eyes widening at Ava's appalled expression. 'My friend Heather tells me it's not appropriate to ask young women that these days, but I forget sometimes.' Clearly eager to fix her faux pas, she went on, 'It's just I've thought about you often over the years and I always imagine you rocking a baby on your hip, the picture of happiness. Or baking with a toddler covered in flour, just like us on our Fridays.' Her eyes shone at the memory. 'It's what I've hoped for you, that you'd have a child to love and cherish one day, to experience the precious joy that was cruelly stolen from your mum.'

Overcome with a powerful surge of emotion, Ava dropped her shopping bag on the ground and lurched forward to hug her old Auntie Kathleen tight, not caring who thought what as they walked past. She smelled exactly the same, and Ava was instantly transported back to afternoons spent crafting or playing, or singing, but always smiling.

'I must go,' she whispered, not daring to speak should her voice crack and betray her inner turmoil. 'But I will see you soon.'

———

Despite feeling buoyed by seeing Kathleen again, Ava's mood nosedived during the drive home. As she put the shopping away, Eadie's claim about Ali being in love with Ethan and taking her for a mug popped to the surface again, as it had been doing ever since their encounter in John Lewis. The same question kept circling: why would Eadie lie? But to say Ali was in love with Ethan was preposterous. Wasn't it? Ava mentally ferreted around for evidence but found nothing concrete. Yes, Ali clearly thought the world of Ethan, but to be in love with him – his own foster brother? No, Ava felt it was a stretch. But yet again she was back to the same question: why would Eadie make up such an outrageous declaration?

In her office, sitting in front of her computer, Ava held her head in her hands. It felt full of prickles and poison. She was married to Rex – an abusive misogynist, who she hated, who made her life an absolute misery. And she was having an affair with Ali – her ex-student, who she believed loved her but who, according to Eadie, was using her as a way to get closer to Ethan, both physically and emotionally.

Ava thought about what action she could take. What could she possibly do? What the hell was she even going to search for? She still had her basic Facebook profile but no other social media presence whatsoever or understanding of any of the other platforms. She tapped her fingertips absentmindedly against the keyboard, and muscle memory had her logging onto Facebook within seconds. She typed Ali's full name into the search bar. No results. She didn't know Eadie's or Ethan's surnames, so she couldn't search for them. She sighed, exasperated at her own ineptness and still unconvinced about Eadie's wild theory, especially in light of Ali's ongoing behaviour to the contrary. He could not have been more supportive since the miscarriage. Did she even want to keep investigating something she still didn't really believe? Out of search options, she typed another name in. She hadn't looked for a while, and she was curious.

The picture pinned to the top of the profile showcased a stunning square cluster of diamonds front and centre, in sharp, close-up focus. The caption announced: *I said yes!* A dazzling smile featuring plump, glossy pink lips was visible in the background, in the top left corner of the photo, just above a bare forearm slung around the smiler's slim, tanned neck. The forearm's wrist bore a TAG Heuer Carrera Porsche Special Edition Chronograph watch with a stitched black leather strap. The very watch Ava had bought her husband after he had lost his wedding ring. She stared at the image for a long time, still and unbelieving, hot tears pooling in her eyes.

With a jerk, she snapped out of her trance and bolted to the toilet where she dry-heaved, the tears streaming down her flushed cheeks. Standing on shaky legs, she ran the cold water, soaked her hands and pressed her fingers against her flaming face, breathing shallowly and trying to calm her fevered mind. Rex and Poppy were engaged? How? He was still married to her; they weren't even separated yet!

All thoughts of Eadie's warning about Ali gone, Ava looked at her reflection in the bathroom mirror. She needed to think. She knew about this now, but Rex didn't know she knew. Yes, he knew about her Facebook account, but he didn't know she had been stalking Poppy since that seemingly innocuous text had flashed up on his phone months ago.

Ava had been instantly suspicious as that bloody phone was normally glued to his hand (an expression which had angered him greatly the only time she had ever used it), but that day he had spilled coffee onto his cuff, dangerously near his precious watch, so the phone had been placed on the counter momentarily.

'Poppy James?' she had enquired, daringly, peering at the screen.

He abandoned the coffee stain, snatched the phone up and stowed it quickly back in his pocket.

'Just one of the head office bimbos,' he said. 'I'm going to get changed, this shirt is fucking filthy now.'

'Poppy' had become a vague shape in her mind, quickly evolving into a prettily packaged and very real, living, breathing Barbie doll once Ava had found her profile online. She had been immediately assaulted with image after image of perfection: glossy lips, glossy hair, glossy skin. The woman spammed her wall with a mixture of pouting close-ups, cleavage shots and videos of herself working out in trendy, skimpy gym gear. Checking the pictures one by one, she saw that her husband had liked them all.

Frantic, she had scrolled through Poppy's posts, going back weeks, until she found what she was looking for, innocuous yet damning. A trio of heart-eyed emojis from him. She had known then, as her gut twisted like electric eels, each zap more painful than the last, that Poppy was more than just a 'head office bimbo'.

And now they were engaged. How could he do this to her? He knew her history. He knew what she had been through with Blake, what her dad had been through after her mum's death, and he was obviously prepared to put her through more grief too. Of course he was, she thought – their entire marriage was diseased, rotten to its core.

Back in her office, as the scarce few remaining scraps of love and loyalty towards her husband took their last breaths, she realised she needed to make a plan. She was damned if she was going to end up savaged emotionally as well as physically. She needed to be strong and savvy, like Eadie. She had the advantage now – Rex didn't know she knew about Poppy, and Rex didn't technically know about Ali. He'd only heard unsubstantiated rumours about that night at the restaurant. There was nothing else he could pin on her, not even getting pregnant with another man's baby, a baby that hadn't survived due to his most recent severe punishment.

Her phone rang. It was a number she didn't recognise – maybe Rex was calling from a different number to check up on her today. She fortified herself and answered.

'Hello, is that Ava Bateman? It's Debra Jones.'

Ava's brows furrowed, not immediately placing the name. 'Sorry, who?'

'The landlady from the flat you viewed earlier this month. The previous tenant has left a few days earlier than expected, so it's ready whenever you are.'

Ava thought for a moment. Such a lot had changed since she viewed the flat a few weeks ago. She no longer wanted to simply escape. She wanted something more than that.

Clearing her throat, she said, 'I'm sorry, Debra, but I won't be moving in after all.'

'What do you mean you won't be moving in? You've paid a deposit, signed a short-term lease.' The landlady's previously cheerful voice became shrill.

'I understand if I have to forfeit the deposit,' said Ava.

'Well, it's not just that, it's the hassle of arranging more viewings, getting someone new in.' She huffed. 'You're putting me out.'

'I really am sorry. Please feel free to bill me for the inconvenience.'

Before Debra Jones could utter another word, Ava hung up, her mind whirring, more active than it had been for months, possibly years. With absolute clarity she knew that if she moved out of the house, she might end up forfeiting that too. She knew that if she divorced Rex, he would fight to the death – probably hers – for at least half of her net worth, which amounted to a substantial sum. He was mercenary where money was concerned. She needed to keep what was left of her inheritance safe to secure her own future. A new type of future. One she could envisage so clearly after overcoming one major obstacle.

A few minutes later, she picked up her phone again. At the sound of Ali's voice, she immediately started sobbing.

'*Habibti?*'

'He's engaged to another woman! How can he marry her

when he's still married to me?' she blurted out, her words tumbling over each other. 'He can't!' she said, answering her own question. 'So you know what that means, don't you?'

'He will be divorcing you?' asked Ali.

'No... no...' Ava cried. 'If he divorces me, he won't get any money... and he loves money, Ali, he loves it more than anything. And he wouldn't shame himself by getting a divorce either. Appearances are everything to him. That's why he punished me so badly after he found out I had been to the restaurant... killing our baby...'

She dissolved again.

'So, what do you think he will do?' Ali asked.

Ava swallowed, calmed herself as much as she could.

'As divorcing me means a legal battle for half my money, he'll need an easier, quicker way to get to it. All of it. And the best way to do that is to get rid of me! It's the only way he can save face and not disappoint his mother. He'll be a wealthy widower free to marry his new fiancée,' she screamed, utterly distraught. 'I have to stop him before he kills me... will you help me?'

CHAPTER THIRTY-FOUR

ALI

ALI WOKE to the sound of his phone ringing. He felt himself float up to the realm of consciousness, the journey nastily intertwined with the vivid replay of Ethan's recent visit.

'Eadie was right, wasn't she?' he had asked, gaping at Ali.

'Please, Ethan, you're my brother and my best friend...'

'We're not brothers, Ali! You were just some kid that Mum and Dad fostered for a bit. They fostered loads of kids before you came along, you weren't special!'

Ali's heart scrunched at his spiteful words.

'No, do not say that! You do not mean that. We were all so happy. If your mother had not left us, we would have been the perfect family!'

Ethan laughed without mirth.

'You're fucking deluded, mate. We weren't happy. Mum was carrying on with Ken well before you were plonked in our house. For all I know, she was so unhappy fostering kids, it drove her to him. Maybe you were the final straw!' Flecks of spit flew from his lips.

'Ethan, please, you do not know what you're saying.' Ali's body trembled with disbelief.

'I know exactly what I'm saying, and I'm seeing clearly now too. I've thought about this a lot. You just want to get back at me, don't you? Ruin my life the way you think yours was ruined when you got sent away? All those Skype calls...' He shook his head. 'You've been playing the long game, pretending to care about me, about Dad. But now you're making up outrageous lies about my girlfriend cheating on me because you know that's the one thing that will hurt me the most! No, you're no brother or friend of mine.'

The words wounded Ali, and he clamped his hands on his head as though trying to keep his skull from cracking open. He had to make Ethan see that he was wrong, so terribly wrong.

'No, please...'

'I hate you.' Ethan spat the words at Ali like they contained the filthiest flavours he had ever tasted. 'And no matter what it takes, I'm going to get Eadie back.' He crossed to the door and turned back for his parting shot, jabbing his index finger mid-air. 'Whatever she's done, I forgive her, but I don't forgive you and I never fucking will!'

Ali dropped to his knees in Ethan's wake and curled his body over in utter despair. He banged his hands against the carpet repeatedly in abject frustration at losing not only the one person he truly cared about, but his dreams for their future too. All because of Eadie. What was he going to do now?

The question had plagued him ever since.

He felt physical pain at the memory of it all but somewhere deep within him still hid a speck of hope, that perhaps it was Ethan calling him to say he understood everything now that he'd thought about it properly.

He reached for his phone and saw Ava's name. The disappointment at it not being Ethan felt like a blow, and he closed his eyes again, wondering if he could ignore it, but he knew he couldn't. He had to maintain the status quo until he figured out his next move.

Accepting the call, he prepared himself for the barrage of emotion that had become the norm, and he was right to do so. Ava sounded distraught. He felt a quiver of empathy for he now understood what it was like for your happiness to be at the mercy of another. Finally, she became more coherent. He listened as she told him about Rex and Poppy's engagement. Her pot-kettle-black story of infidelity.

'I have to stop him before he kills me... will you help me?'

Ali's lips parted at her surprisingly certain claim, his mind whirring. Did she honestly believe Rex was going to kill her? A thought formed then. He sat up. The thought quickly morphed into a sketchy plan, like a graphic programmed into a computer. Perhaps there was a way to solve both their problems in one fell swoop.

'Listen to me, Ava, listen to me,' he said quickly, his excitement building at his lightning bolt of an idea. 'Things always seem darkest just before the dawn but there is something we can do. Yes, I will help you, but you will need to do something for me in return.'

CHAPTER THIRTY-FIVE

REX

September 2018

Rex had something special up his sleeve for Poppy. He had booked another overnight stay, in the Quebec Hotel in the city centre, for their one-year anniversary next month, and to celebrate their recent engagement properly. Poppy had squealed with delight when he had rung her from work to tell her. She had then delighted him by describing exactly what she was going to do to him in that hotel room as his dick had got rock hard under his desk. He had been forced to sneak to the staff toilet and relieve himself to one of her selfies.

His life could be one long overnight stay with Poppy, he lamented, if it wasn't for his goddamn excuse of a wife. Ava was the proverbial fly in the ointment, nothing but an annoying insect that needed to be swatted away from him, from them, forever. Ironically, ever since his mistress had said yes to his recent proposal, becoming his fiancée, he had been consumed by thoughts of his wife.

He recalled their latest tiff two nights ago. He'd got home to a filthy kitchen and found her asleep on the bed under a blanket – at just 7.30pm. Sleeping while the house was in a state! Didn't she realise how hard he worked? He deserved a spotless house in return. And he deserved to walk free of his sham of a marriage with his fair share of her money for all the years he had invested in her. Fuck knows where she'd be if he hadn't taken pity on her. In the nuthouse, probably.

He had watched her sleeping for a few moments. She was lying on her back and her skinny arms were wrapped protectively around her narrow torso. Her long, blonde, wavy hair was fanned out on the pillow and if he hadn't been so full of rage, he might have thought she looked beautiful. He had never viewed her that way though; Poppy was beautiful whereas Ava, albeit objectively attractive, had always been distinctly average in his eyes. His fingers fizzed with the urge to flick her face.

Instead, he yanked back the blanket and pinched her cheeks together. Her eyes instantly popped open, doll-like, as though her head was in a vice. She stared at him for a few seconds and then she smacked his hand away and laughed at him. He was astonished and recoiled as though from a venomous snake. She had never laughed at him before. Enraged, he recovered quickly, took hold of her leg and tried to pull her out of bed, but she kicked out at him like a wild banshee. It triggered his memory of how unstable she had been after her dad died; how increasingly erratic her behaviour had been, for weeks. He had wanted to leave her so badly but even he couldn't bring himself to dump a woman in the throes of intense grief, especially when they were due to be married. He would have looked like a right bastard in his mother's eyes. Besides, Ava had already treated him to a Savile Row suit for the occasion. And then there was the handsome lottery-sized windfall she had inherited, meaning his dream of owning his own showroom was in reach.

However, the months following the wedding had been torturous. She had severely tested his patience, pushing him, needling him, until he had finally snapped. She had fought back then, the way she was doing now, but she soon came around to his way of thinking. They bought the new house, she started looking and behaving more like a wife was supposed to look and behave, and he made sales manager at the showroom. All the while enjoying a few dalliances on the side. She mainly hid away in the house, as per his instructions, but he had allowed her to accompany him to the dealership's Christmas do one year, packing her off in a taxi alone before the after party, obviously. A routine of sorts had been established after that and it was the routine they still followed to this day. She mostly did as she was told and when she didn't, he was forced to show her the error of her ways.

Just like he had two nights ago. After suffering a sharp kick to the ribcage and a stinging slap to the face, he managed to overpower her. He flipped her over on the bed, yanked her arms behind her back and held her down until he felt her deflate under the force of him. Using one hand he deftly unbuckled his belt and unbuttoned his trousers. He hadn't fucked her in months, but surprisingly aroused, he suddenly had the urge. She was still his wife, after all. He pulled down her frumpy pyjama bottoms just enough and forced himself inside her. She whimpered but remained limp. He moved both hands up towards her neck as he thrusted, lacing his fingers around her throat. It would be so easy to just strangle her, to get rid of his biggest problem. His fingers became wet with her tears, and he clenched tighter, enjoying the feeling of his power and her helplessness. He ploughed into her again and again and just as he was about to pull out, she snivelled pathetically, and it sent him over the edge. He swore as he came inside her, grunting with the combination of ecstasy and annoyance. But surely one last time wouldn't hurt; it wasn't as if she'd ever got pregnant before – she knew exactly what the consequences would have been if she had.

'I'm going for a shower,' he said as he withdrew himself. 'Get up, get downstairs, and get this fucking house cleaned up.'

In the bathroom he turned on the shower, pulled off his tie, took off his shirt and surveyed the damage Ava had caused. He winced as he pressed the bruise that was already beginning to bloom on his torso.

'Fucking bitch,' he said, and tutted. Where had that wildcat reaction come from all of a sudden? Well, he'd tamed her this time but what if there was a next time? He didn't want to have to cope with any more crazy outbursts anytime soon. As he stood under the powerful rainfall shower head and let the hot jets soothe his body and mind, he resolved to deal with his wife once and for all.

CHAPTER THIRTY-SIX

AVA

AVA WAS SITTING by the window in the café, thinking about her and Ali's last conversation. She was wearing a cap over her long blonde hair and her sunglasses lay on the table in front of her despite the bleak September day. Her turtle-neck jumper covered the bruises on her neck that Rex had caused when he raped her two nights ago. It was that horrific act that had changed her mind about meeting Ali today.

She had tried to fight back for the second time in their marriage, but things had escalated even more quickly than the first time. She had lost even more weight since her miscarriage and was even less of a match, both physically and emotionally, for his gym-toned body and inner fury now than she had been before. The most worrying aspect of it was that although he had forced himself on her many times, he had never tried to choke her before. She honestly believed, in that moment, that she was going to die, just like her mother, at the hands of a brutal man.

As she waited, she seethed. But despite all the trauma she had been forced to endure recently, the person she was angriest at right now wasn't her violent husband.

'Hello Ava,' Ali said, slithering into his seat with a disarming smile.

Goosebumps immediately pimpled on her skin and she clutched her bag to her body like a shield, glancing around the empty café pointlessly. It occurred to her that they were finally out together freely, in a public place. It had been what she dreamed of, back in July. She had never imagined it would be to discuss what they were about to discuss.

Ali reached out to touch her arm, but Ava shrank away from him. As the waitress approached, he retracted it.

'What're you having, folks?' the waitress asked.

Ali looked over at Ava, but she shook her head. He ordered a black coffee. They both waited until the waitress was out of earshot before resuming their conversation.

'Go on then, say what you've come here to say,' she demanded, remembering how cold and unrecognisable his voice had become when they talked just after she found out Rex and Poppy were engaged. She had rung him with the intention of masterfully manipulating him into exposing Rex's adultery, or perhaps planting something incriminating on her husband's computer somehow, but he had turned the tables on her, offering a more permanent solution to her pressing problem as well as to one of his own. During that conversation, his mask had fallen, and she had been able to see who he really was, the man she had foolishly given herself to completely.

Ali paused, looking at her. Ava stared back, fighting against the tears threatening to fall.

'Remember our calls, *habibti*? Remember your tears, your heartbreak?' Ali whispered, reminiscent of the man Ava had met online a few months ago, before things turned more complicated than she could have ever imagined. 'Remember our whispered words, your pleas for help, your desire for me? Remember making love to me in your marital home, in the bed you share with him?' he added hoarsely. She reddened with a flash of lust despite herself although it was now combined with intense shame. 'I have shown you nothing but understanding and affection. I saved you from your misery.'

'You haven't saved me though, have you? You've caused me even more misery, because of your selfish, twisted motives!' Ava shot back, shocked that he could justify his actions so convincingly.

'No,' hissed Ali, eyes flashing, stabbing his finger on the tabletop. '*He* caused you more misery than you had ever experienced. He caused you to lose your child! Doesn't he deserve to be punished? In Sharia law, the retribution for an injury is an equal injury, or as you say here, an eye for an eye.' He sat back again.

She registered his words like a physical blow. He was right. Instinctively, she clutched her stomach as the waitress returned with Ali's coffee. Smiling, the comely woman placed the mug down on the table, then, obviously reading the atmosphere correctly, quickly walked away again.

Ava took a few slow, deep breaths in an attempt to calm herself down.

'But you misled me, Ali. You used me to get here – to be close to Ethan. Not to be with me. I thought you loved me but you're nothing but a liar! Eadie was right about you from the start.' Ava pressed her lips together, letting her tears spill but, unlike their first meeting, Ali did not wipe them away.

'Eadie certainly does enjoy poisoning minds against me.' He sighed. 'We used each other, Ava. We both wanted a better future, and now we are going to help each other to achieve that. You will finally be free of Rex, and I will finally be free to live a life I choose rather than one my culture demands.' He punctuated his statement by taking a sip of his coffee.

Ava shook her head, still unwilling to accept that the

consequences of her actions had led to this bizarre reality, somehow almost as bad as her pre-Ali existence with Rex. Yet a masochistic part of her still yearned for things to have been different, for Rex to have loved her as he now seemed to love Poppy. For Ali to love her as he seemed to love Ethan. She understood what Ali was proposing and a tiny part of her was secretly thrilled at the prospect, especially after Rex's abhorrent assault two nights ago, but she still couldn't bring herself to agree to what he had suggested, whether it brought them both happiness or not.

'Let us go over it again,' said Ali, moving his cup and saucer aside and leaning forward conspiratorially. 'I am going to deal with Rex while you are dealing with Eadie at the same time. She will be expecting me, ready to welcome me with open arms, but I am sure you will find a way to be invited inside.'

'Wait... why will she welcome you in? She knows you hate her!'

'Trust me, she will be happy to know we will be meeting.'

Ava searched his face, comprehension slowly descending. She gasped as her hands rose to her face.

'You've been *with* her, haven't you? She's Ethan's girlfriend. How could you do that to him?' Various emotions swirled within her; agonisingly, jealousy was one of the most prominent.

'No,' he said, slamming his palm on the table. 'I did not do anything!'

Ava jumped and looked around to see whether the waitress had noticed his outburst, but she was nowhere to be seen. Ali closed his eyes for a moment, composing himself.

'This is what she does,' he said, opening his eyes. 'She seduces men. She is worse than a whore. She conned her way into my hotel room while I was sleeping and I woke up to her using me for her own pleasure!'

Ava searched his pained face while Eadie's words elbowed

their way to the front of her brain and whispered softly: *men fucking lie.* Confusion joined jealousy as Ava wrestled with her thoughts.

He shook his head and lowered his voice.

'I did not agree to have sex with her. I did not want to. She is a rapist!' He stabbed his index finger on the tabletop three times to punctuate his statements.

'Oh my God.' Ava covered her mouth with her hand, eyes wide. 'I saw her, in a shop. She called me your sugar mummy. Was she was trying to turn me against you when all along she really wanted you for herself?'

'Yes!' he exclaimed, becoming more animated. 'She is nothing but a devious witch, *habibti*. I want her out of Ethan's life because he is weak and needs help and I know he is not strong enough to withstand her charms. But now I also want her to pay for what she has done to me – and you. She spreads lies as easily as her chubby legs, without caring about the damage. She is an evil narcissist so desperate for attention that she will manufacture a way to get it. I am so happy you have seen through her. Now can you see why I proposed what I did? She is as bad as your husband. They are both users and abusers. Now can you see why they both deserve to disappear?'

In answer to his question, Ava's eyes filled and overflowed again. This time he did reach out to wipe them away, taking her face in his palm tenderly once more.

'Eadie will welcome my visit because I will pretend that I want her – properly,' he repeated. 'However, when you get there instead, you will pretend to have a drink with her as friends. It is ideal that you saw her again recently as she will allow you to enter readily. You will then do what you have to do. It will all be over in one night.' He sat back, grinning.

'And where will this happen?' Ava asked, sniffing.

Ali took another sip of coffee.

'That is a detail I will confirm soon.'

Ava shifted in her seat, still clutching her bag.

'How will we do it without getting caught, without leaving any evidence that we were there?'

'It will be a simple but effective solution, I assure you.' He glanced around the empty café. 'It will look like they have overdosed.'

'Where will you get the... the stuff from?'

'You do not need to concern yourself with that. I will source what we need.'

'And then what?' Ava asked, her voice breaking. 'Do we just wait around for them both to be discovered and then help the police with their enquiries?' She exaggerated a shrug.

'Yes.' He stated simply, a picture of nonchalance.

'Well, it seems you have everything figured out,' said Ava.

'We will meet again to go over everything in more detail as soon as I have thought everything through and finalised it all. I will be in touch.'

Ava nodded and stood. Ali caught her bony wrist and looked up at her.

'There is one final thing – you will pay me £50,000 for this privilege. I will also require a new laptop up front. I will need better technology than I currently have for what I will need to do.'

Ava blinked, not surprised by the demand.

'And what if I say no?'

He tightened his grip and she saw a sinister glint in his eye.

'You have never said no to me before, Ava. I do not advise starting now.'

CHAPTER THIRTY-SEVEN

ETHAN

HE WAS WELL out of it, he thought. All this time he had treated Ali like a friend, like family, like a brother. No, he didn't believe it. Now he'd had time to think about it, he was convinced Eadie had lied about fucking Ali. She was a self-confessed commitment-phobe, self-sabotaging because they had been falling in love. Testing him. And he had failed the test by believing her fiction and letting her break up with him. He wished more than anything he hadn't said what he said when he left. He was mortified that he had called her that. She wasn't a fat bitch; she was a goddess! Although he had no respect for his mother, he respected females in general, especially Eadie, and he was ashamed of himself for giving his ego a cruel voice. The guilt of insulting her was crippling him but she wasn't answering his apology messages despite posting on Instagram several times daily, as usual.

'Dad, I'm going out,' he said, walking into the living room. 'Here's a cuppa and your medication. Your game-show will be on soon, so you'll be all right, won't you?'

'Is it the episode you're on?'

'No, Dad, that aired a while ago, remember?'

'Oh yes. We watched it when Ali was here, didn't we?'

Ethan nodded and ran his hand through his hair, impatient to leave. He was planning on meeting Ryder and getting off his face. He couldn't get a handle on his thoughts, so he needed to obliterate them instead.

'Will you put it on again? Your episode?' asked Bruce.

Ethan sighed inwardly but picked up the remote and found the recorded programme for his dad. He paused it at the title sequence and handed the remote to Bruce as he headed for the door. He didn't want to see Eadie's face on screen, not if he couldn't see it in real life yet. He didn't want a reminder of where it all began. He was going out to forget all about her, and the whole fucked up situation with Ali, hopefully.

'When's Ali coming to visit again?' asked Bruce as Ethan stepped into the hallway. He'd been asking the same question almost daily since Ali surprised them that Sunday back in July.

Ethan could hear the hope in Bruce's voice and felt cold inside. He shrugged on his coat and continued to the door. How was he meant to explain what had happened between them? At least he hadn't introduced Bruce to Eadie yet. Bruce would be disappointed he hadn't managed to hold on to her. Christ, he was disappointed too. But that was going to change as soon as he figured out what to do, how to mend things between them.

Ali, however, was a different story. Despite trying several times already to block out the awful scene in the hotel with whatever substance he could get hold of or afford, it kept replaying. He closed his eyes, one hand on the latch, ready to leave.

Ali's lies kept coming back to him, like bombs being dropped in his brain: *She came here! She seduced me! She blackmailed me, Ethan. She threatened to tell you terrible lies about me unless I had sex with her.*

And then his so-called explanation for everything that had

happened: *I love you, Ethan, you're my brother and my best friend...*

Ethan had scrunched his fists against his head, so hurt and angry and drunk and pissed off and disgusted that he thought he was going to puke on the patterned hotel carpet.

'Ethan, are you still there?' Bruce called, bringing him back to the present.

'Sorry, Dad, erm... I don't know when Ali's visiting next. I'll ask him, okay?' He had no intention of asking him but one of the saving graces of Bruce's severe depression was that he was likely to lose interest and stop asking soon. Then they'd be able to get back to normal.

Yet the thought of their normal life in their three-bed ex-council semi-detached home stretching out before him propelled Ethan out the door. He was suddenly desperate for fresh air followed swiftly by a varied selection of his vices. Nothing was going right. All he wanted was a break. All he wanted was to escape. To meet Ryder then hitchhike to oblivion. Tonight, he was going to forget all his troubles no matter the cost or the consequences.

CHAPTER THIRTY-EIGHT

AVA

Ava didn't know what to believe but something wasn't sitting right. Ali's claim about Eadie sneaking into his hotel room while he was sleeping and starting to have sex with him without his knowledge or permission rang alarm bells. She had been so shocked when he said it, sympathetic even, and she found it hard to believe someone would lie about something like that, especially to her given all she had experienced at the hands of Rex. He seemed so certain, so righteous. But then, all good liars are.

She thought about how differently she felt now, as though something had shifted in her. Perhaps it was because of the baby she had lost. That, and the terrible days following it, really had been rock bottom. She was amazed by the depth of grief she had experienced – and was still experiencing – for something that hadn't technically existed. Even though she should be an expert in grief by now, after losing both her mum and dad so cruelly, she had decided that, after all this, she was going to seek help. Counselling. Therapy. A retreat maybe. Make a real friend or two. Live a varied, joyous existence rather than a lonely, sorrowful one.

Perhaps the shift had happened because Rex had proposed to another woman. Knowing he had lined up her replacement before ending their marriage properly amplified the uneasiness she already felt. She realised long ago that the only reason he stayed with her was because she was his cash cow, but now he wanted her money to start a new life with someone else. What was he prepared to do to make that happen?

Perhaps it was because of Rex choking her, and the realisation that if she didn't take swift action of her own, she would probably end up dead. Although the thought of him being locked up for life appealed, she didn't want to be erased in the process, like her mum had been. Had her mum's death set in motion a karmic chain reaction that had influenced Ava's life? Since her dad's deathbed confession, Ava had tortured herself with whys and what ifs, concluding that, somehow, she was partially to blame for her mother's secret affair, that having Ava had trapped her into a role, a marriage, a life, that she might not have wanted. And now Ava had a secret life of her own, borne out of desperation, just like her mum. She should have known better. There were too many parallels now. Too many warnings. She needed to heed them. Affairs ruined lives catastrophically. Her own desire for love and affection had resulted in nothing but twisted mess after twisted mess, and now she was going to have to unravel them and clean them all up.

It was this epiphany that had forced Ava to consider Ali's proposal from a different perspective. Perhaps becoming a murderer was the only way to save herself, after all.

CHAPTER THIRTY-NINE

ALI

CLEVER ALI, he thought as he recalled his and Ava's meeting in the café. He had instantly realised his mistake when he assured Ava that Eadie would welcome his suggestion to meet. It had just slipped out. But now she believed that Eadie was no better than a rapist. She was so pliable, so easily manipulated, it was laughable. She was the perfect mark. He felt so smug.

He thought through the plan again. It was all locked in his head, like a puzzle compendium, and he had been replaying it over and over during the past couple of weeks, determined not to rely on a written account, no matter how coded he made it. There would be no paper trail. And now it was time to go through it with Ava.

As if on cue, he heard her knock.

He opened the door and grinned down at her. She looked back at him from under the peak of her cap, a large fabric bag clutched to her long, padded coat.

'Please come in,' he said, stepping back then closing his hotel room door behind her.

She walked over to the seating area in front of the window

and placed the bag on the coffee table between the two chairs. From the bag she pulled a Dell laptop box and handed it to Ali.

'Here – as requested. Let's get this over with.' She sat down stiffly on one of the chairs, clasping her hands in her lap.

Ali turned down the corners of his mouth, impressed with her efficient air. He was only too happy to comply. He sat on the unmade bed, placing the new laptop beside him.

'You must listen very carefully to what I am going to say. You will need to memorise everything, as I have. If our plan is to work, there must be no evidence whatsoever of our plotting. I believe I have thought of everything, but you are free to ask questions or point out anything you think may need further consideration.' He paused for her response and Ava nodded. 'Before I begin, please prove to me that you are not recording this conversation on your phone.'

Ava hesitated for a moment then stood, took out her phone from her pocket, showed it to Ali then placed it screen up on the coffee table. Obviously pre-empting his next request, she took off her coat and handed it to him. He checked the other pockets and nodded. She took the coat back, put it on and sat down again. He glanced at the fabric bag, and she picked it up from the coffee table, held it upside down and shook it. It was empty. She draped it over her knee and looked at him expectantly.

'Very good,' he said, smiling like a teacher pleased with his student. He was thrilled she was behaving so encouragingly. He placed his palms together and took a breath. 'Okay. We are going to execute our plan at the Quebec Hotel two weeks from today. I have been conducting lots of covert investigations and I have discovered that your husband and his new fiancée Poppy are booked into a room on the twentieth of October to celebrate their one-year anniversary. I must thank Poppy for having an open Facebook profile and sharing so many posts about her full and busy life. I was able to deduce this information in seconds despite the fact she is careful never to mention your husband by name.' He glanced at Ava to check whether she appreciated his levity, but her blank face gave nothing away.

'I will book a room in the same hotel and invite Eadie. I will tell her I cannot stop thinking about her and want to meet again. That will feed her insatiable ego and I am confident she will not refuse. You will contact Rex by text while he is on his way to meet Poppy to leave a text trail of your ignorance about where he is. If he replies, that would be beneficial too as he will want to cover up the truth. By the time Rex arrives, I will have placed a sign on the hotel room door informing him they have been upgraded. It will divert him to the penthouse suite, which I have already booked in advance under a false name. I will kill him there by injecting heroin and making it appear an overdose.' Ali concluded his speech by spreading out his hands and smiling proudly.

Ava frowned in response.

'I've thought about that part... Rex has no history of taking drugs. He wouldn't contaminate his body with them.'

'That may be true,' Ali replied, extending his index finger, 'but remember, we are telling a story for the police, merely setting a celebratory scene. He is staying in the penthouse suite of a smart hotel. Penthouse suites are normally used for special occasions. The possibility he will use heroin is plausible. That is all it has to be.'

'Where will you get heroin from anonymously?' asked Ava.

'As I said before, leave that to me. Meanwhile, you will go to the room I have booked to meet Eadie, who will be expecting me. You will kill Eadie using a lethal combination of powdered drugs in her drink. Do not leave until she has ingested it. When you do leave you will hang the *do not disturb* sign on her door, as I will when I leave Rex's body in his room.'

Ava twisted her lips, thinking.

'And what if Poppy texts Rex before he gets to the penthouse suite and he realises the redirect is a ruse?'

'It is a possibility, yes, but the likelihood is that she will merely ask why he is late, and he will assume she means to the penthouse, not the original room, and still head to it. I will be inside already, perform my task and then I will text her from his phone telling her to wait. As I leave, I will remove the redirect sign from her door. When Rex does not arrive, she will think he has stood her up or simply been waylaid. She may be his fiancée, but she is still also his mistress. She will not alert anyone immediately, if at all. I will then discard his phone somewhere in the hotel.'

'But people will see us – the staff and other guests and there are cameras everywhere!' said Ava.

'Aha! This is why the new computer is needed.' Ali patted the box beside him. 'I will hack into the CCTV and create a time glitch to make sure nobody sees me putting the note on the door of Poppy's room or going to the penthouse before Rex arrives. Or you going to Eadie's room. Or either of us leaving their rooms afterward. We will wear cleaning uniforms and wigs so that other guests will not give us a second glance and if they do, they will not be able to identify us correctly.'

'You can hack into a hotel's CCTV system?' asked Ava, incredulous.

'During my upbringing in Saudi Arabia, I was taught how to hack into many systems, when I needed to,' said Ali wearing a smug grin.

Ava blinked several times but did not comment and Ali felt strangely disappointed she did not seem more impressed.

After a moment, she asked, 'What if Poppy does tell someone about her affair with Rex afterwards – won't it look weird that they were in two different rooms in the same hotel?'

Ali sighed softly.

'You are looking for more problems where there are none, Ava. For our purposes, Rex was alone in a penthouse suite and took an overdose. If Poppy does come forward to claim she and Rex were meant to meet at the hotel in a different room, what of it? It could be a mix-up. They could have each booked rooms to surprise the other. She could be a fantasist or a stalker or an escort. It is an irrelevant detail after the fact.'

'And what about when it's all done, what then?'

He smiled.

'We will meet back here, in this room, in this hotel. We will stay all night but check out early, presenting as the normal guests we are. The staff will see us, and we will be each other's alibi.'

Ava glanced out of the window then turned her attention back to Ali.

'When Rex and Eadie are found, won't it look suspicious that we were both in a hotel nearby?'

Frustration rose within him; didn't she realise he had already thought of everything? Forcing himself to keep his tone measured, he spoke words of reassurance.

'A coincidence, yes, but again it is plausible. People conduct affairs in hotels and affairs are not illegal. It can be explained easily enough, and it is not an outright lie. In fact, when you leave today, make sure to catch someone's eye or say goodbye. It will strengthen our history. The police will determine that Rex and Eadie have overdosed. Neither of us have a strong motive to kill either of them, and remember, we will have alibis. The next day, we will go our separate ways. You will be free of Rex, Ethan will be free of Eadie, and I will have £50,000 to start a new life. You will never see me again.'

'It certainly sounds like you've got it all worked out,' Ava said, a note of sadness in her voice.

Ali beamed at her. I certainly have, he thought to himself.

He was excited; his plan was foolproof. It may take Ethan a while to get over Eadie's death, but Ali would be there to support him emotionally. And financially, if necessary, with Ava's money. Maybe he and Ethan would eventually marry, take care of Bruce in his twilight years, adopt a child. Ali felt his heart swell with love and hope and possibility. As far as he was concerned, removing Rex and Eadie from the picture solved all their problems.

He was gratified Ava realised that now too, even if he hadn't been wholly honest with her about his reasons for wanting Eadie dead. She might not have been so easy to convince if she knew for sure that he had been in love with Ethan for years, that Eadie hadn't raped him, that he had been adeptly manipulating her since learning of her violent and unhappy marriage during their online tutoring sessions.

Now they were hurtling towards the climax of their story and Ali was finally going to get the happy ending he dreamed of.

CHAPTER FORTY

AVA

October 2018

THE PAST TWO weeks had been surreal. Knowing that her life was about to change, Ava had spent the time taking stock, tying up loose ends, planning ahead.

Ali had been in touch just once more since their meeting in his hotel. A brief housekeeping call to remind her of a few key details. As if she was likely to forget. He paused before he hung up and in that second of silence, memories of how they used to be in their early tutoring sessions flashed through her mind and she wondered if maybe he was going to apologise. Hoped that he was sorry for it all. But he didn't. He wasn't. If he had shown even the slightest hint of remorse, she might have decided to do things differently.

Afterwards, gripped by the urge to root herself back in reality, she had visited Kathleen. Navigated her way back to what she still thought of as home, even after all these years.

Home would always be where she had lived with her mum and dad. Where they had been a happy family, or so she had thought.

'Why did Mum have an affair?' Ava asked Kathleen as they both nursed cups of tea in the cosy conservatory. 'Was she unhappy being married to Dad, being a mother to me?'

'Oh, my goodness, no!' said Kathleen, leaning forward and transferring her cup to the coaster on the small side table. 'Your mother loved you both, so much. But she was so lonely, Ava. Your father worked all the time, your grandparents were already gone, and she had no siblings either. Obviously, she had me but that was circumstance more than anything because I happened to live next door. She had mentioned a few times about getting a job herself, just something part time, once you started school that September. To give her purpose, you know... not that being your mum wasn't fulfilling but she missed being out and about in the *real world*, as she put it. But September never came, not for her.' Kathleen sighed. 'Whereas me, I would have given my right arm to have had what she had – a husband and a child. A family of my own.'

'That's all I want too,' said Ava, gazing out of the window at Kathleen's well-tended back garden. The planted borders were vibrant against the October drizzle and there was a weeping willow where the apple tree had once been. A taller, six-foot fence bordered the perimeter now and the adjoining gate had gone, but in her mind's eye, Ava could see it all just as it had been thirty years before. Despite the tragic memory attached to Kathleen's home, Ava felt calmer and more peaceful than she had in a long time.

'You will have a child, one day. I can feel it in my bones,' said Kathleen, reaching over to pat Ava's hand before picking up her cup and settling back in the chair again.

'I think I can too.' Ava smiled.

———

Now, Ava knocked and waited, looking down at the familiar hotel carpet. It was hard to believe it had only been three months since July when she had stood right here about to meet Ali face-to-face for the first time. Her cheeks felt hot, a mixture of adrenaline, the exertion from taking the stairs rather than the lift, and the warmth of the hotel after coming in from the chilly October wind.

Knowing he was just on the other side of the hotel door made Ava's stomach bubble and gurgle as though attempting to verbalise its distaste for what he was going to force her to do. He was taking his time to answer. She knew it wasn't because he was otherwise engaged or in any way incapacitated, but because he was reminding her that he was in full control. She would have hated him for it, for all his deceit, if she was not about to benefit from it too.

He finally opened the door with a flourish, and greeted her disguised form with a whistle.

'Red hair suits you,' he said, grinning down at her, brown-black eyes narrowed mischievously. She forced herself to meet his gaze, trying to appear less disgusted than she felt, grateful that the disguise helped her feel slightly detached. He gestured for her to enter, tracking her as she brushed past him to the other side of the stale, airless room; as stale as her feelings for him now. Still, visions flashed like lightning, unbidden and unwanted, making her tremor with shame – whispered declarations, nakedness, pleasure... She blinked them away and forced herself to focus, stilling her body like a sculpture.

She knew he would stay by the door, blocking her escape

until he was ready to let her leave, and she was right. She found it jarring trying to reconcile this master manipulator with the seemingly sweet, unassuming, sensitive man she had met mere months before. A man she wrongly believed would save her and love her and make her dreams of a real love, a real family come true. She still physically ached with the grief of realising he never intended to do any of those things.

After locking the door, he turned to face her, still grinning, incongruously given the circumstances. His handsome face masked his dark, selfish soul.

'All set?' he asked, one black eyebrow raised. No pet names anymore. No names at all. All pretence eradicated.

She nodded once, her face impassive, her mouth set in a grim line, liquid nausea rising.

'I have messaged Eadie and arranged to meet her at the other hotel. As I suspected she would, she readily agreed to a rendezvous. She will text me the room number when she gets there and then I will text you.'

Ava nodded again.

With a magician's swish, he reached into the pocket of his black leather jacket and pulled out a small plastic bag full of powder, holding it out to her in his open palm. A palm that had once caressed her distorted, tear-stained face as though she was adored. She resisted the urge to grimace and batted the memory away quickly; those times were nothing but fiction.

She moved towards him and opened her bag, and he dropped the drugs inside. He smiled victoriously, as though to an adoring audience, yet his eyes remained steely as he then produced the room's spare key card and handed it to her. She took it.

'It is showtime,' he declared with a wink.

He grabbed her arm and looked down at her through half-closed lids. She tried to yank herself away, but he held tight.

'If anything goes wrong, as much as I do not want to, I will make your life even more miserable than it has been with your husband. Do you understand me?'

She swallowed.

'Do you understand me, Ava?' he repeated, tightening his grip.

'Yes, Ali,' she said.

CHAPTER FORTY-ONE

ALI

THROUGH THE CRACK in the en-suite doorway, Ali watched a grinning Rex enter through the already open door, drop his bag on the floor and his phone on the bed, then cross to the penthouse suite's balcony. He pulled back the long, netted curtains and the velvet, floor-length drapes in one fluid swoop, calling for Poppy.

'Baby, where are you? Fucking hell, look at this room! No more than we deserve though, eh?' The disappointment at not finding her hiding in wait for him straight away was evident on his face. Rex turned, scanning the vast, luxurious space, clearly confused about where his fiancée could be. A salacious smile appeared a second later as he looked towards the en-suite bathroom.

Ali felt a thrill of excitement thrum through his body as he tracked Rex. He was wearing a disposable protective coverall that he had bought with cash from a local DIY store as well as shoe covers and latex gloves. He held a one hundred millilitre syringe full of heroin in his fingers. He felt like an actor in one of the sci-fi movies that Ethan liked.

'If you're not coming out, future Mrs Bateman, I'm coming

in,' Rex said, unbuttoning his shirt. Striding towards the en suite, Rex was practically salivating with desire as he threw his shirt to the floor. Bare-chested and belt undone, he pushed on the door and stepped inside the bathroom.

Taking advantage of the element of surprise, Ali lurched forward and body slammed Rex, sending him sprawling to the intricately patterned tiled floor. Rex landed heavily, crying out as his arm twisted beneath him. Swiftly and silently, Ali pushed the door shut, stepped forward and straddled Rex's back, pulling his head back by his well-groomed hair.

'What the fu–'

Angling it carefully, as he'd learnt from his medical textbooks and online research, Ali plunged the syringe into Rex's neck, depressed it and withdrew it before standing up and stepping away. Rex's head immediately dropped to the floor.

Ali headed out of the en suite and over to the bed. With his gloved hands he picked up Rex's phone. There were three picture message alerts from Poppy on his home screen. The thumbnails were small but even Ali could make out naked flesh. He crossed back to the en suite, pressed Rex's thumb to the screen and unlocked the phone to view the messages. All selfies. Poppy hadn't sent anything else asking where he was. Ali smiled and after scrolling through a few earlier texts, he replied to the latest picture message as though he was Rex, making sure to use the same idiosyncrasies:

Stunning. C U soon. Xx

Simple but effective. He pocketed the phone and returned to the bathroom to find Rex spasming, eyelids fluttering and foamy spittle dribbling from his lips as his body jerked and twitched. A minute later he was limp. Ali bent down and hooked the used syringe in Rex's fingers before unzipping his coverall, retrieving his own phone from his pocket and taking a photo. Looking down upon Rex like a wealthy magnate would survey a tramp, Ali smiled again before dropping the empty bag that had contained the heroin onto the floor beside the body. He left the room as quickly and stealthily as he'd entered it.

He'd taken care of the CCTV already, hacking into the system from his own hotel room and setting up a sixty-minute glitch, to cover him going to the penthouse and Ava going to Eadie's room. A technical, sophisticated hack that Ramzi had favoured. If anything failed – not that it should – he would crash the hotel's server completely. He still found it amazing how easy passwords were to crack, how simple so-called impenetrable firewalls were to penetrate. Although Ali still nurtured a lot of hatred for Ramzi, he had to admit that all those years being forced to work for his criminal cousin had taught him a lot of useful skills. Skills that he was now able to use for his own benefit.

Thanks to him, Ava was finally rid of her piece of shit husband who had made her suffer so badly, who had caused her to lose so much. He was a hero for saving her! And he was very much looking forward to listening to her recount of Eadie's death. Although he was desperate to see that witch's dead, fat body for himself, he trusted that Ava had played her part effectively, especially after his warning earlier.

The thought of he and Ava executing their plan – literally – in unison, made him feel a rush of gratitude towards her. Despite the way things had turned out, they were now forever bound.

CHAPTER FORTY-TWO

EADIE

'WHY ARE YOU HERE?' Eadie held the door open, her other hand on her hip.

'Can I come in?' asked Ava.

Eadie tutted.

'I'm expecting someone.'

'Please. This won't take long.'

Eadie would have frowned had her forehead not been frozen with Botox. Instead, after a pause, she moved aside and allowed Ava to slip past her into the hotel room. She reasoned that if Ali arrived while Ava was still here, they could always have a threesome.

'New look?' she asked, purple shaded eyes narrowed at Ava's red wig. She closed the door and crossed her arms over her sleeveless black silk blouse. It had a pussy bow at the collar and red buttons, and she had teamed it with a leopard print midi skirt in a contrasting red and purple colourway. Both items of clothing had been gifted from plus-size brands. By her usual standards, it was quite a demure outfit.

Both women faced each other at the foot of the bed.

'I know who you were expecting,' said Ava, ignoring Eadie's previous question.

'Really? Go on then, who?'

'Ali.'

'So?' Eadie said, shrugging. 'He asked me here. Whatever he does with you is your business. Whatever he does with me is mine.'

'Do you fancy him?'

Eadie huffed out a laugh.

'What are you – twelve? No, I don't particularly *fancy* him, but he was a good fuck and I'm up for another.'

'So you did have sex with him?' Ava asked. 'In his hotel room?' She twisted her bag strap in her fingers.

'Wasn't that clear when I said he was a good fuck?' Eadie rolled her eyes. 'Look, if you're expecting an apology, you're not going to get one. I'm not sorry for doing, and getting, whatever I want. I decided a long time ago to live an unapologetically selfish life. I don't believe in monogamy, and I don't give a shit what anyone else thinks about me.' Somewhere behind her, Eadie's phone pinged. She turned her head in its direction but didn't automatically move to check it. She already knew it was the back-up sex she'd organised if Ali bailed on her.

'I know. I admire that actually,' said Ava. 'But I have one more question: did you start having sex with him while he was sleeping, without his knowledge or consent?'

'What the fuck? No, I did not!' said Eadie, her jaw dropping. 'Wow. That's something I've never been accused of before. He's inventive, I'll give him that.'

Ava nodded.

'That's what I thought. He said you did. He was quite convincing.'

'Men will say anything to cover their own arses,' said Eadie, shaking her head at Ali's wild accusation. She fixed Ava with a stare. 'Listen to me... you need to trust your own instincts and fine-tune your bullshit detector. Look after your own interests over anyone else's, no matter what.'

'You're right. It's time I put myself first,' said Ava. 'I jumped from the frying pan into the fire by thinking Ali was going to save me from Rex. In a warped way, at least Rex was honest in his hatred for me. His beatings made that clear. Ali though... Ali manipulated me from the beginning.' Her eyes shone with tears.

'Rex?' Eadie asked, wondering how common the name was.

'My lying, cheating, abusive husband,' confirmed Ava. 'Ironically, it's our wedding anniversary today.'

Eadie raised one eyebrow.

'What's your surname?' asked Eadie.

'Bateman. Why?'

'Fuck,' said Eadie, and sat down on the bed. 'What are the chances?'

'What do you mean? What are you talking about?' asked Ava, frowning.

Eadie certainly didn't want to have to console an already crying woman, nor add to her evident distress by suggesting that she knew Rex intimately too, but she felt like she needed to know. Although the coincidence was surprising, the type of men Eadie was truly attracted to were usually the bastards.

'I know him,' she admitted.

Ava's stare bored into her, the unasked question hanging between them. If she'd had a conscience, Eadie would have hung her head, but she stared right back at Ava and nodded once.

'Yeah, intimately,' she added, confirming what Ava had clearly realised.

Eadie wasn't sure of the etiquette involved after telling

another woman she had slept with her husband. She considered whether Ava would rage at her, or attack her physically, but she didn't seem the type to do anything violent. Although she seemed a lot stronger than the previous times she had seen her, she still needed toughening up. Ava slumped down next to Eadie on the bed.

'Look, I know most women probably say it, but I really didn't know he was married,' stated Eadie. 'He wasn't wearing a ring and he certainly never mentioned a wife. I'll be honest though – I don't care if any of them are married or not, that's their status not mine, but I genuinely didn't know this time. But I will say this: you're better off out of it. He's not exactly Mr Good Guy. When I first met you in that restaurant, it was obvious some man – or men – had done a number on you. You had that aura all broken women have. And broken women are either victims or survivors. Believe it or not, I want you to be a survivor. It's the only way to take back control.'

Ava straightened her back and looked at Eadie.

'Do you know what?' she said. 'You're right. I am a survivor, and I am going to take back control.'

'Good for you. So, why did you come here – was it just to ask about Ali?' asked Eadie.

'I was supposed to kill you,' Ava replied, without hesitation.

Eadie nodded, unfazed by the confession.

'How?'

'Drugs.'

Eadie turned the corners of her mouth down.

'As good a way as any. Ali's request, I assume?'

Ava nodded.

Eadie cocked her head.

'To agree to it in the first place means he's either got something over you, which seems unlikely, or he's promised you something in return.' She regarded the other woman beside her with a newfound respect. 'So why haven't you done it? Why are you telling me about it?'

'Because men fucking lie; you were right about that.' Ava smiled. 'And because now I need your help.'

Eadie smiled back.

CHAPTER FORTY-THREE

AVA

Leaving the *do not disturb* sign hanging on the door handle, Ava used the key card Ali had given her to enter his room at his hotel, her head clear and calm for the first time in years. The grief she had been carrying over her mother's murder, her disastrous university affair with Blake, her father's death and her unhappy, abusive marriage felt lighter, no longer weighing her down like it had been. Like Eadie had said: it was time to take back control, and that was exactly what she had been planning to do.

She was a bit earlier than scheduled, so she had time. She removed her coat, gloves and red wig, throwing the fake hair down on the bed and scratching her head vigorously. It was thrilling to think that at this very moment Rex could be dying or already dead. That Poppy was alone and probably anxious, waiting for a fiancé who was never going to arrive. That instead of overdosing, Eadie might now be scrolling through her trusty phone looking for company or getting ready to go out, to find another conquest to bring back to her already paid-for room. Perhaps another man just like Rex. Strangely enough, the thought of them together didn't affect Ava at all.

All she felt was an even deeper-seated hatred for her so-called husband.

Ava opened her large bag and took out the bottle of champagne and two glasses she had bought in preparation. She placed them on the table in the seating area near the window and sat down with a satisfied sigh, Ali's scent still in the air, already familiar to her. She gazed around the room. The new laptop she had bought him was open on the desk, the screen filled with a grid of videos which Ava assumed must be the areas the CCTV covered in the other hotel.

Too restless to just sit and wait, Ava roamed the room. The bed was unmade but Ali's only bag of belongings was placed neatly on the room's luggage holder. He certainly travelled light. Ava briefly wondered about the life he had left to come here, what it was really like behind the scenes he had presented. Learning how to hack wasn't exactly synonymous with wanting to train to be a doctor. Was that yet another lie? Curious, Ava crossed to the bedside table and opened the drawer, looking for something, anything to give her some sort of clue about the man Ali truly was. Sitting on the bed, she reached for the passport inside. As she opened it and glanced at Ali's unsmiling profile, a loose photograph dropped onto her lap. It was a sepia-tinted picture of two young boys, both grinning widely. A messily decorated Christmas tree was visible in the background. The photo had been torn in half and carefully sellotaped back together, yet the rip still sliced through the middle of the older boy's image. As Ava stared at it, she realised the boy was Ali. She laughed softly to herself; even the picture indicated he was two-faced.

A short while later, Ali, wild-eyed and exhilarated, returned. She was quite relieved to see this reaction, rather than a worryingly calm demeanour hinting that he had done this sort of thing before.

'Ava!' He looked pleased to see her. 'You are here already.'

'I came straight from seeing Eadie, as planned.'

He crossed over to the open laptop and hunched over it, tapping keys furiously for several minutes without speaking. She watched from afar, fascinated.

'It is done?' he threw over his shoulder without taking his eyes from the screen.

'Yes.'

After a few more minutes he slammed the laptop's lid shut and turned to her.

'Rex too?' she asked.

He grinned.

'Oh yes, it is done.'

A hot jolt of emotion flashed through Ava as he confirmed she was now a widow.

'I want to see the proof,' she stated, raising her chin.

'No, no you don't.' Ali shook his head. 'It was not a pretty sight in the end.'

She was surprised he was concerned about protecting her from it. Or had he forgotten to get it?

'I want to see him and then we can celebrate properly.' She gestured to the champagne bottle and flutes on the coffee table.

'You do not trust me to play my part?' He looked at her quizzically, a hint of amusement on his face.

She stood up.

'You've seen the evidence of what he did to me, and that's only recently. He tortured me for years, Ali. I want to see that he got exactly what he deserved. And I told you: without proof, I can't pay you the £50,000 you've demanded. Please show it to me now.'

A few seconds passed then he nodded once. She exhaled quietly in relief. He retrieved his phone from his jacket pocket, navigated to the photo and turned the screen towards her. As

Ava stared down at her husband's spittle-covered lifeless body, her own began to shake.

'Satisfied?' he asked, sporting a smug smile.

She pounced on him then, taking full advantage of his heightened state. He hesitated, obviously surprised, then returned her kisses with fervour.

'Does this mean yes?' he asked, breathless.

'Yes, I'm satisfied,' she said, kissing him again, slowly and deeply.

'I want to see proof that the witch is dead too,' he said, when they broke apart.

'All in good time. I want to say thank you properly,' she said, rubbing her palm over the outline of his erection. 'One last time.'

His brow furrowed at her questioningly, but his expression soon softened as she began unbuttoning his jeans.

'Your wish is my command,' he said.

Ava pushed Ali back onto the bed. She lifted her long dress to reveal her naked body underneath. His eyes cast over her as she laid down next to him and she didn't care if he was wishing she was Ethan, or Eadie for that matter. All she wanted was one thing. It seemed he wanted it to.

He freed himself and mounted her. It was over in a few ferocious thrusts, and they parted, panting side by side.

After a minute, Ava got up and popped the champagne, carefully poured the glittering liquid, and then carried the fizzing flutes over to the bed. She handed one of them to Ali then held the other aloft.

'To a plan well executed,' she toasted, moving the glass towards her lips.

Ali propped himself up on one elbow, still trying to steady his breathing.

'Indeed.' He took a long glug of the glittering liquid, his Adam's apple bobbing as it slid smoothly down his throat.

'Tell me exactly what happened, and then I'll tell you about Eadie and show you proof of death,' she said excitedly, putting her glass down and lying on her front. She gently traced her finger down his torso. 'And then I will transfer the money.'

'You really want to know all the gory details?' he asked, still trying to catch his breath.

Her eyes glittered mischievously.

'I really do. Don't leave anything out.'

He surveyed her for a moment.

'You seem different, *habibti*,' he said, using his old term of endearment before downing the rest of the champagne, still clearly on a high from the events of the evening. He fell back onto the pillows, not bothering to cover himself up, and stared up at the ceiling, grinning.

Ava took his glass from him and placed it on the floor next to the bed.

'I am different,' she said, grinning too.

CHAPTER FORTY-FOUR

AVA

'MAY WE COME IN?' Detective Inspector Ritchie asked Ava after introducing himself and his colleague PC Smithson. He waited expectantly for her answer.

'Oh.' Ava peered at the blank-faced officers through the crack in the door. She stepped back to permit them entry, a crease of curiosity between her eyes. 'Yes, come in. Go through to the kitchen,' she said, nodding towards the back of the house then closing the door behind them.

'What's this about? Is everything okay?' asked Ava, gesturing for them to take a seat at the kitchen table once they were all situated. The officers remained standing. The taller of the two, the detective, wore a brown suit while the much younger PC Smithson sported a uniform so pristine it looked as though it was made of cardboard.

DI Ritchie cleared his throat and ran a hand down his patterned tie.

'Mrs Bateman, we're here to inform you that your husband, Rex, was found at the Quebec Hotel earlier today. I'm afraid he was dead.'

Ava's lips parted.

'Dead?' she whispered, the word barely more than a breath. 'What do you mean?' She reached out to grasp the back of a chair but was too far away to reach one. Instead, her hand hovered mid-air.

'We're sorry for your loss,' he said, promptly stepping forward, pulling out one of the chairs and twisting it around. Unnecessarily, he indicated towards it.

Ava sank down onto the seat, clasping her hands together in her lap.

'Which hotel did you say?'

'The Quebec Hotel in Leeds city centre,' the detective confirmed. 'Did you know—'

'Why was he at a hotel?' she interrupted, looked up at him.

DI Ritchie raised his eyebrows.

'You didn't know he was going there?'

Ava shook her head, pinching her bottom lip between her thumb and forefinger as she stared at the floor, trance-like.

'When did you last see your husband?' DI Ritchie pulled out another chair, sat opposite Ava and took out a small notebook and pen. PC Smithson placed a glass of water on the table and Ava's eyes flicked towards it.

'Thank you,' she said as he stepped back again, impressed with the stealthy way he had navigated around her kitchen. She reached for it and took a shaky sip. She put the glass back down and exhaled a deep, shuddering breath. The detective repeated the question.

'Erm... Friday,' stated Ava. 'I messaged him last night and he didn't reply. I assumed he was out with work friends.'

'You didn't see him yesterday morning or afternoon at all?'

Ava shook her head.

'No, he left for work early, before I woke up. He works weekends.'

DI Ritchie made a note.

'Was it unusual for him to go out and not return home?'

Ava pressed her lips together and closed her eyes briefly.

'No.'

'Where were you last night?'

'Erm... here, at first, and then I went to see my friend when I realised Rex wasn't coming home.'

'What time did you go out to see your friend?'

'About 7pm.' She nodded, reinforcing her words.

'And what time did you get back home?'

Ava twisted her fingers and narrowed her eyes, considering the question.

'Just after midnight, I think. I was going to stay over, but I wasn't feeling well so I came home.' She paused. 'I... I recently had a miscarriage, and I've not been feeling well since.' Her face crumpled as she repeated the statement.

'I'm sorry to hear that.' DI Ritchie's tone was sympathetic. He looked down at his notes while Ava composed herself enough to continue. She swallowed thickly.

'... which is why I went to see Eadie. Rex has been so distant since it happened, and I... I just needed someone to talk to.'

'Eadie?'

'Eadie Lee,' confirmed Ava.

'And she lives...'

'Park Square. In one of the apartments.'

The detective nodded as he jotted the details in his notebook.

'How were things in your marriage?' he asked gently.

Ava stared out into the garden through the bifold doors. It was drizzling lightly but the late afternoon sun was still trying to pierce through the October clouds. She hoped there might be a rainbow later. She looked back at the middle-aged detective. His weary eyes contained genuine kindness and she wondered how many times he had done this – informed a wife that her husband had been randomly found dead one afternoon. She hoped whoever had told her dad that her mum had been murdered had been as compassionate as DI Ritchie.

'Sorry,' she said, wiping a tear away. 'Umm... not good. It was our wedding anniversary yesterday and Rex had forgotten. Or if he had remembered, he still chose to spend the night away from home. From me. I suspected he'd been having an affair for a while. I guess that explains the hotel...'

'So, things between you and Mr Bateman had been strained?' the detective concluded.

Ava nodded.

'Yes. I thought it was because of the miscarriage... it drove us further apart. He began working late a lot more. Well, that's what he said he was doing.' She shrugged.

DI Ritchie tapped his fingers on his notebook.

'Mrs Bateman, this may be difficult to hear, but we have reason to believe that Mr Bateman may have ended his own life deliberately.'

Ava gaped at the detective; her pale face stricken.

'Killed himself? No. No, that can't be right!' Ava stood and crossed to the island, gripping the countertop as she hung her head. PC Smithson moved towards her, but Ava held out a palm to stop him. Her tears splashed on the marble surface.

'How did he do it?' she asked after few moments.

'The evidence points to a drug overdose. We'll know more soon.'

'I didn't know... I didn't know he was struggling too,' she said, bringing a hand to her mouth and stifling a sob. It was the only sound in the silent kitchen as the police officers waited respectfully for her to regain her composure.

'Are you sure it's definitely him... Rex?'

'The hotel booking was made under his name, and his driving licence was found at the scene.'

'What will happen now?' asked Ava, turning and wrapping her arms around her waist.

'Well, the coroner's office will conduct an investigation to determine the exact cause of death. It may involve a post-mortem examination. After that you'll be invited to formally identify the body.' DI Ritchie stood and pushed the chair back under the table. Ava was reminded of Rex's obsession with having everything 'just so' and felt another wave of relief that he was gone. The detective surveyed Ava for a moment. 'We'll also continue to speak with hotel staff and check CCTV footage to determine Mr Bateman's final movements. As soon as we know more, we'll let you know. Would you like us to call anyone to be with you?'

Ava shook her head then looked at him with a distressed expression.

'Does Barbara know – Rex's mum?'

'No. You're his next of kin so you're the first to be informed. Would you like us to call her for you or pay her a visit?'

Ava briefly closed her eyes, tears tracing her cheeks.

'No. No thank you. I'll tell her myself.'

He tucked his notebook back into his inside pocket and tipped his head in a goodbye. PC Smithson smiled tightly before turning to follow his superior.

'Thank you,' whispered Ava as the men left her kitchen. She listened to the sound of their footsteps along her hallway floor then heard the front door close gently behind them. She was sure she felt the house exhale with relief, its secrets still locked inside. Ava sighed too, suddenly exhausted now that the adrenaline was depleting. The performance had really taken it out of her.

She picked up her phone and as she made her way upstairs, she sent a broken heart emoji to Eadie. It had been Eadie's suggestion and a way for Ava to let her know that the police had been to inform her of Rex's death and would be visiting her soon to check out Ava's alibi for the night before. An alibi that they had constructed together after Ava had asked Eadie for help to double-cross Ali rather than for her to murder Eadie as planned.

Throwing her phone down on top of the covers, Ava curled up on her empty bed. She closed her eyes and replayed the events of the previous evening in her mind...

After leaving Eadie's hotel room she had gone to meet Ali in his, as arranged. He had been surprisingly easy to seduce one last time given his alleged love for Ethan, but he might have felt it was the least he could do given he had screwed her in other ways. Or maybe the adrenaline in his system had simply spurred him on. Perhaps he still desired her deep down. Whatever the reason, she preferred that he had been an active participant during the sex; it made it seem slightly less sordid. Afterwards, he fell unconscious soon after glugging the spiked champagne she offered him, his jeans and pants still around his thighs – an undignified tableau for the cleaning staff to find – as she began to stage the scene.

She dressed in the shapeless, casual clothes she had brought with her and snapped on a pair of latex gloves. She began to move quickly but carefully, following the steps she had choreographed constantly in her mind ever since visiting Kathleen. Talking to her only mother figure about having a child of her own had not only reinforced her desperation, but it had propelled her towards this extreme but necessary course of action. She wiped the champagne bottle and Ali's glass clean of her own fingerprints before wrapping his clammy fingers around them both, leaving his glass next to him and the bottle on the bedside table. Emptying her still-full champagne glass down the sink, she put it in her large bag, along with the dress she had taken off, the red wig she had discarded, and the laptop she had bought.

Next, she put on a short brown wig, her padded coat and a cap, slipping Ali's phone, passport and wallet into her pocket. From her bag, she took out the brief but carefully worded suicide note she had written and placed it on Ali's chest, clamping his hand on top of it, simultaneously shocked and frustrated to find that he was still breathing, albeit slowly and shallowly. This meant she now had one last task to perform, to be on the safe side. Taking the already loaded back-up syringe out of her coat's inner pocket, originally meant for Eadie if her spiked drink hadn't done the job properly, she removed the needle cap, located a vein in Ali's arm and injected him with a generous top-up. Her final parting gift. His jaw jerked open in a silent cry and his fingers splayed before relaxing again within seconds.

Hooking her bag onto her shoulder, Ava clutched the straps tightly as she looked down at Ali's body in the gloom. After a minute or so, she pressed two fingers to his wrist, checking for a pulse. She didn't find one. Ava exhaled, relieved it hadn't been as messy as Rex's demise.

She had some humanity.

Now, in her own bed, she clutched her still flat belly, praying that another tiny heart would soon beat within her. No matter how she became pregnant, whether it was as a result of being raped by her husband or having sex with her husband's murderer one last time before killing him, she would be grateful for the gift of a baby. She knew to most people her drastic plan would have seemed heartless at best and twisted at worst, but she was thirty-five and time was running out. This could be her only chance to have a child of her own, to have the love-filled life she'd dreamed of but had been cruelly denied for so long. Of course she felt an immiscible mix of both guilt and remorse for ending Ali's existence, but being married to Rex had taught her how to compartmentalise effectively, to bury her fear and pain while she dreamed of a better future – that's what she had done while she was in that hotel room with Ali, and that's what she was going to do again.

Ava closed her eyes. Now free of the two men who had hurt her more than she had thought possible – her heartbreak over Blake paled in comparison – she fell into the most hopeful and peaceful sleep of her adult life.

CHAPTER FORTY-FIVE

EADIE

'Miss Lee?' asked the middle-aged detective in the ugly brown suit and patterned tie standing in her doorway.

Eadie looked him up and down before glancing at the younger, stiffer, uniformed officer beside him. She returned her gaze to the suited man.

'It's Ms,' she replied, crossing her arms across her skimpy green negligee and matching silk floral gown and leaning against the wall. The uniformed officer's eyes briefly widened as the movement caused her ample breasts to become even more prominent, barely concealed beneath the lace. He blushed and dipped his head.

'Sorry. *Ms* Lee,' the older man corrected, smoothing down his tie. 'I'm Detective Inspector Ritchie and this is PC Smithson. May we come in? We need to ask you a few questions. We won't take up too much of your time.'

Eadie considered the request then sighed before turning back into her apartment. 'Okay but be quick. I need to finish shooting a campaign,' she instructed over her shoulder, floral gown flapping fluidly behind her as she walked into the open-plan kitchen area.

DI Ritchie followed her inside.

'Thank you. Nice place,' he said, gazing around at the exposed brick walls and curved staircase leading to a mezzanine level. A tripod, camera and ring light were set up on the coffee table in the lounge area beyond, a multicoloured pile of underwear discarded on one of the velvet sofas. PC Smithson closed the door and joined him.

Eadie, as ever, wasn't in the mood for small talk. She stood, hands on hips, waiting for the detective to get on with it. He obliged while his colleague stood silently by his side holding a small black notebook, pen poised.

DI Ritchie cleared his throat.

'Could you tell us where you were last night, Ms Lee?'

Eadie cocked her head and gestured to the space around her.

'Here. Why?'

'Were you alone?'

She regarded the detective coolly for a few moments. He stared blankly back at her.

'Why?' she repeated.

'Please answer the question, Ms Lee.'

Eadie rolled her eyes.

'No, I wasn't alone. Ava was here.'

'Ava...?'

'Bateman,' she supplied. DI Ritchie nodded.

'What time did she arrive and leave?'

'Sevenish until about midnight.'

'And how did Mrs Bateman seem?'

'She was upset.'

'Why was she upset?'

'What's this about?' Eadie bounced her gaze between the two men before smiling coyly. 'Have I been a naughty girl, Detective Inspector, and you're here to arrest me?' She giggled, holding out her wrists, as though ready to be cuffed. PC Smithson's blush reappeared; his swallow audible.

'These are just standard questions,' replied the senior officer blandly. 'We appreciate your cooperation.'

Eadie narrowed her eyes then gave an exasperated sigh.

'She recently had a miscarriage, and her dick of a husband had forgotten their wedding anniversary.'

Still practically glowing, PC Smithson jotted something down in his notebook.

'What state of mind was she in when she left here, would you say?'

'Not great, obviously, but she just wanted to go home. She loves Rex – that's her husband. She wants to try to work things out. Against my advice I might add.'

'Why's that?'

'She was miserable. I thought she should leave him but all she wants is a family, like some women do. More fool her.' Eadie shrugged and her silk gown slipped down, exposing a bare shoulder and more of the lacy negligee. PC Smithson emitted a squeaking sound before clearing his throat and averting his eyes.

'So, she left around midnight?' reiterated DI Ritchie, throwing a frown at the younger officer. 'Can anyone else verify that?'

'I'm verifying it. And this will.' Eadie picked up her phone and swiped and tapped the screen a few times before thrusting forward a photo of herself and Ava that she had posted to her Instagram stories last night. The detective scrutinised the screen and nodded at PC Smithson who then added more to his notebook.

'Did you hear from her again last night? She didn't message that she got home safe, with it being late?'

Eadie tutted as she placed her phone face down on the counter next to her.

'I'm not her mother and we're not *besties*. She needed a shoulder to cry on, so I provided one. Simple as that.' She shrugged again. 'It's up to her if she chooses to stay with him or not but as far as I know it's not illegal to forget your wedding anniversary.'

DI Ritchie raised an eyebrow at Eadie's abrasive tone.

'No, you're right, it's not.'

'She messaged me earlier today though. A single broken heart emoji.' Eadie huffed a soft laugh and shook her head. 'Obviously still obsessing about it. I haven't replied yet. To be honest, marriage drama really bores me, and I don't want to encourage a prolonged agony aunt situation – with Ava or anyone. Got to keep firm boundaries, you know?' She flashed a self-satisfied smile at the two men.

DI Ritchie scratched his forehead.

'Well, as Mr Bateman was found dead yesterday afternoon, Mrs Bateman might be in need of a friend right now.'

Eadie's smile swiftly slipped from her shiny red lips.

'Dead?' she asked, eyes wide. 'Wow. Fuck.'

'Indeed,' DI Ritchie responded as PC Smithson tucked his notebook back in his jacket pocket. 'Anyway, thank you for your time, Ms Lee. We'll be in touch if we have any further questions.'

'Sure. See yourselves out,' said Eadie as PC Smithson turned and practically raced towards the door, DI Ritchie following behind. She retrieved her phone and headed upstairs without a backward glance.

CHAPTER FORTY-SIX

POPPY

SITTING in the car after her early Monday morning Bodyfit class, sweaty, dizzy and still angry, Poppy ran her thumb back and forth over her engagement ring. She had checked her text messages, WhatsApp, emails and social media profiles hundreds of times each but Rex still hadn't replied to any of her texts, picture messages, voicemails or voice notes since his brief message on Saturday telling her he'd see her soon at the hotel. She'd waited for him all night, but at dawn, when she woke with a start from a fitful few hours' sleep with no Rex and no further communication from him, she had checked out in a tearful huff and gone home. Now, she was beginning to worry that he had inexplicably gone back to his wife. Not that he had technically left Ava yet, but he was on the brink of leaving her. This thought, already bad enough, was countered with the irrational fear that she had somehow done something wrong, and he was punishing her for it. She was annoyed if that was the case because they didn't treat each other that way. Yes, he had a quick temper, and a tendency to sulk and swear occasionally, but he wasn't psychologically or physically cruel.

She knew he had taken Sunday off work too – they were supposed to have had each other for breakfast and lunch at the hotel – but he should be back there today. The car dealership was about twenty minutes away from the gym and she was considering driving there to confront him when it opened at 9am. Sod the consequences of an unannounced visit – she was his fiancée now! Wasn't she?

Fresh panic washed over her as she opened Facebook again in the hope that he had contacted her in the last few minutes. She rechecked her messages then began to scroll down her feed when she found nothing new in her inbox. A local news story about a suicide pact had already amassed a lot of reactions and comments and momentarily distracted her.

Poppy's blood chilled as she read some of them – they were a mixed bag of bigotry, sympathy and superiority as was typical for the platform:

Bloody gays, the world is well rid of them...

Such a shame...

Those poor men, driven to suicide because of non-compassionate people like the idiots commenting in this thread... let them rest in peace, together...

Interest piqued, she clicked on the link and was taken to the external local news website. Scanning the copy, she gasped and clapped her hand over her mouth in anticipation of the bile about to rise. She read the story with shaking hands and tears blurring her vision.

Two Men Die in 'Suicide Pact'

Two men are believed to have killed themselves in a lovers' suicide pact, West Yorkshire Police have reported. The bodies of Rex Bateman and an unidentified man were found in the Quebec Hotel and the Royal Hotel respectively, in Leeds, West Yorkshire, yesterday afternoon. They had both seemingly committed suicide in a planned, tandem fashion, albeit in separate locations.

Early reports suggest both men died from deliberate drug overdoses. The unidentified man of Arabian descent left an unsigned suicide note declaring his love for Mr Bateman and that their 'separate but together' deaths were symbolic of what he described as their 'taboo love' for each other.

A spokesperson for Mr Bateman's wife of three years, Ava, has said she is 'shocked and devastated' and that she will continue to help officers investigating the deaths piece together the events leading up to this tragic incident.

A Leeds Police spokesman said: 'This appears to be a carefully orchestrated suicide pact, but our investigation is ongoing. Identifying the unknown man found in the Royal Hotel is paramount.' He added: 'Although our inquiries will continue, we are not currently looking for anyone else in connection with the deaths.'

The note left by the unidentified man was considered 'self-explanatory' by assistant coroner William Wells, who gave the conclusion of suicide. Mr Wells said the deaths 'appeared to be a well-planned event'. Post-mortem examinations will confirm the exact causes in due course.

. . .

Poppy dropped her phone, threw back her head and screamed.

EPILOGUE
AVA

March 2020

'WHO'S HERE?' Ava asked her daughter as she opened the door. 'It's Auntie Eadie!' she said, exaggerating her delight for the child's benefit.

'I told you to stop calling me that,' said Eadie, bustling in bearing a pile of packages and placing them on the kitchen island. 'Here, I signed for these for you. The delivery driver was fit.'

'*More* gifted stuff?' asked Ava, walking into the kitchen behind Eadie and looking at the labels on the boxes, puppy Ralph yapping and scampering around her feet. 'Will you hold Christine while I open them?' she asked.

Eadie sighed and rolled her eyes. 'I suppose so,' she said, her already outstretched arms belying her annoyed tone and expression. She took the baby from Ava and marvelled, as she always did, at her beauty.

'People pay good money for eyelashes like these,' she said, smacking her matte-red lips against Christine's rosy cheek.

Ava smiled at the sight of Eadie cradling her daughter and made enough room on the messy counter to spread out the packages. Instead of being a stark, sterile space, her kitchen was now littered with baby accoutrements, the glass doors showcased sticky fingerprints and wet nose smudges, and a tapestry of Polaroid photographs adorned the fridge. She began to open the packages that Eadie had brought in, oohing and aahing at their contents – personalised outfits for Christine, post-pregnancy active wear, and a new mummy subscription box filled with goodies that she'd need to work off whilst wearing the active wear.

As she frequently did, Ava reflected on how much her life had changed over the past seventeen months. Since Rex's shocking death, it felt like her life had become public property and she was amazed at the amount of sympathy still being sent her way, as well as at the way her new career had exploded. Thanks to Eadie's mentorship, she had become a high-ranking mummy blogger and social media influencer and had been swept into the spotlight via the surge of public compassion bestowed upon her once the news about Rex and his 'tragic gay affair' got out. Of course, Eadie continued to receive a healthy commission out of the business arrangement. It was the least she deserved for providing Ava with an alibi.

Ava herself had also changed; motherhood and pregnancy certainly suited her. Nobody knew about the new baby yet, except Eadie. They had already created the content for the upcoming pregnancy announcement and Ava was excited. She knew that Rex's mum, Barbara, was going to be overjoyed at the prospect of another grandchild too. Two in relatively quick succession. Ava stroked her blossoming bump. She was barely showing yet, but she couldn't stop running her palm over her hardening belly. It was like a compulsion; she had been the same with Christine.

'Have you checked a certain someone's profile lately?' asked Eadie, jiggling Christine against her hip.

'No, why?' asked Ava, knowing Eadie was referring to Poppy, Rex's mistress, or rather, his fiancée. Was someone still a fiancée if the person they were engaged to was dead? she wondered.

'She's engaged again. He's tagged in one of her Facebook posts. Minor celebrity. Nutritionist or something. Loaded.'

'Interesting,' commented Ava. Well, that answered the fiancée question.

'Has she sent you any more messages?' asked Eadie.

'No, not for a long while. Hopefully that'll be it if she's moved on. Some of the messages she sent were really nasty; it was as though she knew a version of the truth.'

'No way. I told you – you did a great job of covering your tracks. Professional level.' Eadie appraised Ava with respect.

Ava tugged on her bottom lip and regarded her friend.

'What?' asked Eadie. 'You've got that look again.'

'I wish you wouldn't compliment me like that, as though I deserve an award or something for expertly executing a staged double suicide. It was a terrible thing to do,' Ava whispered and cast her eyes to the floor. For the first few weeks following Rex and Ali's deaths, she had fully expected the police to connect her and Ali, once they had identified him, either from their online tutoring sessions or from Ali's hotel CCTV. But the months had continued to pass, her growing pregnant belly marking the time effectively, and they never did. Or if they had, they hadn't felt it necessary to question her again. It really had been an open and shut case and unlike her mother's murderer decades before, she had no intention of confessing, not now she had a family to protect. Christine and the new baby needed her.

'Listen to me one last time,' replied Eadie, scowling. 'If you hadn't taken control the way you did, your life would still be a shit show, or you'd have gone to prison, or one of them would have ended up killing you, or Ali might have killed me, or even Ethan, jealous fuck that he was. You prevented all that and saved us.' Ava looked up as Eadie gestured to all three of them. 'You need to remember that.'

Ava nodded, taking one of her daughter's outstretched pudgy hands and kissing her sticky palm. This was a variation of the same discussion they'd had many times over the past seventeen months and although Ava knew Eadie was right, the fact that she'd made such a callous choice, committed such a calculated crime, despite feeling it was a necessary course of action, still plagued her deep down, despite her resolution to compartmentalise her thoughts. Yet if she hadn't have done what she did, Christine might not be here now. Although she was already pregnant when she seduced Ali, she didn't know it at the time, and she felt sure that had she been tried as a co-conspirator in Rex's murder, another miscarriage would have been inevitable. Or worse, she would have had to give up the baby post-birth and spend tortured years in a prison cell with empty arms and a broken heart. Ava physically shuddered at the mere thought of how differently, how badly, things could have turned out.

'Speaking of Ethan, he messaged me the other day,' said Eadie, segueing smoothly away from their well-worn topic.

'Really? What did he want?' asked Ava, surprised to hear Ethan's name again after all this time. She felt a flutter of fear in her stomach, but one glance at Eadie's bemused expression reassured her she had nothing to worry about. She had only ever met Ethan once – at the Italian restaurant with Ali – and if he was going to tell the police anything about them, he would have done it by now. Given how drunk he had been and the brief amount of time she had been there, she doubted he could have picked her out of a line up anyway.

'Mainly just to let me know how amazing his life is now and what I'm missing out on. He's a trier, I'll give him that.' Eadie laughed at the ridiculous notion of her life lacking in anything. Her make-up range had gone stratospheric – it was stocked in Selfridges and John Lewis – and she had a regular slot on QVC. As an early investor, Ava also enjoyed the financial benefits of its immense success.

'There are no hard feelings there though. No feelings at all, actually,' she continued. 'He was a nice enough guy, but you know how I feel about nice guys.' Eadie feigned gagging and rolled her brightly shaded eyes.

'Speaking from experience, nice guys are better than the liars and cheaters,' Ava said sadly. 'How's he doing now?'

'You remember I told you I encouraged him to get help with his gambling and alcohol addiction after his dad got worse when they eventually heard about Ali's death on the news?'

Ava nodded.

'Well, apparently, he's now become an ambassador for two charities: gay mental health and orphaned foster children. Which has boosted his public profile. Which has helped him get a load of TV interviews and auditions. Reckons he's going to be the next male Angelina Jolie or something. Maybe be a bombshell on the next series of *Love Island.*'

'All's well that ends well,' mused Ava, guiltily glad that yet another person's life had improved following Ali's death.

'We need to leave soon. What's happening with pipsqueak here?' Eadie asked, as Christine let out a squeal. Ralph ruffed gently from his bed.

'Barbara's coming to collect her.'

'How's she coping?'

'The more time she spends with this one the better she seems to be,' said Ava, stroking one of Christine's rosy cheeks. 'I'm going to tell her about the new baby tonight.'

'Have you given any more thought to telling her the truth one day?' asked Eadie. 'About Rex's violent tendencies?'

Ava shook her head.

'I think it's better to let her think her son was a tortured closet homosexual rather than an abusive money-obsessed narcissist and sadist who raped his own wife while being engaged to his mistress. It would break her heart to know the truth. Now she has a tragic story to dine out on forevermore as well as a granddaughter to cherish.'

'And what if madam here had been Ali's daughter rather than Rex's?' Eadie stroked Christine's downy hair.

'I would have hoped that Barbara would have turned a blind eye if my genes hadn't been dominant enough.' Ava smiled at her darling daughter. 'And I hope she'll still consider this one her grandchild even though I've used donor sperm this time. A much less stressful process!' She placed her palm on her bump and wiggled her fingers against it. 'I think she would have still loved Christine though, even if she had been Ali's daughter. I know I honestly didn't care either way. I was so desperate for her, I just wanted to improve my chances of getting pregnant in the first place. To turn all the badness into something beautiful.'

'Job done,' stated Eadie. 'I must admit, though, I feel like I should take some of the credit – if it hadn't been for my inspiring pep talk in that hotel room, you would never have dared do it at all.' A wry smile played on her full lips.

'Maybe,' acknowledged Ava, as she always did when Eadie raised this point. She sighed. 'I often think back to what you told me: men fucking lie. And you were right. They all lied to me,

Eadie, and worse. Until seventeen months ago I spent my whole adult life allowing men to withhold information, or to control me, or to manipulate my thoughts and feelings. My dad lied about how my mum really died until his deathbed confession, Blake 'forgot' to mention he was married, Rex lied about, well, everything... and Ali lied about you and his feelings for Ethan.'

'Quite the list of accomplished Pinocchios,' agreed Eadie.

'I've been a victim, mired in grief, ever since I was five years old, when I saw my poor mum lying dead on that kitchen floor. I had to take control instead of continuing to passively accept whatever life threw at me, whatever men used me for, or I would have stayed a victim forever. We're both still here – single, successful women being role models to the next generation. There have been enough deaths, but Rex's and Ali's have set me free. It's time for new life,' she said, gazing lovingly at Christine.

'Amen to that. I've said it before, and I'll say it again: all's well that fucking ends well,' stated Eadie.

A knock at the front door punctuated their conversation and Ava hurried down the hall to let her mother-in-law in.

'Only me!' Barbara announced cheerfully as she stepped inside.

'Hello, only you,' replied Ava, embracing her warmly.

'Where's my special girl?' the older woman asked, moving through to the kitchen. Christine's eyes lit up at the sight of her grandmother and Barbara made a beeline for the baby, immediately taking her from Eadie's arms. Ralph skittered excitedly around her ankles, vying for attention.

'Lovely to see you, Barbara. How are you feeling?' asked Eadie.

Barbara gave her a heartfelt smile.

'As long as I'm with my beautiful granddaughter, I'm fine.

C. L. JENNISON

I've brought some more photo albums so I can tell her all about her daddy. They're in the car. Anyway, how are you both? Are you sure you have to go to work today? You could stay here with us and reminisce.'

Ava and Eadie exchanged a glance.

'Thank you for the offer, Barbara, but I can't let the brand down and I need to keep Little Miss here in the manner to which she's become accustomed. And you,' replied Ava.

'Well, don't work too hard. You know how grateful I am to you for taking up where Rex left off financially, but I don't want to see you running yourself into the ground, even if you are a successful "Instabook" businesswoman or whatever.'

Ava circled her arm around Barbara's shoulder and gave her a squeeze.

'Nonsense. There's no way I was going to let you lose the house. Whatever Rex's faults, that was something he did do right – look after you. You're Christine's only grandparent and my only mother figure now. I want you to be as comfortable and as happy as possible, despite everything that's happened.'

Barbara's chin wobbled and she nodded, emotion threatening to overwhelm her. She clutched Ava to her with her free arm, enveloping the baby, too, within their close bodies. Three unconventional generations of women united in their shared desire for a happier future.

'Bye bye, baby, Mummy and Auntie Eadie are going out now,' said Ava, checking the time on the beloved watch of her mum's she still wore. She stroked Christine's blonde tufts. 'Have a lovely time with Granny. Oh, by the way, Barbara, I've got a surprise for you later!' She kissed her mother-in-law on the cheek then leant down to stroke Ralph.

'Oh, lovely! I'll look forward to it.'

'Stop calling me Auntie Eadie,' said Eadie again as she and

Ava walked down the hall. 'I'm a role model and a strong woman, not a fuddy-duddy auntie.'

'I think we're both role models and strong women now,' said Ava, 'doing whatever it takes.'

'Whatever it takes,' repeated Eadie.

THE END

ACKNOWLEDGEMENTS

Although it's often said, it's very true that a LOT of work goes into writing and publishing a book, and I can honestly say that overcoming the mental hurdles (imposter syndrome be damned!) is the hardest work of all. Therefore, there a few people I would like to thank for helping this author dream of mine finally become a reality, whether they helped physically, virtually or emotionally.

Thank you to the amazing team at Bloodhound Books, especially Betsy, Tara, Ian and Abbie. After entering their #PitchHound blurb contest in August 2022, I was thrilled to be offered a publishing contract for *The Desperate Wife*, and I have felt extremely valued and supported ever since.

Thank you to my husband, Richard, for repeatedly encouraging me to just 'get on with it' – I wish I had got on with it sooner! And to my in-laws who always show such genuine interest in my writing career – I appreciate it so much.

Thanks also go to my old writing group friends for the feedback on the early snippets of *The Desperate Wife* that I shared on those Monday mornings all that time ago, especially Carol and Lynne who are still brilliant writing cheerleaders in general.

Finally, thank you to all the wonderful author podcast hosts who have been informing, inspiring and motivating me on my daily dog walks since 2018.

A NOTE FROM THE PUBLISHER

Thank you for reading this book. If you enjoyed it please do consider leaving a review on Amazon to help others find it too.

We hate typos. All of our books have been rigorously edited and proofread, but sometimes mistakes do slip through. If you have spotted a typo, please do let us know and we can get it amended within hours.

info@bloodhoundbooks.com